NATIONAL NANCYS

NATIONAL NANCYS

Fred Hunter

ST. MARTIN'S MINOTAUR
NEW YORK

ISBN 0-312-25233-1

First Edition: May 2000

10   9   8   7   6   5   4   3   2   1

For Glenn M. Hughes, Village Person

NATIONAL NANCYS

I was not a political person. Despite the best efforts of some of my more militant friends, I managed to remain blissfully apolitical for the better part of my life. Of course, I'd always exercised my patriotic duty and voted, but I left the actual activism to Peter, my husband, figuring that one soapbox in the family was enough.

But it's hard to remain politically neutral when you know as many dykes as we do. Our friends Sheila and Jo were the ones who approached us about volunteering for Charles "Charlie" Clarke, who was one of the Democratic candidates for the senate seat that was being vacated by our retiring elder statesman. Clarke's classically liberal views and his open support of gay rights had made him the favorite son of the community, and galvanized their efforts on his behalf. It also solidified the gay-baiting radical right's opposition to him. Both sides viewed Clarke's run for office as a call to arms.

Sheila and Jo made it sound as if turning down the opportunity to serve Clarke would be about the same as telling Christ you didn't want to be a disciple.

"Do you have any idea how important it is to get involved?" Sheila had said passionately over dinner one night. "Do you have any idea how many setbacks queers have suffered over the past couple of years?"

I inwardly rolled my eyes. In recent days Sheila had become one of those people who use the word *queer* for political empowerment with an insistence that ends up making them sound like children who've just learned a dirty word.

"The Republicans want to take away all of our constitutional rights, and the Religious Reich think it's okay to kill us. We need people like Clarke in office. There's important work to be done!"

Peter had flashed his beautiful green eyes at me in a way that said, "See? I've been telling you that for years." At least he didn't say it out loud.

After a while my reluctance to get involved was overwhelmed by the Borgian pull of the entire gay community. Resistance was futile. I had to succumb. Which is why I found myself stuffing envelopes in the Chicago branch of Charlie Clarke's campaign headquarters.

The headquarters was located in a storefront on Lincoln Avenue just north of Fullerton. It was crammed with folding chairs and tables at which volunteers were engaged in a variety of menial tasks. The far end of the room was partitioned off as cubicles for our office manager and her assistant, and the back room had been turned into offices for the candidate and his campaign manager to use whenever they were in town.

It wasn't a heavily funded campaign, but it was sincere. The belief that kept us going was that once Clarke won the Democratic nomination in the primary (and we were given daily doses of blind assurance that he would), there would be an infusion of money into his campaign from the party, whether or not the party actually liked him. Many of them didn't. Clarke had a reputation for being straightforward, which could make even some members of his own party quake in their boots. But personal feelings aside, they would throw their support to their most bitter enemy rather than relinquish the seat to a Republican.

Peter volunteered when he could, but I was the one with "free time on his hands," as Sheila had so quaintly put it. She didn't know just how accurate she was. Since taking up our occasional work with the CIA, I'd let the business I'd built up as a freelance graphic artist dwindle down to one steady client, who I'd kept on more as a courtesy than anything else. But over the past year our CIA assignments had also evaporated. I wasn't hurting for money yet. I had a decent though not inexhaustible savings. And Mother always told me that I didn't have to worry, because through shrewd investments she had parlayed the considerable inheritance my late father had left her into an even more considerable nest egg. But I could feel my genitals receding at the idea of being in my thirties and supported by my mother. At that point, I felt like stuffing envelopes was about all I was good for.

"Here's some more," said Jody Linn-Hadden as she hoisted an enormous box of fliers onto the table where I was working.

Our office manager had been born Jody Linn, and had hyphenated herself after falling in love and forming a permanent partnership with her familiar, Mary Hadden. I've been told that meeting Mary had softened Jody, an idea that I find horrifying because I hadn't worked with Jody for an hour before I was thinking of her as the Rosa Kleb of local politics. Only Jody was bigger. She was a huge Teutonic woman with long blond hair she wore viciously twisted into two braids, then rolled up and pinned to each side of her head like a pair of unglazed cinnamon buns. She might not have physically resembled Kleb, but I still believed that if she clicked her heels together a blade would pop out of her shoe.

"You don't look happy," she said, her lips forming a disapproving triangle.

"I'm fine."

She clucked her tongue. "You obviously don't understand how important it is that we get Charlie Clarke elected. . . ."

My brain reeled as Jody launched for the hundredth time into a tirade about the ills of the world and the solutions that Charlie Clarke had to offer. I'm sure she was using actual words, but my mind was registering only a hollow gurgle, like the sound of water swirling down the drain. I drifted back into focus when it sounded as if she was wrapping it up.

". . . so everything, no matter how insignificant it seems to you, is important! If just one person doesn't get that flier, that may be the one vote that decides this election."

"Yes, sir!" I said, snapping a crisp salute.

Jody pulled back slightly and scowled. I thought she might bite me, but instead she just shook her head with disgust and walked away.

"Too intense for words, isn't she?" said David Leech, the blue-eyed nymphet who was working at the end of the table.

"I wish," I replied.

I spent the last hour answering phones, which I found only slightly less tedious than stuffing envelopes. It's hard to believe that irate phone calls could become boring, but they did.

"You tell that pansy-ass faggot-lover that if he gets elected, he's a dead man!" snarled one caller.

"I'll do that, sir," I said wearily. "And can I give him your name?"

Click.

"Can you tell me, what is Mr. Clarke's position on garbage cans?" asked another caller, this time an elderly woman.

"So far he has not positioned himself on garbage cans," I replied, casting aside the response sheet on which we were supposed to rely. "I'm sure the minute he gets into office, he'll be dealing with your garbage."

Click.

"I've got it! I've got it!" cried Shawn Stillman, one of the other volunteers. He jumped up on his chair, put his hand over the mouthpiece and merrily waved the receiver in the air. "It's today's bomb threat!"

The workers broke out in cheers and applauded. The office had been receiving bomb threats for the past month—some times three or four a day. To most of the volunteers it had almost become a game. We were thinking of holding an office pool, betting on who could rack up the most threats in one week.

"Hello? Hello?" Shawn said into the mouthpiece. "Aw, he hung up!" He jumped down from the chair and replaced the receiver.

Despite all the joking around about it, some of the volunteers were worried about the threats. There was fear behind their smiles. In my own present frame of mind I felt that after defeating evil foreign agents, crooked American agents, and crazed religious zealots, it would probably be fitting if I was blown to bits while stuffing envelopes.

"It's like I've told all of you before," Jody Linn-Hadden announced in her booming voice, "these threats are a badge of honor! A threat to Charlie Clarke and his campaign means that he's really making headway as we move toward the primary. We have victory in sight! We've got them scared and all they can do is come back at us with cheap threats!" She paused to punctuate this with a triumphant smile. "Now, pick up the pace, people! We still have a lot of work to do!"

She clapped her hands together twice, then went back to her cubicle. Shawn finished a whispered conversation with the volunteer to his left, then got up and followed Jody, casually brushing the sandy locks out of his eyes as he crossed the room. I'd never had much in the way of dealings with him, but he struck me as the type of person who believes the world is his Red Sea and it needs to part for him.

"What do they do about the threats?" asked David, who had wandered over to the bank of phones during the hubbub. He was a bit newer to The Cause than me and looked rightly confused by the celebration surrounding the phone call.

"They just log it and turn it over to the FBI."

His eyes widened. "That's all?"

I shrugged. "We're getting them every day. What more can we do? I'm sure they follow them up. It's easy enough for them to get phone records."

"But shouldn't somebody check the office for a bomb?"

"There's no bomb here," I said reassuringly.

"How do you know?"

"If there was, Jody would have sniffed it out."

He laughed without looking happy, then went back to his work before the commandant could catch him sloughing off.

By five-thirty I was no longer listening to the callers at all. While they droned on I was mentally singing:

> *Go down, Moses, way down to Egypt's land*
> *Tell old Pharaoh, let my faggot go . . .*

Moses finally arrived in the form of Peter Livesay, my husband, lover, and at that moment my liberator. He had fallen into the habit of stopping in at campaign headquarters on his way home from Farrahut's, the men's clothing store at which he worked, and then we'd walk home together.

It's a testament to just how bored I was (and how much I adore him) that when he appeared in the doorway he seemed to be bathed in a bright white light and float toward me in slow motion like a blue-suited guardian angel.

"Are you ready to go?" he asked.

"I assume that's a rhetorical question," I said as I got up from the table and grabbed my jacket from the coat rack by the door. I didn't wait to put it on before going out onto the street.

"What's your hurry?"

"No hurry," I replied, slowing down. "I just feel like I've been locked in a cage all day."

"Come on. It can't be as bad as all that."

"That's easy for you to say. You've been helping young men in and out of their clothes. I've been listening to the huddled masses yearning to spew anti-gay bile."

"Well," he said with a heavy sigh, "it's all in a good cause."

"Oh, please! You're not going to start telling me what a worthy candidate Charlie Clarke is, are you?"

"Well, he *is* a worthy candidate."

"I know, I know, I've heard about it all day—again! Especially from Jody. That dyke is so damned political every time she opens her mouth I can feel my brain trickling out of my ear!"

Peter laid his hand gently on the small of my back. God, how I loved his touch.

"Honey, every day you sound more unhappy with this volunteer gig. If it's making you so miserable, why don't you just stop it?"

I produced my most dramatic, world-weary sigh. "Because getting Charlie Clarke elected is really important to myself and to my community."

He laughed. "You don't want people to know you actually believe that, do you?"

"I do believe it," I replied with a smile. "That's the trouble."

It was a nice walk down Fullerton to the town house we shared with my mother—or rather, that she shared with us, since she was the owner. When we got there, we found her setting the table for dinner.

"There are my darlings!" she said, sweeping over to us and giving us each a peck on the cheek. "How was your day?"

"Not half as good as yours, it seems," I said. This was a bit effusive, even for her. "Have you been in the cooking sherry?"

"Not at all!" she said as she breezed into the kitchen. Peter and I followed her. She was humming a tune as she stirred a pot of boiling potatoes.

"Mother, the table's only set for two."

"I know. I won't be joining you. I've got a date."

"You what?" The words popped out of my mouth before I was able to eliminate the tone of shock.

"You needn't sound so surprised," she said, shooting a comic squint at me over her shoulder. "Rumor has it that I'm not deformed."

"I didn't mean that. I just didn't know you were seeing anyone."

"I wasn't. I went downtown to shop today and I ran into him at Marshall Field's."

"At Field's?" said Peter. "Are you sure he's straight?"

"Don't be daft, darling," she replied. "I was in ladies' accessories, or whatever they call it nowadays. And there he was, completely up a tree, trying to choose a scarf to take home to his mother."

"How sweet," I intoned.

"Yes! Simon—that's his name, Simon—is from England! He was born in the north country, but he spent most of his life in London. He's here doing some sort of business. I helped him pick out a scarf, a nice deep blue one with a muted paisley print—it's really, really lovely—and he was so grateful for the help he asked me out to dinner." She turned back to the stove and resumed stirring the potatoes.

"Do you mean to tell me you allowed yourself to be picked up in a department store?"

"Yes!" she exclaimed with delight.

"And you're going out to dinner with him? Are you crazy? You hardly know anything about him! He could be an axe murderer!"

"Darling, he's British."

"So was Crippen!"

"Gawn!" she said, taking a playful swipe at the air. "Simon was a proper gentleman. He's ever so nice."

"Gawn?" I turned to Peter "I don't believe this! Ten minutes with another Englishman and she turns into Eliza Doolittle!"

"Well, I think it's great," said Peter. "But you didn't need to cook dinner for us. We could've fended for ourselves."

"Nonsense! I enjoy doing it. But if you wouldn't mind, I would appreciate it if you'd finish it up so I can get ready for my date. He should be here soon. Now, there's a lovely bit of beef in the oven, and it should come out in about twenty minutes. The potatoes will be done about the same time. There are salads in the refrigerator."

She bustled toward the doorway, pausing just long enough to pinch my cheek. "Do try not to look quite so much like a blowfish, dear."

With this she scurried through the house and up the stairs.

"Oh, this is great," I said once she was gone. "I spend all day being brow beaten by the Beast of Belsen, and Mother's dating Jack the Ripper."

"She's a level-headed woman. You don't have anything to worry about."

I looked at him as if he'd lost his mind. "This is *my* mother we're talking about, right? The woman who once set fire to a building that we were in to try to rescue us?"

He shrugged. "It worked."

I looked heavenward for help. "That was only one example of her little antics! Do you want to hear the whole list?"

Peter stared at me in silence. "Honey, what's wrong?"

"Nothing!"

"Of course there is. You know your mother can take care of herself. What's going on with you? You seem so unhappy lately. I don't mean just about your mother and this volunteer thing. There must be more to it."

There's something inherently comforting about being known too well. It brings a shorthand quality to your relationship that even at the worst of times can make you feel that everything will be all right. I suddenly felt like crying, and Peter must've sensed it, because he slipped his arms around me. I buried my face in his shoulder.

"I feel so worthless!"

"Why?" he said, stroking my hair.

"I've practically ruined my business. . . ."

"No you haven't."

"Yes I have. And it's my own damn fault!"

"That's silly," he said quietly. "You could build it back up in a minute if you wanted to, and you know it. You're a damn good artist. That can't be all that's bothering you."

I swallowed. "We haven't heard from Nelson for months."

Agent Lawrence Nelson was our boss from the CIA on our occasional forays into the world of espionage.

"I see," Peter said with a smile in his voice. "You know, I'd hate to think you were this unhappy because it's been so long since our lives have been in danger."

I laughed halfheartedly. "You don't understand. You're gone all day. You have something to do. I'm just sitting around here like a worthless lump of nothing waiting for the phone to ring."

"So all of this is work-related?"

"I guess. I feel like a housewife who's been told all she's good for is volunteer work. Nobody needs me."

Peter pushed me back slightly so that he could look into my eyes. "*I* need you."

The sincerity with which he said this knocked a couple of pegs out of my self-pity.

"No, you don't," I replied, hoping he'd say it again.

"Oh, yes I do." He gathered me back into his arms. "If you weren't around, I don't think I could go on living. You're what keeps my heart beating."

I pulled back and looked at him. The corner of my mouth curled. "That is the soppiest thing you've ever said to me!"

He laughed. "That doesn't make it any less true."

Our lips came together and for a few moments all of the cares I'd been feeling disappeared. We were interrupted when Mother called from the top of the stairs:

"Alex! I think I smell something burning."

"Don't worry, Mother," I called back. "It's just me!"

The lovely bit of beef Mother planned for our dinner did get a little singed while Peter and I engaged in a spontaneous spot of necking. But when we got around to having dinner, it was pretty good nonetheless. We were clearing the table when the doorbell rang.

"Would you get that, darling?" Mother's voice floated down from the second floor. "I'm not quite ready yet."

I opened the door and was faced with an absolutely striking man of around my mother's age. His hair was jet black and flecked with bluish gray at the temples. His skin was rather light, and his eyes were light blue. He wore an expensive-looking three-piece suit.

"Hello," he said in a deep, pleasing voice. "My name is Simon Tivoli. Does Jean Reynolds live here?"

"Yes," I replied. "Please, come in. Mother will be down in a minute. I'm Alex, her son."

He stepped in and I closed the door behind him.

10

"I'm very pleased to meet you," he said as he reached out and gave me a firm handshake.

When I disengaged myself, I said, "And this is my husband, Peter."

Tivoli reached for Peter's hand, but stopped short. "Oh? Oh!" He smiled broadly and gave Peter's hand a hearty shake. "You must forgive me if I sounded surprised. Your mother didn't mention that you were a Nancy boy."

"It seldom comes up at the first meeting," I replied.

"Oh! I'm so sorry!" He looked properly abashed. "I've really put my foot in it. My dad used to say 'Nancy boy,' but he did it quite nicely. I've never thought much about it. It is a term you fellows find offensive?"

"Only when it's preceded by 'kill the fucking,' " said Peter.

Without a hint of sarcasm, Tivoli said, "You're really very gracious. This is my first visit to the States, you know, and ever since I arrived I've felt rather like I'm tripping over myself. D'you know what I mean?"

"Yes," I said. "How long will you be in town?"

"About a fortnight, altogether," he replied amiably. "I've already been a week. My company sent me over."

"What company would that be?"

Peter applied some not too gentle pressure to my left shoulder blade.

"Oh, it's just a computer company. Nothing you'd ever have heard of. The main office is in London, and they've sent me here to the American branch for some seminars."

"Sounds interesting."

" 'Tisn't really," he said with a smack of his lips. "But it got me a trip to a place I've never seen. The only thing really interesting that's happened to me so far was meeting your mum. It's rather lonely, you know, being in a country where you don't know anybody. It was awfully nice to run into someone from England. It made me feel right at home."

"Is that you, Simon?" said Mother as she came down the stairs. She was wearing a long pearl dress with a white, loose-knit

11

shawl wrapped around her shoulders. She didn't exactly look dressed for the ball, but with her natural beauty and bearing, she had about the same effect as the transformed Audrey Hepburn descending the staircase in *My Fair Lady*.

"It's so nice to see you again," she said, extending her hand. He lifted it to his lips and kissed it lightly.

"I suddenly feel like her wicked stepsister," I whispered to Peter, who responded by jabbing his elbow into my ribs.

"I've made reservations at a restaurant called Mon Petit. I'm afraid I don't know anything about it, but one of the fellows at my company says that it's very good."

"I'm sure it will be lovely."

"Don't you mean loverly?" I said under my breath. Peter gave me another jab.

Tivoli turned to Peter and me. "You'll excuse us, won't you? We don't want to be late."

He smoothly maneuvered Mother to the door, where she paused long enough to say, "Have a nice evening, boys." As the door closed, she added, "Don't wait up."

After a lengthy silence, Peter said, "Well, he seems nice enough."

"Yes, he does," I replied. "I hate him."

I didn't purposely wait up for Mother—I was kept awake by the sausage-curled, pasty-faced image of Bette Davis standing beside the bed, staring down at me with a bright red smile painted on her face and saying, "Butcha *are* a failure, Blanche! Ya' are!"

Although he was asleep, Peter seemed dimly aware of my wakefulness. He rolled over on his side and stretched a comforting arm across my chest. Tears formed in my eyes. He had told me that he needed me, which did make me feel better (even though I'd already known it), but at the same time it added a little pressure. There's nothing like being deeply in love for making you want to succeed in life, not just for yourself but for your spouse. It wasn't so much that I wanted Peter to be proud of me—he already was. It was that I wanted his pride to be justified.

It seemed like I'd been lying awake in the dark for several years before I finally heard the sound of the front door opening and closing. I glanced at the clock on our bedside table. It was 1:57. There was a jaunty quality in Mother's step as she came up the stairs, and she was humming when she passed our door. So she'd had a good time. I knew if I contemplated how much of a good time I'd never get to sleep. I decided to dwell instead on the fact that she'd arrived home safe and sound, and cast aside any question of why a simple dinner at a French restaurant had taken over six hours.

TWO

When I awoke the next morning I was feeling so cranky from the lack of sleep that I didn't even get my usual warm fuzzy feeling from watching Peter get dressed for work. Sure, I still registered how beautiful he is and how lucky I am to have him, but that was about all.

The TV at the foot of the bed was tuned to a local morning news program on which a broad-mouthed white-bread anchor was interviewing The Candidate of the People, Charlie Clarke. Clarke and his wife, Wendy, sat close together on the opposite side of a small round table from the anchor.

"I'm sure you know," said the anchor, "that with your pro-gay, pro-choice stance you've earned the wrath of the religious right as well as some members of your own party."

"Yes," Clarke replied with a coy smile that implied that this was a joke that we were all in on. "They need to demonize someone. In this election they've chosen me."

"And yet, despite your openly liberal views, you have a very large following among conservatives. What do you attribute that to?"

Clarke shrugged. "Well, I like to think it's because I'm basically an honest person. People may not agree with my positions on the issues, but at least they know what my positions *are*, and I think they find that refreshing. Everybody's sick of equivocating politicians." He managed to say this all with an air of self-effacement that made him seem embarrassed to be forced into the position of singing his own praises.

"Are you aware that some of your detractors accuse you of being gay?" the anchor asked.

I was astonished by the brashness of the question, but Clarke was not. In fact, he was so unfazed that I suspected he might have suggested the question himself before the interview had begun.

"I don't know that having someone say that you're gay should be considered an accusation," the candidate replied as he gently laid a hand over his wife's.

Oh, good move, I thought.

The anchor smiled toothily. "All right, but does it bother you when your opponents say that?"

"No. First of all, because there's nothing wrong with being gay. Second of all, I think it's a sign of how desperate my opponents are."

"What do you mean?"

"Well, that's the type of 'accusation' that's unanswerable. The object of spreading rumors of that sort is to put you in the position of not being able to say anything. If you deny it, then half of the population thinks you're lying, and the other half is offended because a denial makes it sound like you're saying there's something wrong with homosexuality. My opponents know that I have a strong following in the gay community, and they'd like nothing better than to get me to lose that support. But I'm not going to give in to that."

"He's really good," said Peter, who had crossed to the bed and now stood beside me, knotting his tie.

"I know. I'm sure he has answers already prepared for any possible question, but he really does make it sound like he's answering off the cuff, doesn't he? I don't know whether or not we should find that scary."

Peter looked down at me with a wry smile. "Are you saying that the fact that he seems honest should worry us?"

After a beat I said, "Well, of course it sounds paranoid when you put it like that!"

Peter laughed and I took hold of his tie and gently pulled him down to me. What started out as a peck quickly turned into something deeper.

"Hey," he said, pausing for a breath, "this is a school day."

"I know, I know." I heaved a sigh.

We went downstairs together and found Mother making breakfast. She was clad in a fire-engine-red kimono that had a gold dragon embroidered on the back. It was one of the several silk gowns she'd brought back from the trip she'd taken to Japan to celebrate my father's death. Well, not his death, but the inheritance. She was "la la"-ing a disjointed tune as she scrambled some eggs. Duffy, the Westie we inherited, sat nearby looking up at her and with his tail wagging frantically. Apparently he thought the excessive good humor might send a few tidbits his way, as if he wasn't spoiled enough.

"Good morning, darlings!" Mother said when she saw us.

"Morning," Peter replied with a grin.

"Mother," I said, "please don't take this the wrong way, but I think I prefer it when you're not quite so happy."

She narrowed her eyes and "la la"-ed pointedly in my direction.

"What time did you get in?" Peter asked innocently as he poured out some orange juice.

"Oh, around two o'clock."

"One fifty-seven," I answered simultaneously. Both Peter and Mother turned and looked at me with raised eyebrows. I blushed. "That's the trouble with having a digital clock."

"We had such a lovely time!" said Mother as she placed a plate of buttered toast on the table. "We had a beautiful dinner at Mon Petit, and then Simon took me dancing."

"Dancing? Where?" I asked.

"At the Fairview."

I set my juice glass down with a slight thump. "That's a hotel, isn't it?"

"I do believe it is," she replied with an unreadable smile.

I looked to Peter for support which was not forthcoming. He seemed to be having a very difficult time keeping himself from laughing. I frowned at him before looking away.

"Is that the hotel where he's staying?"

"Heavens no! That's far too expensive for a company junket. He's staying at the River Edge Motel." She came back to the table carrying a pan from which she began dishing out the eggs.

"Really? Then how did he know there was dancing at the Fairview? He knows an awful lot about Chicago for someone who's only been here for a week."

She tapped the serving spoon against my plate. "Everyone knows there's dancing there. It's listed in the weekend papers. Honestly, Alex, you're acting like you're *my* mother rather than the other way 'round!"

"I'm sorry," I said, somewhat abashed. Mother doesn't often take that tone with me. Then again, I like to think I seldom give her reason to. "I didn't sleep well last night."

"Ah," she said sympathetically. "Well, you'll be relieved to know that Simon and I had dinner, went dancing, and then he brought me home. And for all that the only thing he received in return was a very chaste kiss."

"Where?"

"On the stoop," she said flatly. "I had a marvelous time, and Simon was a perfect gentleman all evening."

"I'm glad to hear it."

She pursed her lips and her eyes took on the playful quality that always means trouble.

"Then again, maybe tonight will be different," she said with a half-smile as she took the pan back to the sink.

After the rather inauspicious start, I wasn't surprised that my day went downhill the minute I got to Clarke's office. My heart sank when I walked in the door and found the walls lined ceiling to floor with newly delivered cartons of fliers and envelopes.

"Looks like another bright day in the drudge mine," said Kerry Fiedler, a lanky, dark-haired volunteer, as he hung his coat next to mine on the rack.

"Maybe today will be better," I replied with mock enthusiasm. "maybe today I'll get to collate."

It wasn't until then that I noticed the lack of activity in the office. Several of the volunteers were sitting around drinking coffee and chatting, only interrupting themselves to answer the occasional phone call.

"What's going on?" I asked Dave as I took a seat at the table where we'd been working the day before.

"Jody's not here yet."

My jaw dropped. "What? It's after nine o'clock!"

"I know. We figure she must be dead. I don't think she's ever gotten here later than eight."

"Mary's not here either?"

Dave shook his head.

"Who opened the office, then?"

"Annie Watson. She's a good friend of Jody and Mary. She has a key in case the two of them can't make it. Not that anybody ever thought that would happen."

"Didn't they tell Annie why they were going to be late?" I asked.

He shook his head again. "Nope. They didn't call anybody. The place was locked when Annie got here, so she just opened up."

"Hm." I took a sip of coffee, then Dave and I continued our envelope-stuffing assignment of the previous day while speculating on the whereabouts of our fearsome leader.

Our conjecture was brought to an abrupt halt about twenty minutes later when Jody Linn-Hadden burst through the front door, stopped, and slowly surveyed the room with a particularly nasty scowl on her face. She looked like a bargain-basement Brunhilde on the verge of waging war.

Mary followed closely on her heels, but Jody had stopped so suddenly upon entering that Mary was left propping the door open with her body and looking vacantly at Jody's back as if she were afraid of what was about to happen, and anxious for it to be over.

"Well!" Jody boomed. "Did you all see Charlie Clarke on the *A.M. Show* this morning?"

There was a stunned silence. We'd all been expecting some sort of tirade about our work performance, or some new campaign atrocity perpetrated by one of Clarke's opponents. To have such an innocuous question yelled in your direction was like having Muzak blared at you.

"Well, did you?" she demanded when nobody answered.

A few of the volunteers tentatively murmured "Yes."

"He acquitted himself really well, didn't he!" she continued as she walked slowly through the room between the tables. "That guy that was interviewing him, he tried to trip up our Charlie, but Charlie was too quick for him!"

Though what she was saying was inherently positive, her tone of voice made every word sound like a scathing accusation.

"I suddenly feel like I'm in *High Noon*," I whispered to Dave, who made the mistake of laughing.

Jody stopped in her tracks by our table and reared back in a way reminiscent of Maleficent changing into the dragon in *Sleeping Beauty*.

"You think something's funny? You find something funny about this, little man?"

"I . . . I . . ." Dave looked stricken. His eyes became saucers and his skin paled.

"You pissant little . . . little . . ." She faltered short of an epithet, apparently fighting to keep from crossing a line. "I know your kind and you make me sick! The whole damn world's some big, funny joke to you! Nothing is serious! While your own people are being murdered, you just flit through your worthless life laughing at everything and never caring about anything! You don't make a damn bit of difference to this world!"

"Hey, now wait a minute, Jody," I said, rising from my chair. It was one thing for her to behave like a sergeant in the Gestapo to the volunteers, it was another thing to abuse them. "There's no need for that."

"And you!" she yelled, turning on me. "You're another funny man, aren't you! You think everything's funny! Well I'm going to tell you something. . . ." She leaned across the table, her reddened face stopping about six inches from mine. I'm embarrassed to admit that I recoiled. "I'm going to tell you something, Mr. Funny Man! I don't think it's fucking funny!"

"What on earth are you talking about?" I asked.

Mary had followed Jody into the office. Just as Jody was about to let me have it—verbally, I mean—Mary placed her hands lightly on Jody's shoulders and said, "Please, don't . . ."

Jody continued to glare at me for a moment, then shook herself free of her partner and stormed into the back room, slamming the door behind her.

"What the hell was that all about?" I said to Mary.

Mary Linn-Hadden was nothing like her partner. She was nondescript almost to the point of nonexistence. I didn't think she'd been bullied into submission through her relationship with Jody, I thought it went deeper than that. Mary had the air of someone who'd learned at an early age that the world was too big for her, and had surrendered rather than fight.

She turned her perpetually doelike eyes to me, brushed her auburn locks back over her shoulder, and said, "We've had a little trouble this morning."

"Oh. I'm sorry. I didn't mean to—"

"Not me and Jody. It was . . . well . . . it was something else. I really can't say."

She looked down at the floor, then without another word went to the back of the room and disappeared into her cubicle.

There had been a shocked silence during Jody's outburst, and now that it was over the volunteers slowly started to resume their work, although with a lot less enthusiasm or discussion than there had been a few minutes earlier.

I was about to sit back down when I glanced at Dave. He'd

gone back to stuffing envelopes, but looked as if he were fighting to hold back tears. This really got to me. There's nothing sadder than a weepy faggot. I decided that for the sake of office harmony, I'd better try to find out what was going on. As I approached the door to the back room it crossed my mind that Peter might be right about my enjoying putting my life in danger. Mary's cubicle was right by the door, and her eyes were absolutely terror-stricken when she saw me put my hand on the knob.

"I wouldn't," she said in a choked whisper.

"It's all right. I've had my shots."

I opened the door and stepped through, closing it behind me. Although the back room had been done up as offices, it still retained its dank, basementlike smell. On the back wall there were two small, barred windows so caked with dirt that they didn't admit much light. The area to the right had been walled off to form a private office for the candidate, and the open area into which I had walked served as the work space for John Schuler, Clarke's campaign manager.

Jody was sitting in Schuler's chair, staring straight ahead as if she were angry at the air, and drumming her fingers. She hadn't bothered to take off her coat.

"What do you want?" she barked without looking at me.

"What's the matter?" I asked, knowing full well that I was intruding and the likelihood of her answering me was very limited.

"What's it to you?"

"Do you have any idea how bad you made Dave feel, yelling at him in front of everyone like that?"

"What do I care!"

"Jody, we're volunteers. You can't abuse volunteers and expect them to stay on. We could go work in an office somewhere and get paid to be abused."

"Don't you have work to do? I saw a lot of work out there!"

I sighed. "Are you going to keep snapping at me like a little bull dy—" In the heat of anger I caught myself in the middle of a Freudian slip. I quickly correctly myself. "—bulldog, or are you going to tell me what's wrong?"

"Why the fuck should I tell you?"

"I might be able to help."

"Help? Huh!" She glared in my direction, and the sneer on her face was perfectly frightful.

"Look, I know I don't know you very well, but I would like to help if there's anything I can do. I'm assuming that whatever it is isn't personal."

"Oh, it's personal all right!"

"But Mary said—"

"That bastard *made* it personal!"

"Who are you talking about?"

"When I get ahold of him, I swear to God I'm gonna deep fry his balls and eat them for breakfast!"

Aside from the vividly unpleasant visual image this conjured up of a rather distorted steak-and-kidney pie, I was completely puzzled. The only person she'd mentioned since walking in the front door was Charlie Clarke, and I found it hard to believe she was talking about him now—although it's certainly not uncommon for a person's feelings to swing wildly when a hero gets knocked from his perch. It occurred to me that as militant as Jody was, Clarke might have said something on that morning program that had rung the death knell for her affections. Perhaps in his comments about homosexuality he'd somehow managed to hit on the one word or phrase that would turn her against him.

"I still don't know who you're talking about. Do you mean Clarke?"

"No, you idiot!" she yelled. "Not Clarke! This bastard!" She pulled an audio cassette out of her pocket and slapped it angrily on the desk. She tapped her rigid index finger against it as she continued. "It's not enough that those bastards call here every day, making their threats! Now they're calling me at home!"

"You're kidding," I said blankly. "Someone's calling you at home and threatening you?"

"Didn't I just say that? I got him on this tape! I can tape calls with my answering machine. The minute I heard the voice, I hit the button!"

22

"It was a man?"

"He tried to disguise his voice, but it sure as hell was!"

"What did he say?"

She let out a snort, then delivered what I imagined was a verbatim recital of what the caller had said. According to Jody, his mildest suggestion was that she use gasoline for a douche and let him strike the match. As she related this, she turned the tape around and around in her hands all the while.

"Jody, that's disgusting. I'm sorry that happened to you."

"Not as sorry as that asshole is going to be if I get my hands on him!"

"Did you call the police?"

"No, I called that Will Henry guy from the FBI. He's the one we're supposed to turn over all the threats to. When Clarke became a viable candidate, he became a national problem, not just a local one."

She slapped the tape back on top of the desk. She looked like it was taking all her willpower to keep from crushing it with her fist.

"The threats that come into this office, they're aimed at Charlie, and they're all just nuts. There isn't any way they can harm him. But this!" Again she angrily tapped the tape. "This was directed at *me!*"

I watched her for a moment, then said quietly, "You're afraid, aren't you?"

"Wouldn't you be?" she yelled defensively. "Wouldn't you be if you had this filth on your phone?"

"Yeah. I would be."

Once I'd realized that fear was the problem the way she was acting made more sense, and in a way I felt sorry for her. Like a lot of strong people, Jody liked to think of herself as invulnerable and completely in control. The fact that something had scared her made her furious, not just at the perpetrator, but at herself.

I don't know what I'd hoped to achieve by going back there to talk to her, but at least getting her to open up about it seemed to have relaxed her a bit.

"Look," I said, "if there's anything I can do for you, all you have to do is let me know."

"There's something you can do all right," she replied.

"What's that?"

"Get back out there and finish stuffing those damn envelopes! We've got to get them out before the primary!"

She almost smiled when she said it.

When I went back out into the work area, I wasn't surprised to find that Dave had gone. Joe Gardner, another of the volunteers, told me that a couple of minutes after I'd gone into the back room, Dave got up, retrieved his coat and walked out of the office without a word.

"He didn't say anything?" I asked.

Joe shook his head. "No. He didn't even look at anybody. I think he was too humiliated."

"He doesn't have any reason to feel that way."

Joe pursed his lips for a moment, then leaned into me and whispered. "I think he was embarrassed because she scared him."

"Really?"

"Yeah. You know the type." He eyed me significantly, then added a shrug as if to say, "What can you do?" as he went back to the phones.

I returned to my job, the tedium of which was relieved somewhat by my contemplating that fact that fear seemed to be contagious. The nasty piece of work who had made the obscene phone call to Jody was operating out of fear: fear of the unknown, fear of what he couldn't understand. Fearful bigotry. In that fear he lashed out at Jody and infected her, and she, in turn, infected Dave. I wondered who would be next.

Later that morning there was an influx of volunteers, mostly from the gay community. Jody must've exerted all the force of her evil powers to get people in that day to make a good showing for Clarke, who was in town and scheduled to spend a minuscule part of the day at the Chicago headquarters (most of his time would be spent meeting with civic groups, courting other politicians, and doing most of the other things that candidates do when they want to get elected).

In addition to Jody's efforts, the sudden surge in staff was also due to the community's genuine concern about getting a homo-friendly candidate in office, and to their desire to get a glimpse of the man who many took to be our savior.

It was just after eleven o'clock when the Great Man himself arrived, with John Schuler in tow. They were followed by an entourage that seemed to circle him like the debris on the edge of a tornado.

The experience of seeing Charlie Clarke in person was rather like meeting any celebrity in the flesh: There was something surreal about it, as if something that doesn't really exist has just stepped into the real world. Clarke was slightly shorter than he appeared on television, and a good deal better-looking. I don't like to disparage my own people, but I'd be willing to bet that the latter was the main reason for a good deal of the gay following. And he managed to be handsome without being extraordinary. He didn't look like he had an array of makeup artists and hair stylists following him around; it just seemed to come naturally to him. He had very dark hair which he wore slicked back, friendly brown eyes, and a smile that made you feel as if you were being undressed in the nicest possible way.

"Hello, everybody!" he cried cordially as he walked through the door. He made his way through the room, shaking hands and thanking people for their work. I had to hand it to him. He sounded pretty sincere for someone who couldn't possibly have any idea exactly what work we were doing. He made a special point of waving a greeting at the volunteers who weren't close enough to physically touch him, making it clear that nobody was forgotten when it came to his gratitude.

It took less than two minutes for Clarke to make it across the length of the room. When he and Schuler disappeared into the back room, they were followed by Jody and Mary. I suppose they were going to report on the progress of our work. The rest of us were left feeling that if we weren't in the inner sanctum, at least we had touched the Hem of the Holy. There was just no denying that Charles "Charlie" Clarke had *presence.*

While he was in his makeshift office, the entourage stood around the now severely congested room making small talk with each other and basically looking bored and confused, as if once Clarke was out of sight, they didn't quite know why they were there.

They barely had time to wonder, though. Less than fifteen minutes later Clarke and Schuler emerged from the back and the whole parade was performed in reverse. He waved and called out general thank-yous as he made his way toward the door, this time preceded by the human debris.

"Isn't he wonderful?" said Mickey Downs, one of the other volunteers, once our leader had gone. "I would do him in a minute!"

I allowed my forehead to drop onto the table with a loud thunk.

While the dust was settling I noticed Jody standing nearby, her arms folded across her chest and an oddly twisted smile on her face.

"You don't look happy with your hero," I said.

She scowled down at me. She might have been Clarke's most ardent admirer, but Jody wasn't the type of woman who'd appreciate being thought of in terms of hero worship, no matter what the object. "Of course I'm happy. Charlie just . . . He was going to spend more time here, but had to run because of that moron Schuler."

"Why? What did he do?"

"He forgot about a radio interview Charlie's supposed to do in a half an hour. He forgot to put it on the schedule. If I hadn't reminded him of it, he would've missed it, and that would've made him look bad. That Schuler is such a fuck-up!" She gave a dry spit and went back to her cubicle.

After the furor died away there was a bit of a letdown, but that was to be expected. When you've just had a brush with greatness, it's hard to go back to the mundane task of folding letters and answering phones. A few of the volunteers disappeared after the event, but most stayed to help with the work. With some new faces on hand, the slight valley was followed by a period of work that was really quite congenial.

At about one o'clock the mail carrier, a fortyish African-

American gentleman, arrived with a sack of mail which Mary Linn-Hadden received in her cubicle. On his way out of the office, he grumbled amiably about how light his load used to be before Clarke's office moved into the neighborhood.

A few minutes later the playful chatter of the volunteers was brought to an abrupt halt by a blood curdling scream from Mary's cubicle.

Jody was out of her own cubicle in a shot and crossed the narrow aisle to her partner's so quickly I almost didn't see her.

Several of us ran back to see what was wrong, but I managed to reach the doorway first. Mary was in Jody's arms, weeping hysterically while Jody tried to simultaneously comfort her and find out what was wrong.

"Shhh . . . shhh . . ." Jody said more gently than I thought possible for her. "Just tell me what happened."

"There! There!" Mary exclaimed, pointing a shaking finger at the padded envelope that was lying on the top of the pile on her desk.

Jody started to move toward the package, but Mary clung to her more tightly. Jody shot a glance at me. I came into the cubicle and circled the desk, then carefully picked up the envelope by the edges. Mary had used the pull-string to tear open one side of the package, so all I had to do was press the sides to get the slit to flex open. When I saw what was inside, my hands jerked involuntarily, and I dropped it. The contents spilled out onto the desk.

It was an enormous dead rat.

Mickey, Joe, and a couple of the other guys were crowded in the doorway, and when the contents were revealed they fell back from it like ripples radiating away from a pebble dropped in a pond. Shawn Stillman was visible from the nose up as he peered over the cubicle's short wall. His forehead creased sharply when he saw what was in the package.

"Now *that's* gross!" said Mickey.

An hour later a man I'd never seen before walked into the office. He was tall with dark hair parted on the left, a hard line for a mouth, and skin the color of sand. He was wearing a two-piece navy blue suit and a red and blue striped tie. He looked like a graduate of Moody Bible Institute. I recognized him immediately as a Fed. Although he passed through the room without looking left or right, I got the feeling he was checking everything out. He went directly into Jody's cubicle. I was a little disappointed that he didn't show any sign of recognizing me as a fellow agent, but I don't know what I could expect. I guess I thought maybe there was a government equivalent of gaydar, and our eyes would meet and he would think, "Oh, yeah, you're one." But he didn't even look at me.

"It's about time you got here," I heard Jody exclaim angrily.

Her chair slammed against the none-too-stable wall of her cubicle, then she showed the Fed into the back room. He came out a few minutes later with a bag that I assumed carried the envelope with its disgusting contents. I suppose he had the tape in one of his pockets.

Jody followed him halfway out, and once he was gone she started back for her desk.

"Was that the FBI agent you were telling me about?" I asked quietly as she passed by my table.

Jody nodded. "Will Henry. And I'll bet he doesn't do a fucking thing!"

I clucked sympathetically as she walked away.

When Peter picked me up later that day, he was surprised to find me bubbling with excitement. Well, maybe not bubbling, but at least excited enough that I'd been partially lifted out of my depression.

"We were visited by various forms of vermin today," I said. "A politician, a Fed, and a rat."

"Who was the rat?" Peter asked with a laugh.

"It was a *rat!*"

He stopped in his tracks. "You mean an actual rat?"

"Uh-huh."

"Oh my God!"

"You ain't heard nothin' yet!" As we walked home I filled him in on the events of the day.

"This doesn't sound good to me," said Peter, whose expression had grown more concerned as he listened to my story. "Doesn't it seem like whatever's going on is escalating?"

"Well, the rat was a change, but we get threatening calls every day. Of course, usually they just threaten to blow us up. They don't normally personalize it like they did for Jody. You might be right, though. This is the first day I've actually seen a Fed on the premises. I think he came to pick up the evidence."

"You've never seen him before?"

"No. The calls are so frequent that Jody just calls them in to the Feds after they happen."

"But with this rat and everything, it does seem like it's getting worse. It makes you wonder just how much worse it can get before the election is over."

"And we're not even at the primary yet," I smiled. "You know, if you're really, really worried, I can give up my volunteer work. It'll really tear me up, you know, to not be able to help in such a worthy cause, but for you I'd do anything."

"Oh, I wouldn't think of taking you away from work you love so much," he replied wryly.

When we got home we found a note from Mother waiting for us on the kitchen counter:

Darlings—Simon is taking me out for dinner and to a film. I probably won't be home till late. I've thrown together a shepherd's pie for your dinner. It only wants heating.

I smiled when I read it. For Mother, throwing together a shepherd's pie meant mashed potatoes made from scratch, arranged neatly in a crust of meat and decorated with fork-made tracks. Not to mention the fresh boiled vegetables that would be at its center. Mother has a Disneyesque effect on a kitchen. She snaps her fingers and ingredients dance into bowls of their own accord, mix themselves together, throw themselves in the oven and emerge fully cooked. Watching her prepare a meal is a bit like watching the tidying-the-nursery scene in *Mary Poppins*.

"I can't believe she's going out with that guy again," I said as I crumpled the note and tossed it in the dustbin.

With a broad smile on his face, Peter took me in his arms, intertwining his fingers at the small of my back. "Sweetheart, last night we had the place to ourselves, and you spent the entire evening worrying about your mother. We have the place to ourselves again. Now, how would you like to spend the evening?"

His left hand traced its way up my spine, then caressed the back of my head as he pulled me toward him. Our lips locked in a kiss deep enough to send sparks radiating through me.

When our lips parted, I made a show of thinking it over, then said, "I suppose worrying is a waste of time."

There's nothing like losing yourself in someone else to really bring you back to yourself. Peter and I had been together long enough to know every nook and cranny of each other's bodies, but that only made reexploring them more meaningful. At times our lovemaking is so much fun that we're as likely to dissolve into laughter as we are to climax, but that evening there was a tenderness to it that made me remember—as if I could ever forget—why I love my husband so much. The gentle passion with which he kissed me as he stroked my naked skin told me, more than any words could have, how completely my love was reciprocated. For the first time in days I felt like I mattered.

When we finished we laid there together, our bodies intertwined, in sort of a pink haze that shielded us from any potential troubles. There was only Peter and me.

I don't know how late Mother got home.

THREE

When I awoke on Saturday morning Peter's arms were wrapped around me. I was still experiencing enough of an after-glow that for a time I was blissfully unaware of the troubles or depression I'd been feeling in recent days. I gently dislodged myself from his embrace, propped myself on one elbow, and watched him sleep. There's a dreamy sensuality about him when he's asleep. His hair was tousled attractively and one wrist was drawn across his forehead so that he looked like one of those underwear ads with perfect models sprawled out on rocks by the ocean.

I gently stroked the hair that trails down from his chest to his stomach. There was movement beneath his eyelids, and a lazy smile spread across his face before he opened his eyes.

"Good morning," I said.

"Good morning. What time is it?"

"A little after eight."

He groaned. "Oh, let me go back to sleep."

"Not a chance. We've got work to do."

"I'm off today."

I smiled and shook my head. "From Farrahut's, maybe, but *not* from the Charlie Clarke campaign."

He groaned more loudly and turned over on his side. "I just want to sleep."

"Hmm. Should I remind you about how important it is to get involved, or that Charlie Clarke is a vital candidate and the best thing to happen to the gay community since The Puppy Episode?"

He craned his head around and squinted at me over his shoulder. "You're enjoying this, aren't you?"

"Ho, ho, you bet I am!"

I gave his naked butt a slap and he grabbed my arm and pulled me down to him.

When we came into the kitchen Mother was making breakfast and softly singing "I Could Have Danced All Night." I know I'm in trouble when she reverts to Lerner and Lowe. She was happy. Too happy, in a Raymond Chandler wives-eyeing-their-husbands'-necks kind of way. She didn't offer any explanation, and I didn't ask since I figured anything she said would make me want to lock her in her room.

Duffy sat in the corner, next to his doggie bed rather than in it, staring up at her. For once his expression was quizzical without being adoring. There isn't a dog on earth that can look as thoroughly confused as a Westie. He blinked occasionally, as if he were beginning to wonder whether or not his mistress had slipped a biscuit.

We carried on with a superficial conversation during breakfast, while Mother maintained that irritating glow. When I worked up the courage to ask how her date had gone, she looked across the table at me with insufferable innocence and said, "I enjoyed the movie." I didn't even want to begin to think what she meant by that.

Peter and I arrived at campaign headquarters at about nine-thirty and set to work at the endless envelope stuffing. There were a lot more volunteers than usual, probably because it was the weekend and more were available. But despite the general good humor, the mood was somewhat subdued. Details of the personal threat made to Jody had leaked out, and the rat was common knowledge. Those who hadn't been there to witness the event had certainly been told about it. There was a tentativeness about the way everyone was working, as if we were all wondering from which can of peanut brittle the next coil snake would leap.

Everyone bridled when the mail carrier brought in his delivery. Jody emerged from her cubicle for the first time that morning and ordered him to deposit it in her space rather than Mary's, adding that that would be the procedure from then on. She seemed angrier than she had the day before. There would be no repeat of the former incident.

Clarke came into the office at about eleven o'clock, this time without the entourage. He was wearing crisply pressed chinos and a plaid shirt, and Peter rolled his eyes at my whispered suggestion that the look would be more effective if it wasn't quite so obviously "Man of the People."

He passed through the workers, creating the usual buzz but only tossing a couple of mild hellos at us before disappearing into the back.

"What was that thing attached to his hip?" Peter asked.

"What? Oh! That was John Schuler, his campaign manager."

"Hmm. He sticks any more closely to Clarke's back and those gay rumors are going to get worse."

I smiled.

"What?"

"Nothing. It's just for a few days there I thought I'd lost you. It's nice to have you back."

He handed me an envelope. "Stuff it, honey."

Not long after the candidate arrived, Jody knocked on the door of the back room and was promptly admitted. She was gone for quite a while, and during that interval I glanced over at the phones a couple of times and caught Shawn Stillman watching the door while answering his calls. He seemed inordinately interested in Jody's absence. You would've thought she was a teacher seeing the high school principal about his low test scores. When she finally reemerged, Shawn quickly looked away and acted as if he'd never been distracted from his work. Jody then did her usual swing through the room to see that all the volunteers were keeping busy.

"That was a long meeting," I said when she stopped by our table.

"Huh?" she replied absently as she scanned the piles of fliers.

"With Clarke."

"I wasn't with Clarke, I was with Schuler."

I was genuinely surprised her tone. "Is everything all right?"

"Of course it is!" she snapped. "He just wanted to know about all the crap that's been happening. And he told me he appreciates everything we're putting up with. . . . I mean, everything we're doing."

She stumbled slightly on the word *appreciates,* which made me wonder if he had appreciated it quite as much as she thought he should.

"You sound like you don't like him."

"Schuler? He doesn't know what he's doing. He was an accountant, for chrissakes. What does he know about running a campaign?"

"Then how did he get the job?"

She snorted disdainfully. "He's had his nose up Clarke's ass for years. They've been friends since college. Schuler's one of those guys who hangs onto people just in case they might go somewhere some time. He lucked out with Charlie."

I shrugged. "It sounds to me like Clarke's a good friend."

"Charlie's a great candidate but he's a soft touch. That's going to cost him someday. Schuler's not qualified for that job. He's . . . he's just not."

"Well, just as a point of interest," I said with an alarming lack of caution, "how exactly are you qualified to be office manager of a political campaign?"

Jody turned deep red. "I have passion for something other than myself!" She went back to her cubicle without another word.

Clarke and Schuler left about an hour later. I laughed when the door closed after them. Peter was right. Schuler kept so close at

Clarke's heels that he was giving new meaning to the phrase "dogging his tail."

The low point of the day came just after noon, when Mother arrived unexpectedly with Simon Tivoli in tow.

"What are you doing here?" I asked as nicely as I could.

"I'm showing Simon around," Mother said.

I turned to him. "Aren't you supposed to be at a seminar?"

"Oh, I'm fluffing off today," he replied cheerily. "I suppose I could be sitting in a stuffy room listening to stuffy lectures, but I'm having much too much fun with your mother."

I waited a beat, then said, "There's got to be a better way of putting that."

"I told Simon where you were working," said Mother, "and he wanted to see it."

"I've never seen a campaign headquarters before. I thought it would be exciting."

"Well, here it is," I said with a shrug.

Simon's eyes traveled around the dingy, cramped, unkept storefront.

"In't exactly the Ritz, is it?" he said.

"It serves its purpose," I replied crisply.

Peter surreptitiously gave my butt a sharp pinch. I winced but managed not to cry out.

"Is there a loo?"

"In the back."

He left us and I wheeled around to Peter. "What was that for?"

"Are you aware that everything you say to that man sounds like a challenge?"

"What? I didn't mean it that way!" I looked at Mother who had folded her arms and was eyeing me with a peculiar smile on her face. "I didn't!"

She reached out and placed her hand on my cheek. "Alex, you are a darling." She gave me a peck on the forehead. I felt not unlike a puppy who had just found himself mysteriously dropped in the middle of a lake and had no idea in which direction the shore was.

When Simon rejoined us, he said, "Well, Jean, let's be off!" He looked at me. "I'm taking your mum to lunch, and then she's taking me to . . . ?"

"The Art Institute," Mother offered.

"Oh, yes. I understand the collection is amazing."

"Ta, luvs," Mother said as Simon slipped an arm around her waist and ushered her out of the office.

I looked at Peter. "Ta, luvs? She's getting more British by the minute."

Peter smiled. "And you're getting more darling."

We had another Motherless evening, and although Peter had been able to distract me the night before by offering himself as a willing sacrifice on the altar of our mutual sex drives, he wasn't as successful that night. After several attempts to engage me in conversation while we watched television, he ended up spending the evening doing crossword puzzles while I sat with my face pointed at the TV set.

Truth to tell, I don't know that I could've explained what there was about Simon Tivoli that bothered me (other than the obvious). Part of it was that he seemed too slick for his own good. I don't know what he was like while he was out with my mother, but during the brief times I'd spent with him he registered as an overly pleasant façade. I came away from these encounters feeling that I knew less about him than before. Not that anything but light pleasantries had passed between us. In my saner moments, I reminded myself that Peter was right: Mother was a good judge of character. Of course, my next thought was always that that didn't mean she couldn't be blinded by a pretty face. And Tivoli was nothing if not pretty. I tried to chalk these feelings up to the general malaise I was going through.

Television that night was dominated by news on the upcoming primary. Try as I might, flipping endlessly from station to station, all I could find were reports on the candidates. And if it wasn't reports, it was a deluge of commercials, each more negative than the last. Except for Clarke's. His commercials focused on his successful law practice and all of the good he'd done in the course of his private career.

His opponents' commercials were another story. Clarke was roundly vilified by the Republican party and the religious right (two groups that had long since become synonymous with each other in my mind). Clarke met all accusations and recriminations, no matter how outrageous, with an almost superhuman grace that even his opponents had to find admirable, if not frustrating.

By the time we went to bed, I had sunk so far back into the blue haze I'd been experiencing of late that I didn't even wonder what Mother was doing.

I woke up suddenly in the pitch-darkness, feeling like I hadn't slept at all. The luminous red numbers on our clock read 5:07. I groaned inwardly at the thought that I might have reached the insomnia stage of depression. Then I realized that I'd been wakened by a noise. A steady stream of screeching sirens was rapidly headed our way. I tensed as they neared our house, then breathed a guilty sigh of relief when they passed us by and faded a bit.

Peter hadn't stirred during the commotion. He was lying on his side, his breathing slow and steady. He emitted a light whistle on every third exhale. I wrapped my arms around him and tried to go back to sleep, but it was difficult. I just couldn't seem to keep my brain from running through my shortcomings. After a while that song from *Oliver!*, "Reviewing the Situation," crossed my mind, at which point all hope of further sleep was lost. The lyrics went through my head with maddening precision, and when I finally came to the end of the song's many verses, I would begin to feel a sense of relief only to have the whole song start over again.

I'm not sure what time it was when I'd finally exhausted myself and started to doze off, but I was roused almost immediately by the phone. I fumbled for the extension on our bedside table and pressed the receiver to my ear, barely managing to mumble a groggy "Hello."

"Alex! Are you awake?"

"Um-hm."

There was a pause. "Are you sure?"

"Sure I'm sure," I breathed. "Who is this?"

"It's Sheila! Did you hear what happened?"

"Um?"

"Did you hear what happened?" she asked more insistently.

"What?"

"Clarke's campaign headquarters blew up!"

"That's nice," I sighed, but I could feel my face creasing with confusion. My eyes popped open. "What?!"

"Charlie Clarke's campaign headquarters—there was an explosion there!"

"You're kidding!"

"Whaaa . . . ?" Peter said, rolling over and looking at me. I motioned him to wait.

"How did it happen?"

"I don't know yet," said Sheila. "The police or the fire department—I don't know which—they called Clarke right after it happened, and one of Clarke's aides called Annie Watson and asked her to notify all the volunteers to let them know not to go there. She called me and I said I'd call you."

"They notified Annie? Why didn't they call Jody?"

"I don't know. I didn't ask. I was too stunned by the news to think! You live right by there, though. Didn't you hear anything?"

I had this weird sensation that I was dreaming. I put my hand on my forehead, and the minute flesh touched flesh I realized I was really awake. "Yeah. Yeah, I did. A couple of hours ago. I heard sirens."

"That was probably it," said Sheila.

"Was it a bomb?"

"I don't know. I don't think anyone does yet. Anyway, I needed to let you know. Headquarters is closed for the time being. I guess someone will call you when we're set up again."

By the time I hung up, Peter was wide awake. He'd been snapped into consciousness by the tone of the conversation. I told him what had happened.

"Jesus!" he said.

I jumped out of bed. "Let's get dressed. I want to go over there."

"You're kidding!"

"Oh, don't play the voice of reason with me now! The place we were working yesterday just blew up! Are you going to tell me you don't want to see it?"

He pursed his lips, then tossed back the covers and climbed out of bed. Apparently some of the familial thrill-seeking shared by Mother and me was beginning to rub off on him. Either that or he was too tired to mount any serious objection.

We threw on some clothes and raced out of the house, but not so fast that I didn't notice that not a creature was stirring, not even my mother.

The office was a few blocks away, but we could smell burned wood and ash before we'd gone very far. When we rounded the corner onto Lincoln Avenue, we found the street blocked off at both ends by squad cars. A fire engine was parked in the middle of the street just north of our former office, and several unmarked cars where spaced around it. I was surprised to see that Mary Linn-Hadden was seated in the open door of one of these vehicles. She was staring, distraught and saucer-eyed, at the wreckage. There was no sign of Jody.

There was a gaping hole where headquarters used to be. The blast had swept outward, taking out half of the mini-mart on the left, and the entire empty storefront on the right. It had been about two hours since the explosion, but there was still a lot of activity. A crew from the fire department was hosing down the neighboring buildings, the remains of which were still smoldering. There were a few men gingerly poking their way through the charred remains of the office, and several others standing in the street watching their progress. On the opposite side of the street three separate news crews were jockeying for positions in which their field reporters could get the most dramatic backdrop to use in telling their stories. I imagined that more would be coming.

Frank O'Neill was leaning against one of the unmarked cars. Frank was a commander at Area Three Headquarters, and coincidentally had dated Mother for a while after they met while taking a night course in English literature at DePaul. You have to love a literate cop. Mother had long since decided that she and Frank weren't meant to be as far as romance went, but in a typical show of British loyalty insisted on maintaining a friendship with him, which only succeeded in keeping his little torch alive. But that came in useful to us now and then.

Peter and I stood with the small crowd by the blue police line sawhorses, and I waved to Frank to try to get his attention. He looked less surprised to see us than I would have liked. In fact, as he came over to us he looked as if our appearance on the scene meant more trouble than he already had.

"I don't suppose you guys just came to gawk," he said.

"As a matter of fact, we've been working there," I replied, jutting my thumb at the hole where the office had been. "We've been volunteering for the Clarke campaign."

Frank sighed. "It figures."

I couldn't tell if he was referring to the fact that Clarke was known to have a gay following, or because in the past we'd been known to be involved in some ridiculously awkward situations. Either way, I didn't like the way he said it.

He pushed aside the sawhorse and admitted us as he added, "If you were working there, we'd better talk."

"Who are all these people?" Peter asked as we followed Frank back to where he'd been standing.

"Well, the guys with the hoses are from the fire department."

"Very funny," I said.

"The guys going through the rubble are from the bomb and arson squad."

"So you think it was a bomb?" said Peter.

"And those guys over there," Frank said, ignoring the question and gesturing toward two men standing on the periphery of the activity, "I think you know."

"Why would we . . ." I started, but stopped when I recognized one of the men. "Oh. The one on the left is Will Henry, the guy from the FBI."

"Uh-huh." Frank folded his arms across his chest and stared at me.

"Wait a minute! We're not working with those guys!"

"But you know them by name."

"I know the one on the left because he's been in the office before."

"Uh-huh."

"Really! We've been getting a lot of threats, and he's the one they were turned over to." There was a pause during which Frank didn't flinch. In fact, I wasn't quite sure he was still breathing. "I'm telling you the truth, Frank! We are not working with those people!"

He continued his silence just long enough to let me know he was finding me very hard to believe—which I would've found truly offensive, were it not for the fact that we'd had to lie to him so often—then he showed signs of relenting. He turned to Peter. "To answer your question, yes, it looks like it was a bomb."

"God!"

"I'm surprised Jody isn't here," I said.

"You mean Jody Linn-Hadden?" Frank asked.

"Yeah. She's Clarke's most rabid supporter, and our office manager. Her partner's over there, but I don't see Jody."

Frank cleared his throat. "Yeah, well, she may be here."

"Huh?"

"Her partner showed up here an hour ago, after getting the call about what happened. She flew over here. Said when she got up this morning, Jody was nowhere to be found."

"You mean she might . . . Oh, God!"

Frank nodded.

We watched the men from the bomb and arson squad for a while as they continued to survey the wreckage, then one of them stepped his way carefully through it and headed toward us.

"Commander," he said to Frank, "hate to make your life more miserable, but there's no doubt about it—there was somebody in there when she blew."

Frank swore and gave a kick at a small stone that had been lying at his feet. My eye was caught by movement far to the right. Mary Linn-Hadden emerged from the car and was headed toward us like a woman in a trance. Her pace quickened as she neared us, until she was almost running.

"What? What did he say? What is it?" she demanded.

Frank looked at her and said with a kindness that made me proud of him, "He said that there was someone inside when the building went."

Mary stared at him blankly for a moment, then her breathing began to speed up and deepen.

"Miss Linn-Hadden, that doesn't mean it was your friend. It could be anyone. . . . It might even have been—"

Mary didn't hear him. She stared wild-eyed at the remains of the building and screamed "Jody! Jody!" She scrambled toward the ashes, but Frank and the other guy caught her by the arms and held her fast. She continued to scream and struggled to free herself for a few moments before collapsing.

The guy from bomb and arson picked her up and carried her back to the car in which she'd been sitting. He tried to be careful with her, but once he had placed her on the seat in a sitting position she flopped backward like a rag doll. Frank, Peter, and I had been watching this, so none of us noticed the approach of Will Henry, the FBI agent.

" 'Scuse me." He directed himself to Peter and me. "What are you doing here? Why are you in the cordon area?"

Frank answered for us. "Agent Henry, this is Alex Reynolds and Peter Livesay. They've been volunteering in the office."

"I know who they are," Henry replied tersely.

Frank looked at me as if he thought this was proof that I'd been lying to him again. I said, "They must know everybody who's been working for the campaign."

Henry continued. "My question was, what are you doing here? Weren't all of the volunteers called and asked not to come here?"

I verbally shuffled my feet. "Yeah . . . but . . ."

"This is a restricted area. I'll have to ask you to leave."

"Well, all right, but . . ."

"Now, please."

Apparently Henry's tone was harsh enough that Frank realized we weren't working with him. He said, "I thought since they worked here they might be able to help us out with some information."

Without looking at him, Henry said, "We'll be interviewing everyone connected with this office later. At their homes. Now, please . . ."

I caught myself just short of saying, "Do you know who we are?", which would've sounded hopelessly melodramatic, and would've been unwise given the fact that we weren't supposed to tell anyone that we did occasional work for the CIA.

"Come on, Alex," said Peter.

As he led me away, I heard Henry say, "Commander, I'd like to have a word with you."

Mother was up and about when we returned home. We went into the kitchen and found her in her white satin kimono—the one I like the least, because it makes her look like an angel in a cheesy Christmas pageant—sitting at the table and sipping a cup of tea.

"Good Heavens!" she exclaimed when she saw us. "You're up and about early! I didn't know you'd gone out."

"Didn't you hear us?"

"I heard a bit of a ruckus, but I didn't realize you'd gone. Would you like some breakfast?"

We both declined, opting for tea. While I fixed it Peter explained to Mother what had happened.

"Good Lord!"

"And there were FBI agents there," I added indignantly, "and one of them fairly threw us off the street! He wouldn't listen to a *word*, he just insisted that we leave!"

Mother set her mug down on the table. There was a sly smile on her face and a glimmer in her eye. "There were federal agents there?"

"What's so funny about that?"

"Nothing, darling, it's just that I'm surprised you made it home before they did."

"What do you mean by that?"

"Well, normally when you involve us in your little peccadillos, I end up entertaining government agents—a devilishly hard thing to do, by the way, since they simply refuse to be entertained—while waiting for you to show up to explain yourself."

"That's not fair!" I whined.

She raised a palm, signaling me to stop. "Think before you speak, my luv."

She really wasn't being fair, but I did as she said because I have a very hard record to argue in favor of. But I wasn't prepared to let it slide entirely.

"You can't believe that that building was blown up just because of my presence."

"Of course not, dear."

Her expression had melted from amusement to concern. It threw me a bit off balance, and I thought it best to get back to the matter at hand. "The FBI will be by later, though. At least I think they will. The agent that threw us out said they were going to question everybody connected with Clarke's headquarters."

Mother pushed back her chair. "Oh, I'd better get dressed, then."

"They're not coming to question you," I said, "and we have no idea when they'll be here."

"I still can't let them into the house in nothing but a kimono! What would the neighbors think?"

She left the room and Peter and I fell silent. Finally, Peter said, "Is something bothering you?"

I looked up, startled out of my reverie, and realized that for several minutes I'd been staring pensively down into my mug as I stirred the tea.

"Huh? Well, yeah. I was just thinking . . . if it really was Jody who was in the building when it blew up, then this bombing might not exactly be political."

"How do you mean?"

"I told you about that threat she got at home—the obscene phone call. And the rat." When I mentioned this Peter shuddered slightly. "I mean, the envelope it came in was addressed to the office, but whoever sent it must have known that Charles Clarke doesn't open the mail there."

"Yeah," Peter said slowly, "but it arrived the day he was going to be in the office."

"Still, would anyone think a candidate would be opening the mail himself? The timing might've just been a coincidence."

"Who usually does open the mail?"

"Mary."

"Well, if whoever sent the rat knew anything about the office, wouldn't they know that Jody wasn't the one who would get it?"

"Maybe. But if they wanted to get to Jody, it was a good way to do it. Those two may have been an odd couple, but they were devoted to each other. Fiercely devoted, if you go by Jody. I think she was angrier about Mary being upset like that than she was about the threat to her own life."

Peter set down his mug and eyed me with one raised brow. "You realize you just spoke of Jody in the past tense. It could've been anyone in that office when the bomb went off."

I shook my head. "Who else would've been there at five in the morning?"

It was another two hours before the Feds showed up at our door. When the bell rang, Mother came down the stairs wearing something that looked like a peasant dress tied with a thin brown belt just beneath her ample breasts.

She flung open the door, took one look at the pair of blue-suited men on the top step and exclaimed, "You must be the agents! Do come in!"

"Dear God," I whispered to Peter, "she's gone from Eliza Doolittle to Auntie Mame."

He poked me in the side as the men came into the living room. Mother closed the door behind them.

"I'm Agent Henry," said the one I already knew, "and this is my partner, Agent Raymond."

Mother shook his hand, a puzzled look on her face. "Are those your first names?"

"No," Henry replied with a smile that I found uncharacteristic in a g-man. "I'm Will Henry, and this is Phillip Raymond."

"Willie and Phil?" I blurted out. Mother and Peter both looked at me as if they couldn't take me anywhere, including our own living room.

Henry's smile disappeared. "We'd like to talk to you about what's happened."

"Have a seat," said Mother, motioning them to the couch. The three of us pulled up chairs and sat facing them.

"First," said Henry, "let me tell you that we know who you are."

"Well, we figured that," I said.

"No, I mean we know *what* you are."

Mother's face hardened on Peter's and my behalf. "I beg your pardon?"

"My partner is putting this badly," Raymond cut in. "What he's trying to say is that we know you work for the government. I should say that you *have* worked for us. I believe you report to an Agent Lawrence Nelson?"

"How do you know that?" asked Peter, who is always inclined to be a bit more suspicious than I am.

Raymond explained, "When it became apparent that Charles Clarke was a serious candidate for senator—and when the threats began—we did background checks on all the people who are working for him. The paid staffers and the regular volunteers, both in the Springfield office and here. Of course, there are a lot of other volunteers in and out of there, just in for a couple of days and then gone. We really couldn't keep track of all of them. But the ones that are considered regulars, we did check on. The two of you qualify in that category."

"If you knew we were connected with the government," I said, "then why did you run us off this morning?"

"We didn't want anyone to think you were working with us," Henry replied. "I understand from Nelson that your participation in government activities is strictly on a covert basis."

"Covert?" I said with a glance at Peter. It sounded so under-handed when he put it like that.

"So, you've talked to Nelson?" said Peter. He sounded as if he was liking this less and less.

"Of course," said Henry. "And he assured us of your coopera-tion."

"What's all this in aid of?" said Mother.

Raymond sighed. "Well, it's now obvious that the threats that have been made against Clarke and his campaign are quite serious."

"Didn't you always take them seriously?" said Peter.

"Of course. However, people who phone in bomb threats don't usually carry them out."

"Now that this one has," Henry chimed in, "security around Clarke is going to have to be increased, and our investigation into the bomb threats will have to be intensified."

"As well as your investigation into the death that occurred this morning," said Peter. His voice was beginning to take on his soap-box tone. And with good reason. We'd seen before the lack of enthusiasm with which various authorities pursued the murder of gays, and how where the Feds are concerned murder could take a back seat to political expediency. The office that had been destroyed may have been Charlie Clarke's headquarters, but the only person killed had been a dyke. Peter and I were both jaded enough to believe the Feds might not take Jody's death as seriously as we would like.

"Of course," Henry replied tersely. Peter's tone hadn't been lost on him.

"Do you know for sure whether or not it really was Jody Linn-Hadden who was inside when the office blew up?" Mother asked.

"No. There is unfortunately not a lot left from which to do an identification. Forensics has a lot of work to do before we know anything, and even when they're done, we may not know defini-tively. We are going to proceed on the assumption that is was Ms. Linn-Hadden."

"Why?" I asked. "I mean, if you don't know, why would you assume it was her?"

"Partly because her partner is so sure it was."

I had to give Henry one thing: He didn't flinch when referring to the relationship between Jody and Mary, as we'd seen some Feds and police do in the past.

He continued. "Mary Linn-Hadden seems convinced that it was Jody who was in the office. Do you have reason to believe it could've been someone else?"

I shook my head. "No. No, I can't imagine anyone else going there that early. And it would be like Jody."

"Has she done that before?"

"Not that I know of. But the thing is, it wouldn't have surprised me to find out she was getting there at five in the morning. It wouldn't have surprised me to find out she was living there. Didn't Mary know why Jody was there?"

"She claims she doesn't."

"Hmm," I replied, trying not to sound as surprised as I felt.

"Now," said Henry, sitting up a bit straighter, "here's one area where you can help us. As you saw this morning, the office was completely destroyed. We have no way of knowing if somebody broke in to plant the bomb, or if it was planted by someone who was in the office while it was open. Can you tell us if there was anybody *unusual* there in . . . say . . . the past day or so?"

"Oh, God!" I said, rolling my eyes. "It has to be the past two days!"

"What's wrong with that?" Raymond asked.

"Just that absolutely *everybody* has been in the office in the past two days! The day before yesterday Clarke himself was there along with John Schuler, his campaign manager. There were dozens of reporters and there were volunteers I'd never seen before, who came in to get a look at Clarke."

"Would any of them have had a chance to, say, place a package under one of the tables?"

"They could've bred livestock under the tables without anyone noticing. The place was jammed with people."

Henry cleared his throat. "Yes, well, what about yesterday?"

"There were fewer people."

Peter added, "But we were kept pretty busy, so somebody could've planted a package without us noticing. Do you know that that was where the bomb was? Under a table?"

Raymond shook his head. "We don't know that for sure. The center of the blast seems to have been pretty far back. It might have been in the back room. Did you see anyone go into the back room? Anyone who didn't belong there?"

"The bathroom was in the back room," I explained. "Everyone went back there at one time or another. And Clarke and Schuler's offices were back there. They were in again yesterday."

"Anyone else unusual?" Henry asked.

I thought for a moment, then suddenly had a sickening thought. Mother and her new beau had been in the office yesterday. And Simon had gone into the back room.

"Not that I can recall," I said, feeling uncomfortably like Ronald Reagan. Or at least how I thought he should've felt.

The agents both stared at me as if they could see right through me. I turned to Mother. Not only did she not look exactly forthcoming, she looked as if she had no idea what was up with me. So I looked at Peter and said, "Can you think of anyone?"

"No," he replied simply.

"All right," Henry said doubtfully, turning back to me, "We understand that there was a blow-up—excuse me, bad choice of words—that there was some kind of argument between Jody Linn-Hadden and one of the volunteers, a David Leech."

"Dave?" I said. "She yelled at him for laughing, that's all."

"We were told that he left right after this happened."

"That's true."

"Do you know if he came back at all?"

"No," I said, wrinkling my nose. "You don't think Dave did this."

"She fought with him," Henry said.

"She *embarrassed* him, for Christ's sake! You don't kill somebody just because they embarrass you!"

"Murders have been committed for less than that," said Raymond without emotion.

"You don't know Dave. I can imagine him throwing a hissy fit, but a bomb? Hell, Jody yelled at *me,* too! Are you going to suspect me of bombing the place because I might have been embarrassed?"

The two of them stared back at me with a complete lack of expression. My stomach dropped as I realized that that was exactly what they would do.

Peter rescued the moment. "So you guys think maybe Jody was the actual target of the bomb?"

Henry nodded. "She was the only one caught by it. We have to consider that possibility, yes. Especially in light of the fact that she had recently received some personal threats."

Raymond added, "This is a matter of being thorough. She may have been the target, or Clarke may have been, or just the office. Right now there're too many possibilities."

"How could Mr. Clarke have been the target?" Mother asked. "The bomb went off at five in the morning."

"That's just it," said Henry. "We don't know anything yet. It went off at five, but that could've been a mistake. It could've been meant to go off later . . . or earlier."

"You mean when *we* were there?" I exclaimed.

"Uh-huh. But more to the point, when Clarke was there."

"Excuse us if that's not the point to us," said Peter.

Henry smiled sheepishly. "I was only talking in terms of motive."

"So you have absolutely no idea who planted the bomb, or why?" said Mother, always one to bring us back to the matter at hand.

Raymond took a deep breath. "Well, most likely it's the simplest explanation: Someone, a terrorist of some sort, planned to blow up the office when nobody was there as a scare tactic, and it was only a fluke that Ms. Linn-Hadden happened to be in the office at the time. Her presence was a shame because it really complicates matters."

Mother replied in her haughtiest *Masterpiece Theatre* accent, "Her presence was a shame because she's *dead!*"

I was surprised she beat Peter to that one.

Raymond managed to look abashed. "Point well taken, Ms. Reynolds." He paused and cleared his throat. "As I said, we have to explore all avenues, and that's one of the reasons we decided to talk to you first."

"First?" I said.

"Well, second. We did question Mary Linn-Hadden. But we want to enlist your aid in exploring one of those avenues."

"Really?" I replied, perking up. "What would that be?"

Henry said, "It's possible that the bomb was planted by someone within Clarke's organization. One of the staffers or one of the volunteers."

"You're kidding," said Peter.

He shook his head. "Clarke is very popular in the polls, but he's also pissed off a lot of people . . . and a lot of groups."

"You mean religious groups?" I asked.

"Yes. Religious groups, and militias."

"Militias?" Peter said, his tone becoming more disbelieving.

"Several militia groups have been really vocal about their hatred of Clarke. We believe that some of the threats may have come from them. They've come very close to making threats publicly. But we also believe that some of the threats have come from the radical right. Religious extremists. These kind of groups are very dangerous. Some of them disavow their place as American citizens—they feel they should be considered a different country. When you're that far outside the norms of society, there's no telling what you'll do."

"That's funny," Peter said through flat lips, "I get the impression sometimes that the American government thinks that *we* belong in a different country."

Henry looked at him as if he wasn't sure whether or not Peter was going to be more trouble than he was worth, and I wondered for a moment if he'd just throw up his hands and leave. But instead he went on as if Peter had said nothing.

"Those are just some of the possibilities. Someone from one of these groups may have infiltrated Clarke's office for the express purpose of causing mischief."

Mischief, I thought sardonically. *Strange way to look at a bomb.*

"Now, you guys have been working there. Is there anyone who you think might not be what they seem?"

Peter and I glanced at each other. He looked as dumbfounded as I felt. I said, "You're asking if we think one of our coworkers might secretly be a member of a militia?"

"Right . . . or some other group."

"Most of the guys working in the office are gay. How in the hell would we tell them from someone in a militia? Check them for camouflage underwear?"

He shrugged. "Maybe somebody is a little less enthusiastic about Clarke than they should be? Or maybe a little *too* enthusiastic? Overcompensating?"

There was something very McCarthyesque about the tone in which he'd put this. I didn't like it at all. At that particular moment I don't think I would've told him if one of my coworkers had been walking around with a ticking box.

"You want to know if there's anybody who is enthusiastic, or isn't enthusiastic . . . ?"

"Yes."

"Nope," I said, spreading my hands helplessly.

Henry sighed heavily. "Well, this brings us to the real point of our visit. We will, of course, be placing agents in Clarke's Springfield office to keep tabs on what's going on down there, but we thought we'd enlist your aid in covering the Chicago office since you've already infiltrated it."

"Infiltrated it?" Peter said, bristling. "We've been doing mailings and answering phones, not photographing secret documents with a tiny tie-clip camera."

Henry stared at him a moment, then turned to me. "Since you're already a part of Clarke's campaign, what we'd like you to do is keep your eyes and ears open. See if you can ferret out any information on the people working for him. See if anybody there isn't what he or she seems to be."

I smiled. "So you want us to be undercover agents."

"Lawrence Nelson told us that you could be trusted," said Raymond.

"*Paid* agents," I said.

There was a long pause before Henry replied. "Of course. Now, it may be that this is a dead end. It probably is. But we need to cover everything, and as long as you're already there, and as you said, there're a lot of your people working in that office, we thought you might be the best ones to do it."

"Your people?" said Peter, his voice hardening. "You want us to spy on our own people?"

"Yes. Like The Mod Squad," I said. "Mother can be Julie, and I suppose since you're already Peter I have to be Linc!"

"I don't like the sound of this," Peter said, ignoring me.

Henry replied, "Whoever planted the bomb just killed one of 'your people.' Do you like the sound of that?"

"Look, that's just the thing," said Mother. "If someone in the office was the bomber, do you think they'd keep going there? Wouldn't they just disappear?"

"No," Raymond answered. "Not necessarily. It would look too suspicious to disappear right now. And . . . his work might not be over."

"Now I really don't like the sound of that," said Mother.

"We'll do it," I announced quickly, before she could complete her protests.

Henry looked at me doubtfully. Although he was the one who'd proposed this arrangement, he didn't seem any too pleased with my eagerness to comply. He turned to Mother and said, "There shouldn't be any danger, Ms. Reynolds."

"I can't tell you how little comfort that gives me! I also can't tell you how many times government agents have said the same thing to us in exactly the same situation." She paused for a breath, then narrowed her eyes in my direction. "Well, not exactly the same situation, but bloody near close to it!"

Raymond said, "We're not asking them to track down the bomber and arrest him single-handedly. All we want them to do is talk to people. Ask around a little bit, and see what they can see." He looked directly at me and added pointedly, "If they find anything suspicious, they will report it back to us. Under no circumstance are they to confront anyone or try to apprehend anyone. They are just to report their findings. Is that clear?"

"Are you talking to me?" I said.

"Oh, he understands," Mother said, looking daggers at me. "I'll see to it!"

She made it sound as if she was going to stand over me while I did my homework.

"Good," said Henry as he and his partner rose. "They'll be reestablishing the office within the next couple of days, and you'll be called and given the location as soon as possible." He handed me a business card. "Here's our numbers. When you have something to report, you can reach us there. You are to report only to me or Agent Raymond."

"Understood," I said. I took the card and stuffed it in my pocket.

The three of us had risen, and the agents started for the door.

"Oh, just a minute," I said. They stopped and turned back to us with eerie symmetry. "You said that Mary was the only one besides us that you questioned."

"Yes?" Henry said.

"You haven't questioned David Leech yet?"

"No, but we will."

"No," I said tartly, "*we* will."

"I hardly think you're qualified—"

"When it comes to questioning David Leech," I said, cutting him off, "I hardly think *you're* qualified. You'll scare him to death. We can talk to him without doing that."

There was a beat before Henry said, "I thought you understood that your involvement in this was to be covert."

I shrugged. "So we'll do it covertly."

Henry looked as if he was unsure whether or not our cooperation hinged on his agreeing to this. Finally, he said, "All right."

"I mean it, Henry," I said. "You badger him and the deal's off."

"I said all right," he replied without emotion.

They left, and Mother closed the door after them. She then

wheeled around and exclaimed, "Are you out of your bloody mind? I don't want you working in an office that's been blown up!"

"We'll be in a new one, Mother."

"You know what I mean!" she said through clenched teeth.

"Why did you agree to this?" Peter asked.

"I don't believe you!" I said loudly. "For weeks the two of you have been telling me how important it is to do your civic duty, and the minute the government actually *asks* for our help, you don't want to do it! Apparently when you said 'your' civic duty, you meant *my* civic duty, not *your* civic duty!"

Both Mother and Peter folded their arms across their respective chests and stared at me.

"What?"

"Well," said Mother, "that sounds very rational and patriotic of you, darling, but I've the feeling that deep down inside you're saying 'Oh goody, I get to play spy again!' "

"That's not true!" I exclaimed. A slight pause elapsed before I added, "All right, it's partly true, but there's more to it than that! One of our very own people was killed, and I think we should participate in finding out who did it."

Peter said, "It's the emphasis on 'our people' that bothers me."

"What do you mean?"

He sighed. "An extremist group infiltrated that tiny office? I think Henry and Raymond have seen one too many Bruce Willis movies. Has it occurred to you that maybe the FBI wants our help because they think one of 'our people' is the bomber?"

Actually, that hadn't occurred to me. "Putting your paranoia aside for a minute," I retorted more angrily than I normally would with him, "do you think that means we shouldn't help catch him—or her?"

He stared at me blankly for a second, then lowered his eyes. "No, I don't."

"I'm sorry. I didn't mean to yell."

He looked up. "But that doesn't mean I would like finding out that we'd been used by the FBI, or lied to."

"Agreed," I said.

He smiled. I felt relieved, and thanked the powers that be that Peter and I seldom experience a rift in our relationship, and when we do it rarely lasts more than a few seconds. I hoped it would be the same with Mother, but I knew she really wasn't going to like what was coming next.

"Mother, darling," I said, lightly mocking her propensity for using that word. "Before you start accusing me of getting us involved in something dangerous again, may I ask you a question?"

"Yes?"

I took a deep breath. "How much do you know about Simon Tivoli?"

"What?" she exclaimed in her best Lady Bracknell.

"Simon. You've dated him, what? Three or four days running? You've spent a lot of time with him. How much do you know about him?"

"I know you don't much care for Simon," she replied broadly, "but have you completely gone 'round the bend?"

"Mother, when those two agents asked us if anyone out of the ordinary had come into the office in the past couple of days . . ." I let my voice trail off and spread my palms.

"What?"

"I didn't mention that *you* had been there . . . with your friend."

She looked puzzled for a moment, then said, "Oh yes, we were! Why didn't you mention it?"

"Why didn't *you?*"

"I didn't think of it. Why didn't you?"

"Because I didn't want to get you involved. They're looking for a bomber!"

She curled her lips and said crisply, "Well, it's nice to know you wouldn't shop your own mother."

"You know I'm talking about Simon! Look, he comes into your life out of the blue, and then the office blows up!"

"It was a chance meeting," she said incredulously. From the expression on her face it was clear she thought I really had lost my mind. And Mother's expressions are vivid enough that it was difficult to press on without doubting myself.

"Chance meetings can be arranged," I countered. "He was in the office for no good reason the day before it blew up!"

"He just wanted to see it!"

"*And,* he went to the bathroom!"

"You can hardly have someone arrested for making water," she replied witheringly.

"Mother!" I said with increasing exasperation, "They believe the bomb was planted in the back room. We have someone here who's an almost complete stranger, who wheedled his way into your life and came into that office for no real reason, *and* was alone for a time in the back room."

"With a bomb concealed about his person?"

"It's possible."

"Alex," she said patiently, "what possible interest could Simon have in American politics?"

I had to think about that one. "I don't know. Maybe it has something to do with trade."

"*With England?*" Her voice slid up an octave on the last word. She was sounding more and more like Dame Edith Evans.

"It might not be his politics at all," I said irritably. "He might have been paid to do it."

She heaved a sigh. "Do you think it possible that Simon may have had a 'real reason' for coming to the office?"

"Like what?"

"Perhaps he didn't want to see the office at all. Perhaps he wanted to see *you.*"

"Me? Why?"

"Maybe he would like to get to know you better," she said simply.

"Why?"

Peter said, "Maybe because he thinks you don't like him."

I could feel my face getting hot. "Even if that were true, what the hell does it matter? He's going back to England in a week." I suddenly had that sinking feeling again. I turned to Mother and added, "Isn't he?"

It was one of those rare moments of hesitation on her part.

"Well, as a matter of fact, he's been talking about extending his visit a bit."

"Why?"

"Maybe he'd like to get to know *me* better . . . and if you say 'why' again, I'll send you to your room!"

"I wasn't going to say that!"

"And the fact that Simon is thinking of extending his visit rather puts a damper on your theory, doesn't it? If he was the bomber, he'd *hardly* be staying longer, would he now?"

"Unless he's afraid leaving so soon would make him look suspicious, like Agent Henry said."

"Oh, tosh!"

"Tosh?" I exclaimed. "Mother, whether you like it or not, Simon was in that office and in that back room, and that makes him a suspect! Now, either we can look into it or those agents will. They're going to ask other people who was in the office. Somebody's bound to remember Simon having been there."

After a pause, she said wistfully, "That's true, he is rather memorable."

I chose to ignore the tone in her voice. "So what are we going to do about him?"

"*We* aren't going to do anything. If there are any questions to ask Simon, I'll be the one to ask them!"

With this she turned on her heels and swept up the stairs. There was a touch of Joan of Arc on the way to the pyre about it.

"I know what you're thinking," I said, once Peter and I were alone, "and you're wrong."

"I'm not sure you do know what I'm thinking," Peter replied in that deep, comforting voice of his. "You know, your mother is positively amazing. Most parents have some difficulty accepting it when their children announce they're gay, let alone the prospect of accepting a same-sex spouse when he comes along. Jean not only offered you her full acceptance, she offered it to me, too. And a place in her home. Why can't you do the same thing for her?"

"It's not the same as you and me," I said, trying not to sound as defensive as I felt. "It's that this guy popped up out of nowhere. We don't know anything about him. I'm worried about her."

Peter came over to me and gently linked his fingers behind my neck. He searched my face with his beautiful green eyes. "Do you remember how we met?"

"Yeah. At Marco's birthday party."

"At Marco's birthday party," he repeated, then softly kissed me. "I'd never clapped eyes on you before, but I was sitting there and you walked into the room . . . and it was love at first sight." He kissed me again.

I pulled back slightly. "Jesus! You don't think she's in love with him, do you?"

He dropped his head on my shoulder and laughed. "You are a nut."

"I really am only worried about her."

He lifted his head and faced me. "I know."

FOUR

Since I'd made such a big deal out of it, I thought our first move should be to talk to David Leech. According to the phone book he lived just off the bar strip in the neighborhood affectionately known as Boy's Town.

Even though parking can be really difficult up there, we took the car with Mother's blessing, and drove up to Belmont. From there we went north up Halsted to Cornelia. David's building was about halfway down the block. We lucked out and found a parking space conveniently located by a fire hydrant, and walked back to the big red brick complex.

"I still think we should have called first," said Peter.

"I don't know him that well," I replied.

"You don't know him well enough to call him, but you know him well enough to drop in on him?"

"That makes perfect sense to me."

He threw up his hands. "I'm married to Gracie Allen."

"I can't explain it. It just seems more plausible to me that we'd be in the area and drop in than it would for me to call him."

"What if he doesn't think it's plausible?"

"Then we'll have to play it by ear."

There were four vestibules in the courtyard of the building. Fortunately for us, in the first one we tried we found the names "Leech-Whitefield" (which sounded like a Dickensian law firm to me) taped under one of the doorbells. I pressed the button, and a few seconds later the inner door buzzed and we went through.

Before we could begin to mount the winding stairs, we heard a door pop open overhead, and a voice called out, "Who is it?"

"Dave? Is that you?" I called back.

"Yeah?" was the tentative reply. "Who is it?"

"It's me. Alex."

"Who?"

"Alex Reynolds. You know, from Clarke's office."

"Really?" There was a noticeable brightening of his tone. "Come on up!"

Although Peter and I are both pretty light on our feet, the brown carpeted stairs creaked and moaned beneath us, so we sounded like an herd of asthmatic buffalo. We found Dave standing in the doorway on the right on the second landing. He wore a glistening, tight white T-shirt with the short sleeves lopped off, showing off his slight but well-toned torso, and a pair of royal blue shorts. On his feet were a pair of those foot-massaging sandals that remind me of a bed of nails.

"There's two of you!" he exclaimed when he saw us.

"This is my husband, Peter."

"Oh! You're the one he's always talking about," Dave said with a sly glance at me as if he was letting out an embarrassing secret. "Come on in. My boyfriend's out at some potluck thingamie at church. I don't indulge, so I'm here all by my lonesome."

From the way he put it I couldn't tell if he was talking about the potluck or the church in general.

The apartment was one of those spacious older ones. There were hardwood floors with matching molding and floorboards that were thick with lacquer. The room was sparsely furnished— apparently Dave and whoever Whitefield might be didn't have nearly enough furniture to make a dent in the space—which made it look even bigger.

"I'm really sorry to drop in on you like this, but we were going over to the Melrose for lunch, and I remembered you lived up here and I thought I'd stop in and see how you were doing."

"I'm doing just fine," he said, looking somewhat perplexed.

"I mean, I didn't see you after that dust-up with you-know-who the other day, and I was a little worried about you."

At my mention of the incident, his expression froze.

"I'm fine," he said flatly.

"It's just you were gone before I came out of the back, and you didn't come back."

"What are you, the truant officer? I don't have to work there!"

"No, no," I said placatingly. "I was only worried about you. There was no excuse for the way Jody acted, and I went back there and told her so."

"You did?" he said, gratefully. "That was . . . I should have done that myself. That bitch didn't have any right! I didn't do anything. I just laughed! What was wrong with that? And she chewed my ass off, right there in front of everybody!"

"She shouldn't have—"

"It's just like one of them! You know *why* she did it? You know why she treats us like shit?"

I shrugged. "That's just the way she is?"

"Because we're *men!* It doesn't matter whether you're gay or not, she's one of those goddamn dykes where, if you're a man, she just fuckin' tolerates you, and then only if she has to!"

"But she supports Clarke."

He shook his head vehemently. "Only because she thinks he can get her what she wants. If there was a lezzie running for senator, she never would've gone near Clarke! It wouldn't matter if it was a flannel-wearing, jack-booted, baby-eating lesbian, she'd support her!"

I wasn't going to offer a protest to that one, partly because I didn't think it would help get information, and partly because I agreed. Maybe not with the baby-eating part, but with most of it. I know far too many people who will vote for a candidate in their own food group, regardless of the candidate's character.

"Did you hear what happened?" I asked.

"What?"

"Campaign headquarters was blown up," Peter said.

Dave face lit up at the news. He looked more thrilled than shocked. "Aw, man! I miss all the good stuff!"

"It happened before the office was open, so you didn't exactly miss it," I said.

"You didn't hear anything about it on the news?" Peter asked.

David puckered his face up with distaste. "The news! I never watch the news. Way too depressing!" He turned to me. "So what happened?"

"Well, it looks like somebody bombed the place."

The blood drained from his face. "You see? I told you! Nobody took those bomb threats seriously! I told you they should have!"

Actually, he hadn't exactly told me that, although he'd acted like he was worried because they weren't being taken seriously. But I wasn't going to argue that point, either.

"Do they know who did it?"

"I don't think so," I replied.

Peter said, "It happened at five o'clock this morning. They don't know anything yet. They've just started asking questions."

"So what happened when Jody found out about it?" David asked gleefully. "I bet she went to pieces!"

Peter and I glanced at each other. I said, "David, they think Jody was in the building when it blew."

"What?!" he exclaimed again. His eyes widened, making him look sort of like a short-haired kewpie doll, but he still seemed more excited than shocked.

I nodded. "They're not absolutely sure it was her, but they think it was."

"Wow! That's incredible!" He clapped his hands together and laughed openly. "Just think of it! Little bits of bitch blown all over the neighborhood! I'll bet the property values go down!"

"Dave!" I said, genuinely shocked. "I know you didn't like her, but come on!"

"I know, I know!" he said, waving a limp hand at me. "Respect for the dead and all that. But she was a beast and you know it! Do you expect me to be sorry she's gone?"

"No," said Peter, who looked more appalled than I did, "We were just hoping you wouldn't be quite so happy about it. It doesn't look good."

"What do you mean?"

"The FBI is looking into this," I explained. "They'll probably talk to you." Of course, I'd seen to it that they wouldn't—at least initially—but I thought scaring him a little might help. Besides, I was so completely turned off by his attitude that I wanted to make him squirm a little. "They know you were upset with her."

"How do you know that?" he said.

"Because they've already started questioning people. When they talked to us, they asked us about the incident."

He looked panic-stricken. "What did you tell them?"

"I told them it was nothing."

"He also told them he thought the idea that you had anything to do with it was crazy," Peter added.

Dave's head swiveled back and forth between the two of us for a moment. He looked like an animal who'd been locked in a cage with two enemies, and didn't know which would attack first.

"It would be just like that bitch to cause me trouble from the grave!" he said at last. "This is why you really came here, isn't it? To warn me!"

Peter looked at me over Dave's head and raised his eyebrows. I almost laughed. Here we'd wondered how we'd explain coming to see him out of the blue, and he'd offered us a perfectly good excuse.

"Yes, that's it," I said quickly. "And I can tell you those FBI guys didn't have much of a sense of humor, so I wouldn't let them think you're so happy about Jody dying. Especially since they think she might have been the target of the bomb."

"Really?" he said. His eyes widened again, but more soberly this time. He looked down at the floor for a moment, and shifted from one foot to the other like a little boy who has to compose himself to keep from laughing before speaking in front of the class. He looked up at me. "I'm not really *happy* happy. I'm not! I mean, you don't want to see anybody get killed. I would've liked to slap her once or twice—only if she was on her leash, mind you—but I wouldn't kill her for cryin' out loud! Who would do a thing like that?"

"That's what the FBI wants to find out," said Peter.

"The other thing is," I said, adapting the tone of the warning friend Dave took me to be, "you should be ready to tell them where you've been since you left the office."

"It's been two days!" His voice took on an unattractive whine. "I don't know where all I've been!"

Peter said, "Well, since nobody's seen you in the office since that incident, they'll probably be more interested in where you've been the past two nights. Overnight."

"Oh, that's easy!" David said, his relief palpable. "I was here, in bed, with Sammy."

"Is he your boyfriend?" I asked.

He nodded.

I cocked my head slightly to the side. "I don't know how good an alibi the FBI will think that is. You must've been out of his sight sometime. You could've gotten up in the middle of the night while he was asleep and gone out."

Dave's smile broadened. He went to the mantel over the fake fireplace and retrieved a photo in a small, red wooden frame. He handed it to me.

"That's Sammy," he said, tapping on the glass. "Would you have gotten out of bed?"

The man who stared back at me from the frame was one of the most ostentatiously handsome men I'd ever seen. And he appeared to know it. I imagine he was able to hold Dave in bed, even when fast asleep, by the sheer power of his beauty.

I showed the picture to Peter, who replied with a "Huh," which in this case served as a wolf-whistle.

"Very nice," I said simply as I handed it back to Dave. "But would he lie for you?"

"Of course he would!"

"What?" Peter and I replied in unison.

David look momentarily confused, then said very quickly, "Oh! I don't mean *that!* I mean he would do anything for me. But he doesn't have to lie about this!"

As we walked back to the car, Peter was noticeably pensive, which is usually a sign that something is really troubling him.

"What are you thinking?" I asked.

"That that young man is lucky you stopped the FBI agents from questioning him. What a nasty piece of work he is!"

"He wasn't like that at the office. I don't think we should make too much of it. Lots of people talk like that."

We'd gotten to the car, and Peter went to the passenger door and looked at me over the roof. "Really? Alex, I'm not sure you should be so quick to write him off. He sounded awfully bitter where Jody's concerned. He sounded downright vindictive, no matter what he says about just not being hypocritical. You'd think when he hears that somebody just got blown up that he'd have the sense to hide the fact that he's happy about it!"

I gave him a sly smile. "You're thinking like a middle-aged man."

He growled at me as I disappeared into the car. I leaned over and popped the lock on his side. As he got in, I said, "Look, I realize you think Dave's attitude is offensive. So do I. But can you imagine him being able to build a bomb?"

Peter thought for a moment, then laughed. "I can't imagine him being able to operate an EasyBake Oven! Where to next?"

"Mary Linn-Hadden," I said with a heavy sigh. "Hopefully she's back home now."

"Alex, she just found out her partner was murdered. I hardly think this is a good time."

"If we're going to be covert then this is the best time. We can go in the guise of offering her support."

Peter stiffened and slowly turned his face to me. " 'In the *guise* of offering her support'? You're beginning to sound just like those FBI agents, and I don't like it."

His tone was enough to reel me in and make me feel a bit ashamed of myself. I was letting the excitement of actually being assigned to a case get the better of me. Thankfully, Peter was there to set me right. "I didn't mean it like that," I said. "I meant *while* we're offering her support, maybe we can find out something."

"That's a little better. But you think we can get information from Mary? I can't believe she kept anything back from the agents."

"I can. Henry said that Mary didn't know why Jody went to the office at that ungodly hour, but I'll bet she does know. As close as they were I can't believe that Jody kept anything secret from her."

He shrugged. "Maybe you're right. You know them better than I do."

I looked at him for a few seconds, then leaned over and gave him a kiss.

"What was that for?" he asked with a smile as we righted ourselves.

"For keeping me on the gay and narrow."

Jody was one of the few people working on Clarke's campaign whose address I knew. She had held a couple of "strategy meetings" at her home. There was really no reason to have had them there rather than the office, other than the fact that Jody had wanted to put herself forward as a one-woman source of gentrification. It didn't matter to her that the dilapidated house she and Mary had bought together was in the North and Clybourn area, which was already being redeveloped by a lot of individuals and companies. She had proudly shown us around the little white house that she had single-handedly brought up to code, while providing a constant stream of disdain for Boy's Town, which she contemptuously referred to as the gay ghetto. Unfortunately, that happened to be where a lot of the volunteers lived. It didn't make her any more endearing.

The house was on Billings, a short side street just off Clybourn about a block north of North Avenue. When we pulled up onto the gravel indentation that served as a parking space, Mary Linn-

Hadden was standing in the center of the picture window, staring out forlornly like an orphan waiting for her lost dog to return home. She showed no sign of noticing us as we got out of the car and went up the walk to the front door. There was no doorbell, so I opened the outer screen door and rapped with the small brass knocker on the inner door. It was about thirty seconds before Mary opened it.

"Alex . . . Peter . . ." she said faintly. "I thought maybe . . ." Her voice trailed off, and her eyes were beginning to tear up as she lowered them.

"We wanted to see how you were doing," I said.

"Come in." She stepped aside and we crossed the threshold.

The interior of Mary and Jody's home was so much like a country house that it gave you the feeling a tornado had picked it up and dropped it in the middle of Chicago. The furniture was masculine, all tans and browns, with a large beige couch shoved up against one wall. But there were feminine touches as well: lace doilies, no less, on the backs of the chairs and a hand-made afghan folded neatly on the couch. Oil landscapes in dark frames dotted the walls. There was a large square rag rug on the floor. The living room opened into the dining room, where the huge mahogany table that served as the centerpiece was matched by a sideboard on the far wall. Almost everything in this home was large and heavy. The air was a mixture of lemon polish and stale cigarette smoke.

Mary paused to look out the window again, then turned around and said, "Please, sit down."

Peter and I sat apart from each other at either end of the couch, as if we'd both sensed that any show of closeness on our part would be painful to her.

Mary wandered over to the only chair that didn't match the rest of the furniture: an armless seat with a heart-shaped back that sat at an angle to the couch. It seemed almost as out of place in the room as Mary herself. She folded her hands in her lap and crossed her ankles.

"It's really nice of you to come by," she said. I couldn't help feeling a twinge of guilt, remembering our purpose there. "There hasn't been a great outpouring of love for Jody."

"It's early yet," said Peter. "I don't think a lot of people know what happened yet. You'll start hearing from them once word gets around."

There was a slight movement of her head as if she'd been about to shake it but caught herself in time.

"Jody's not the most popular woman in the world. I know that. She's very passionate about her beliefs, and very outspoken. People don't always understand that. Or like it. Especially in a woman." This last she added halfheartedly, as if repeating something she'd been told, but didn't quite believe.

"But she had friends," Peter said, carefully modulating his voice so that there would be no doubt he meant it as a statement of fact.

Mary raised her grateful eyes to him. "Yes. She did."

There was a long pause during which none of us seemed to know how to proceed with each other. After all, we didn't really know her very well. Finally, Mary said, "I keep thinking it wasn't her. I keep thinking she's going to drive up and come bursting in the door and have no idea why I'm so upset."

"Has she ever disappeared before?" Peter asked.

Mary shook her head sadly. "I know it was her. She was the one in that office. But I don't think I'm really going to believe it . . . I mean *really* believe it . . . until the police prove it was her." She stopped and sniffed. "The men from the FBI, when they talked to me, they told me it could've been anyone. That it might even have been the person who planted the bomb. Maybe it went off by accident when he was putting it there. . . . Things like that. But . . ." At first she'd sounded as if she were trying to manage a bit of optimism, but she quickly began to falter. "But I know it was Jody."

"How can you be so sure?" I asked as gently as I knew how.

She looked up, somewhat startled. "What?"

"How can you be so sure? This morning, when you found out someone was in the building, you were positive it was Jody."

"I just know. I can just tell that something's happened to her."

"But the FBI could be right. It could've been someone else," Peter offered.

"Then where is she?" Mary said with a catch in her throat. "It had to be her."

"I don't know how you can be so sure . . . unless . . . unless you know for a fact that she went there."

Mary's eyes glazed over as if she didn't want anyone to see inside them. "I don't know what you mean."

"The FBI came and questioned us," I said. "They asked if we knew why Jody would be at the office at five in the morning. We told them to ask you, and they said you didn't know."

She averted her eyes. "I don't know. . . ."

"I can't imagine Jody doing anything without telling you." I tried to sound nonchalant even though I was getting perilously close to asking direct questions. "I mean, the two of you never made a move without each other, did you? I thought you could practically read each other's minds."

I added the last bit because I thought it possible that Jody hadn't told Mary exactly what she was doing, but Mary might have thought she knew anyway. I was trying to give her an opening through which she might feel more comfortable sharing her suspicions, if that's what they were. But it certainly didn't work. She shifted uneasily in her chair and fixed her glazed eyes on my knee.

"I don't . . . I didn't always know what Jody was doing. . . ." she said with a startling lack of conviction.

Peter said, "Mary, if you know for a fact she was there you should probably tell the authorities. It might help them find out who did this."

She looked up at him and her expression slowly changed. Apparently she had reluctantly come to a decision. After sniffing once or twice, she said, "I told them I didn't know, but I do."

"Why not tell them?"

"Jody wouldn't have wanted me to." She fought to hold back tears, I think because she'd forced herself to refer to Jody in the past tense.

70

"Why not?" Peter asked gently.

There was a long pause, then she took a deep breath and responded on a sigh. "I suppose it's all right to tell you. You guys aren't with the FBI."

I could imagine the internal commotion that one was causing my husband.

Mary looked at me. "You know how she is—was—about the opponent."

"By 'the opponent' you mean Fritz Peterson, the Republican candidate?"

She nodded. "Even though Charlie doesn't have the nomination yet, Jody didn't see the other democratic candidates as a threat, because he's so popular. But she was just . . . obsessive about Mr. Peterson. She was trying as hard as she could to find something on him."

"Find something on him?" said Peter. "You mean some sort of dirt?"

She nodded again. "Anything that could be used against him."

"But that's not the kind of campaign Clarke is running," I said.

"I don't think he knows anything about it. You have to understand, Jody really believed that we *have* to get Mr. Clarke elected. She used to say it was for the 'preservation of the species.'"

"Would she go to lengths that Clarke himself wouldn't?"

"Uh-huh." She pulled a small white handkerchief from the pocket of her dress and dabbed at the area just beneath her eyes.

"But Mary," said Peter, "that doesn't explain what Jody was doing in the office at five in the morning."

"We . . . we were woken up by the phone this morning, about four o'clock. Jody picked it up. It was someone . . . it was someone who said he had a tape that she might be interested in."

"What kind of tape?"

"A videotape."

"What was on it?"

"I don't know. She didn't say. All she told me was that he wanted to meet her at the office at five."

"He?"

"That's what she said. I didn't want her to go. I've been so afraid ever since . . . ever since . . . they started calling here. But you know how Jody was." She paused for a moment to wipe away some tears, then straightened herself in her chair and cleared her throat. "Sometimes there was no arguing with her. She really wanted dirt on Mr. Peterson. So she went. There was nothing I could do to stop her." Mary sounded like she was trying to convince herself of this.

"But why not tell the FBI about this?" I asked. "If it's true, then there's any number of people who might have wanted to stop her, including Fritz Peterson himself. If the FBI can solve this, and it involves dirt on Peterson, then whatever it is will become public knowledge."

Mary shook her head emphatically. "Jody *never* would've wanted me to do that! She didn't trust the FBI. She thought they were just as likely to bury it up as they were to air it."

I had no doubt Mary was telling the truth. That sounded exactly like something Jody would say.

Peter was even more pensive as we walked back to the car this time. He wasn't just silent, there was a stoniness about the silence that made me feel as if it was directed at me. Once we were in the car, he rested his arm against the passenger window, shifted himself sideways so he could face me, and took a deep breath.

"I'd like to go on record as saying just how much I object to this little case of yours."

"Of *mine?*" I replied. "We're all on this case."

He raised his right eyebrow at me. "You were the one wagging his tail when the FBI approached us. And look at us now! I feel dirty!"

"Why?"

His left eyebrow joined the other. He looked absolutely astonished. "We haven't been doing this for ten minutes and already you've questioned your own mother and gotten a grieving widow to compromise herself!"

"Compromise herself how?"

"Alex, she told us what she knew because she didn't know we were working for the FBI!"

"Well, to be perfectly accurate, you were the one who got her to do that."

"What?!" he exclaimed, his jaw dropping open.

"I tried, but she wouldn't tell us anything. You were the one who got her to talk."

"I told her to talk to the FBI!"

"Well, she did, only she didn't know it!"

Several seconds elapsed before he shook his head and exhaled through slightly parted lips. "All I'm saying is when she opened up, I felt like we were betraying her."

"We've questioned people before."

"Openly. Not like this. Not while pretending to be their friends."

I looked out the windshield and sighed. I knew he was right. Somehow it never occurred to me when we first started our on again–off again relationship with the government that we would ever be put in the position of investigating our own friends. There was something seedy about it. I'd like to think that Peter doesn't have more scruples than I do, just that I'm a little slower to acknowledge them. But I'm probably flattering myself.

I said, "I don't suppose it helps to know it's for a good cause."

"Not much."

"How about this one: We're the best people to do it."

He turned back to me. "How do you mean?"

"You didn't like the way Henry and Raymond kept referring to 'our people.' I didn't either. Look, I'll admit I was gung-ho about taking on this job for selfish reasons, but that doesn't mean we're not the right people to do it. I'd much rather we were the ones looking into our friends and acquaintances than those guys from the FBI, wouldn't you?"

"I guess," he agreed reluctantly.

"Besides, we haven't betrayed anybody. We haven't reported back what Mary told us."

"But that's exactly what we're supposed to do. I don't feel right about telling Henry something that was told to us in confidence. Something that Mary purposely didn't tell the FBI."

"Oh, I don't either," I said with a smile. "And there's no need to."

The corner of Peter's mouth slid upward. "What are you thinking?"

I shrugged. "We're just supposed to report if somebody in Clarke's camp isn't what they seem to be. So far we don't know anything about that, do we?"

Peter laughed with genuine amusement. "You can split a hair closer than anyone I know. It amounts to the same thing. They wanted us to do that in hopes of finding the bomber. We're all looking for the same person."

"That doesn't mean we have to report any extraneous information that Mary gave us. Nothing she said gives me the impression that somebody in the office isn't who they say they are. How about you?"

He shook he head. "Nope."

"There! We're saved by semantics!"

We both laughed this time, and it was good to find ourselves coming back together. But I was beginning to worry that this case might cause us more problems than it was worth.

"Oh, God!" I exclaimed, sobering quickly. "I just thought of something!"

"What is it?"

"Given what Mary said, Jody really must've been the target of the bomb. I mean, if somebody called and lured her to the office just before it went off, then it looks like she was what they were after. And what better way to lure her there than by telling her that they had dirt on Peterson."

"That's true," Peter said slowly. "Except there's another possibility. The meeting could've been legitimate—"

"As legitimate as a clandestine meeting to get dirt on somebody can be," I interjected.

"Yeah. The timing could've just been really bad. After all, they haven't even been able to identify Jody yet. Maybe there was more than one person in the office when it blew."

74

"That seems awfully coincidental to me. I mean, that a bomb placed by a third party would go off just when the secret meeting is taking place."

We were silent for a few moments, mulling this over. Then I sighed. "Five in the morning is just such a weird time to do it. I thought clandestine meetings were always supposed to happen at midnight."

"Only in Charlie Chan movies, sweetheart," Peter replied with a smile.

FIVE

I wasn't quite sure what mood Mother would be in when we got home. I hadn't exactly handled things very well when I confronted her about Simon. I suppose I could've been more circumspect about it, but I excused myself somewhat with the reminder that it's natural to be on edge when you think your mother is dating a bomber.

As usual, she surprised me. If she'd been Dame Edith Evans when we left, she was Gertrude Lawrence when we returned.

"Darling," she said grandly as she glided up to me and gave me a peck on the forehead. " 'ow was your detecting? Was it productive?"

If her manner wasn't suspect enough, her missing aitch told me something was up.

"Our detecting was fine," I said warily. "We managed to get a bit of information." I explained what we'd learned from Mary.

"That sounds very promising, doesn't it?" she said when I'd finished.

I leveled my gaze at her. "What's up with you?"

"Whatever do you mean?"

"This is *me*, Mother! I know you. You were angry when we left and now you're acting like something out of Noel Coward. What are you up to?"

"Nothing at all," she said with a shrug. She was only lacking a cocktail in one hand and a foot-long cigarette holder in the other. "What gave you the idea I was angry?"

Peter was unsuccessfully covering a wide grin with the fingers of his left hand, and he seemed to be vibrating.

"The way you acted when I asked you about Simon," I said.

"Oh, that!" she replied with a flip of her hand. "I was a trifle put out about that at first, but I decided you were perfectly right in what you said. Simon is virtually a stranger, and he was in the office at the time in question, so it's only right that we investigate him."

"It is?" My wariness had pretty much gone through the ceiling.

"And since we're agreed on that, and since he *says* he would like to get to know you better . . ." she emphasized the word *says*, mildly mocking my suspicions, "I've decided we should all go out to dinner."

"What?!" I exclaimed in disbelief. If I hadn't particularly wanted my mother dating this guy, I wanted even less to accompany her on one of her dates.

"I talked to Simon this afternoon, and he thinks it's a marvelous idea. He's taking us all out to dinner this evening."

Peter couldn't hold it in any longer. He laughed and said, "You're right, that's wonderful."

"You're joking," I said to Mother.

She spread her palms. "It's perfect. You'll get to know him, he'll get to know you . . . and as long as he's a suspect, I'll get paid for going out with him! You see, darling? Everyone's happy!"

Despite any personal feelings I had in the matter, I couldn't deny that Mother's idea was a good one, whatever her own motives might have been. Dinner together would allow us to conversationally probe her new boyfriend, hopefully without appearing to be anything more than naturally interested parties. Which is why at seven o'clock that evening Peter and I found ourselves dolled up in suits and ties, out on a double date with my mother.

We were seated at a table in the center of the room at Mon Petit, the restaurant Simon had chosen because it was the first place he'd dined with Mother. He explained that because of this, it held a special place in his heart. It was all I could do not to grimace when he said it. Peter and I sat at a discreet, old-married-couple distance from each other on one side of the table, while Simon sat close beside Mother on the other side with one arm casually draped across the back of her chair.

I had to admit that Simon was, if nothing else, suave in the extreme. His navy suit was immaculate, and he sported a black tie that fanned out from a small knot at his throat down his crisp white shirt. The gray hairs on either side of his head were slicked back, along with the rest of his dark mane. He oozed British charm. He paid close attention to Mother's wants and needs, and listened intently to every word she spoke. He was so perfect a companion to her he could've done it for a living.

"So," I said, taking a sip of the champagne that Simon had ordered before we'd even reached the table, "how are your seminars going?"

He screwed up his handsome face. "Deadly dull. I'd much rather spend the time with your mum."

Mother beamed and wrinkled her nose at him like a rabbit in heat. If I'd had a grapefruit, I would've squashed it in her face. Simon opened a menu which he shared with her.

"It was nice of your company to foot the bill for a trip like this," I said. "Which company was that again?"

"I work for a large computer company," he said in a slightly tired tone designed to let me know he didn't relish talking about work during his off hours.

"Yes, but which one? I'm very interested in computers."

"Are you?"

"Yes. Peter and I keep meaning to get one, don't we, honey?"

"Uh-huh," Peter said dully. I got the feeling he didn't want to participate.

"Oh, yes! I keep meaning to get one," I continued, ignoring the fact that there was currently a computer sitting on the desk in my home office.

"What would you use it for?" Simon asked.

"Oh, a million things. Mother might have told you that I have my own graphic art business. I could use a computer to keep the books."

"You're a freelance artist," he said, apparently impressed. "That must be fascinating."

Mother sat smiling across the table at me. It wasn't until I saw her expression that I realized Simon had managed to turn the tables and we were now talking about my work instead of his.

"Not really," I replied. "Your work is probably much more interesting. You know, I was thinking that, since I want to get a computer one of these days, maybe you could get me a deal on one."

"Actually," he said smoothly, "we don't really sell computers. We don't sell directly to the public at all, as a matter of fact."

"Oh really? What do you do?"

There was a bit of a sigh: just enough to reinforce the idea that he didn't like talking about work when he was away from it. "We develop new microchips. Far too difficult, really, to describe to the layman. And most of it is rather hush-hush, you know." He lowered his voice and said in an amused, conspiratorial tone, "Industry spies, secrets and all that. I can never really discuss what we're doing."

How convenient, I thought.

"Really?" I said with interest. "I'm sorry, which company was that again?"

He hesitated for a split second before answering. "It's called Cyberdyne. I'm sure you've never heard of it."

Actually, the name did sound familiar to me, but I couldn't call to mind where I'd heard it before. I tried to comfort myself with the fact that I'd finally gotten the name out of him.

"All quite silly, really," he continued. "All this hush-hush business. But I do have to abide by the company rules."

Peter looked at me with a half-smile and a raised eyebrow, as if to say, "Are you satisfied?" I wasn't really, but couldn't see a way to press on without appearing unduly inquisitive. I was saved from the embarrassing pause by the arrival of our waiter. Of course, since Mother was the only female at the table he addressed her first. She looked to Simon in a way so annoyingly feminine I almost asked the waiter for a grapefruit. Simon asked him for a recommendation, then ordered the suggested entrée for the both of them. Then Peter and I gave our orders.

As we handed the menus back, Peter leaned over to me and whispered, "You might want to wipe that look of horror off your face."

Once the waiter had scurried away, Simon said, "Jean tells me you've had a bit of excitement in your lives."

"Which bit?"

He laughed. "I hope your lives don't get much more exciting than having your office explode!"

"Oh, that!" I said. "Well, we weren't there at the time. It's funny, though. It happened the day after you were there."

"Really?" he said with surprise, his accent deepening. "Fancy that! Good job you weren't there when it happened!"

"It happened at five in the morning," said Peter, "at a time when nobody was supposed to be there. But somebody was."

"That's dreadful!" Simon exclaimed. "Who would do a thing like that?"

"That's what we'd all like to know," I said pointedly. "There've been a lot of threats leveled at Charles Clarke, so it seems as if one of them has been carried out." He looked across the table at me with such innocent interest that I couldn't help but try to shake his composure. "But all it is now is a matter of sorting through the threats and following them up. Check up on all the people who were in the office. I'm sure the authorities with be able to track down whoever did it."

"Well, that's comforting at least. I don't fancy the idea that there's some maniac bomber running around."

"Oh, it's not necessarily a maniac," I said slyly. "It could be someone who was hired to do it. For political reasons."

Mother laughed. "Alex, you have such an imagination!"

Simon shook his head and smiled. "I'm afraid American politics is just beyond me. I never can straighten out all those different levels of government and positions and things. If someone wanted to hire me to bomb someone, I wouldn't even know what it was for."

"Would that matter?" I asked. I then cried out, drawing the attention of everyone in the restaurant, as a sharp pain shot through my ankle.

"Oh, I'm sorry, sweetheart," Peter said with barely believable sincerity. "I thought that was the table leg."

"What were you trying to do," I snarled under my breath, "kick the table over?"

"Excuse me for a moment," said Mother, trying to keep from laughing as she rose from her seat, "I'm just going to powder my nose."

Simon rose with her like a perfect gentleman, and his eyes followed her as she crossed the room. He resumed his seat, and there were only a few seconds of silence before he leaned in toward me.

"I know what you're after."

"I beg you pardon?" I said with a glance at Peter, who couldn't have looked more surprised than I did.

"I haven't failed to notice the tone of your questions."

"I . . . I'm sorry if I . . ."

"No, no, no!" he said expansively as he sat back. "Nothing more natural! I've been squiring your mother around the town like an aging suitor. Of course you would be concerned about my intentions."

"Your intentions?" I said after a beat. "I didn't realize you had any."

"I can assure you they're completely honorable."

"I'm glad to hear it."

He sighed wistfully. "I've never had this happen to me before, you see."

"What?"

"I've never met a woman quite as smashing as Jean. I'm afraid she's hit me like a ton of bricks."

"She has that effect on most men," I intoned.

"Oh, not like this," he continued with a shake of his head. "I never expected when I came over here that I would meet someone like her. I tell you, it's fair knocked me for a loop! And I daresay she feels the same way about me."

"You do?" I replied, hoping I didn't look as perfectly aghast as I felt at what I was hearing.

"Oh, I realize it's only been a few days, and we're only at the beginnings of having a relationship develop. But how long should it take, anyway? That's the reason I've decided to stay on a bit once the seminars are over. I know it may seem like I'm rushing into things, but I was really only expected to be over here for a fortnight to begin with, and I'm not going to be able to stay over much longer. I shall have to go back to work, you see?"

I sputtered something ineffectual.

"I know everything seems to be happening very quickly," he continued, "but I've only so much time. I can understand your reticence, but I do hope you wouldn't think of standing in the way of your mother's happiness. Would you?"

"I . . . I . . ."

"Lor', Alex!"

I almost jumped out of my skin. I'd been so astonished, I hadn't noticed Mother's approach. "You look like you've just swallowed a tack! Are you all right?"

I looked up at her for one shocked second, then shook my head briskly to clear it and snatched up my glass. "I'm fine. Don't worry. I haven't swallowed anything."

I downed my drink in one gulp.

The rest of the dinner was subdued, at least on my part. Mother nattered away while Simon made very dignified cow eyes at her—

or whatever the male equivalent is. Bull eyes, I suppose. Peter bravely kept up our end of the conversation, although I could tell he was as nonplussed by Simon's professions as I was. I spent the evening trying my best not to gape at Simon. Occasionally I caught Mother looking at me as if a prescription drug disclaimer was written on my face and she was having trouble reading it.

After dinner, Simon drove us home in his rental car. There was an awkward pause when he parked in front of our house. He and Mother made no move to get out of the car. At first I thought Simon's manners had finally failed him, and he didn't realize that Mother was waiting for him to come around and open the door for her. But I was proved wrong when she slued sideways, looked at me over her shoulder and said, "I'll be in in a tick."

"Oh!" I said stupidly. Peter and I popped open our respective doors and climbed out of the car.

On the way up the steps to the house, Peter said, "Well, *that* was embarrassing."

"I'm not the one nuzzling in a car," I replied.

He stopped beneath the porch light and looked me in the eye. "We've nuzzled in our share of cars."

"We're half their age."

"Right. And when we're their age, I for one intend to go on nuzzling. Was it your plan to stop sometime?"

I sighed. "You know, I really hate it when you're so damned reasonable!"

We sat in the living room, switched on the television and watched the news while waiting for Mother to finish . . . whatever she was doing.

The news, of course, was full of the bombing. A reporter stood in front of the rubble offering some of the speculations that had been put forward over the course of the day: that terrorists had been responsible, or zealots, or the ever popular militia theory.

There were clips of press conferences. Clarke decried the use of violence and the senseless loss of life. He sounded both saddened and disgusted by the event. Fritz Peterson seized the opportunity to denounce radicals. He seemed to genuinely disparage anyone who would resort to violence, while at the same time managing to make it sound as if his opponent had brought it on himself with his ultra-liberal views. The candidates' appearances were followed by a clip of the Reverend Nat Albertson, head of a right-wing church located on the northwest side, who expressed his disappointment that anyone would kill to get their way. Then he explained that he could fully understand the frustration and fury that people feel toward potential legislators like Charles Clarke, who condone perversion and would try to make it socially acceptable. And that when people are confronted with evil, sometimes they might feel that violence was the only recourse.

"Then again," he added none-too-quickly, "we don't condone murder."

"The Lord giveth and the Lord taketh away," I said. "This jerk doesn't condone murder unless it's against someone he doesn't agree with."

It was almost half an hour before Mother joined us. She sat down near me on the couch and let out a contented sigh that I'm sure was meant to irritate me. I switched off the television.

"That was nice," she said. "Dinner, I mean. Simon is really a charmer, isn't he?"

"Why is it I always think of 'charmer' and 'snake' together," I said.

"I don't know, dear." She wasn't exactly smirking, but she certainly looked as if she was finding something very amusing.

"Mother, we need to have a talk."

"Coo, this sounds serious!"

"It is. How do you feel about Simon?"

"I should think that's obvious. I like him."

"You do?" I couldn't help feeling just a little heartsick, but hoped I didn't sound it.

"Of course I do. He's very handsome. He's great fun. And he's a marvelous companion."

"Are you serious about him?"

Her smile disappeared and she knit her brows. "What kind of talk is this?"

"I think he's serious about you."

"Alex, you sound just like a teenage girl! What's gotten into you?"

"Simon, that's what! While you were away from the table, he said some things that . . . that make me believe he's . . . well, serious about you. I don't know how else to say it." I looked over at Peter and turned my palms up in a plea for help.

"Actually, Jean, as much as I hate to agree with Alex in this—since I don't think he has any business nosing into it—Simon really did sound as if he was smitten with you."

Her face opened up like a happy flower. "Smitten? Is he *really?* I like that!"

"And I just wanted to make sure," I said soberly, "that you weren't going to allow yourself to get rushed into anything."

She beamed at me with one eye narrowed for a very long time. Then she leaned over and kissed my cheek.

"Don't you worry yourself, darling." She got up and smoothed her skirt. "I'd never get rushed into anything I didn't want to be a part of, and I assure you, I know how to handle Simon."

She went up the stairs without another word.

I turned to Peter and said, "Why is it I worry more when she says things like that?"

Peter sighed and came over to the couch. He sat close beside me and took my hand.

"Well, are you at least satisfied now that Simon is only after your mother and is not the one who planted the bomb in Clarke's office?" He whispered this in my ear as he rubbed his nose against it.

I thought about this for a moment, then said, "Not so fast."

"What?" he replied, pulling back in disbelief.

"Think about it for a minute. If Simon really was the bomber, if he'd wanted to infiltrate the office, what better way would there be than to get involved with Mother so it wouldn't seem odd if he went there with her . . ."

"Come on, Alex!"

"*Then,* the best way for him to avoid suspicion afterward is to express this sort of over-the-top affection for her."

"Ignoring the fact that your Mother is inherently loveable."

"That's what makes it all so perfect! What better cover? Anyone would believe he'd fallen in love with her!"

Peter's face was a picture of incredulity. Then he uncurled his lips and broke into a wide smile. "Come here."

"What?"

He put one hand behind my neck and drew me toward him. "Come here."

"What are you doing?" I said, totally baffled.

"I'm kissing you, you idiot!"

He planted his lips on mine and gave me a long, deep kiss. When our lips parted, he said, "I don't know why, but the goofier you get, the more I love you."

I hesitated for a moment. The stirring below my belt told me where this was going, but I wasn't sure I was ready to drop the subject yet.

I said, "Yeah, but I'm really—"

The end of my sentence was lost as Peter touched his lips to mine again, his tongue gently darting into my mouth.

Somewhere in the back of my mind I was dimly aware of having been worried about something, but it would be hours before I could remember what it was.

SIX

Our investigation was temporarily sidelined by the fact that there was no place to pursue it. We got a call Monday morning telling us that Clarke's new office would open on Wednesday in a building on Wabash on the south side of the Loop.

So on Monday and Tuesday I engaged in some anxious moping, while Peter worked at his day job and Mother flitted around the house like a latent, lovesick Joanna Lumley, which I tried very had to ignore. Somehow Simon managed to find the time in between seminars to take her to lunch and dinner both days. Although I still had my suspicions about him, his attentions to Mother were so obvious that I had to accept that his intentions were romantic rather than anarchist, however much I would've preferred the latter.

The only news on the bombing over those two days, according to the media, was that there was no news: only the mounting concern that it had been the work of some terrorist group with the usual amount of verbal garment-rending over how this might be the beginning of the kind of terrorism so familiar overseas coming to our native shores. Controversy raged over Rev. Nat Albertson's remarks, which some felt had implied that he had some sort of inside information about the bombing. He held another press conference in which he expressed his outrage that the FBI would include him in their investigation, claiming this was just another instance of the government trying to extend their wily grasp into the affairs of the church. He actually said "wily grasp," which of course made him look guiltier.

Peter arranged with Arthur Dingle—the most understanding store owner in the city of Chicago—to take a few days off. So Wednesday morning we rode the El downtown to the Madison Street stop.

"Exactly how are we going to do this?" asked Peter as we walked over to Wabash.

"What?"

"Well, Agents Henry and Raymond said we're supposed to be looking for someone who isn't what they say they are, right?"

"Yeah," I replied. "They think the office might've been infiltrated by a member of a militia or something."

Peter made a noise that sounded something like "Feh!"

"I'm not the one who came up with that!" I said.

"Okay, okay. But like you said, most of the people in this office are gay, so doesn't this come dangerously close to trying to find out who's really gay and who's not?"

"Maybe, except in this case it would be the closet breeders who're in trouble. But look, the FBI wants to know if there's anyone who isn't what they seem. Meaning anyone. There *are* some straight people working for Clarke, for Christ's sake!"

"And how exactly are we supposed to find out which is which? Hit on guys until somebody bashes us, or just report the first person who can't recite all the words to 'Younger than Springtime'?"

"Are you going to be like this all day?"

"I just want to repeat for the record that I don't like what we're doing. First of all, it's probably impossible. If somebody's been clever enough to get into the Clarke camp without blowing their cover, I doubt if they'll be stupid enough to slip in front of us. And second, it's probably a wild goose chase anyway. These g-men have come up with some strange ideas in their time, but this one is completely nuts."

"Thirdly?" I prompted.

He stopped suddenly and looked at me gravely. "What if we're wrong? What if we think somebody's suspicious, and we're wrong? Do you have any idea how much trouble we could cause somebody if we reported them?

"You mean falsely accuse somebody of being straight?"

He gave a little huff of exasperation. "You know what I mean! If we tell Henry and Raymond that we suspect anybody of anything, they're going to be all over whoever it is."

"I know," I said seriously. "So we're going to have to be very careful. Honey, I know I seemed really excited about getting this case, but I'm not blind. We can't report anything to the FBI unless we're sure of it."

"And how are we going to do that?"

"I don't know," I said as we started to walk again. "Nose around. Keep our eyes and ears open. I think Henry's idea is stupid, too. What we really need to do is find out if anybody knows about that tape."

"Nobody said anything about looking for that tape, if there really is one!"

"Somebody has to. The FBI doesn't know about it. We do. And we can't tell them about it, remember?" I tried not to sound as if I was enjoying trapping him in his own scruples.

He sighed with frustration. "If Jody was trying to find dirt on Peterson, she wouldn't have been doing it at Clarke's headquarters, would she?"

"I don't know. Where would you find dirt on a politician?"

"Probably everywhere you look, but that's not the point."

I laughed. "Well, the thing is, if there is a tape of Peterson doing something scandalous, I would think *somebody* at Clarke's office would know about it. Maybe if we find out who has the tape, we can find out who killed Jody."

"Alex . . ." Peter said warningly.

"I'm not going to get us in trouble."

The new office was in the middle of the block in an older building that was the color of Farina and dotted with soot and grime. Just inside the revolving door there was a set of newly installed metal detectors through which you had to pass in order to proceed. Just past the detectors was a guy in a khaki uniform and wearing a holstered gun, sitting behind a desk and reading the *Sun-Times*. To his right was a huge black building directory with the names of the resident businesses listed in white press-on letters. Peter and I stood for a time staring at the board, looking for Clarke.

"It's not here," I said.

"Can I help you?" the guard said without looking up from his reading.

"We want Charles Clarke's office," I said.

"Five."

"Five what?"

He looked up for the first time. "Fifth floor." His tone implied I was a halfwit.

A sign over the elevators on the left side of the hallway indicated that they were the ones that serviced floors one through twenty. We got on the first one that opened and went up to the fifth floor.

The decor in the hallway was enough to turn an interior decorator's heart to stone: dark brown, deep pile carpet and walls a sort of vomit tan painted in thick coats over a layer of wallpaper. We were silent as we went down the hall looking for the office. I felt as if the walls and floor would snap shut on me if I said anything. A piece of computer paper—the kind with perforated edges—was taped to the door at the end of the hall. On it was printed a message informally announcing CHARLES CLARKE'S CAMPAIGN HEADQUARTERS.

"This is it," said Peter.

"Happy hunting," I replied as I opened the door.

"Hold it!" a voice commanded as we stepped through the doorway. It came from a guard in a blue uniform. Like the guard in the lobby, he had a gun holstered on his right hip, but this one was also carrying a clipboard. The ensemble made him look like an overly strict school principal.

"Who are you?"

"I'm Alex Reynolds, this is Peter Livesay."

His gaze slowly traveled from me to Peter as if he were memorizing our faces. Then he scanned the list on his clipboard and checked off our names.

"Okay," he said.

Despite the age and state of the building, the new office was a definite improvement over the old one. At least it looked liked we were working in an office rather than squatting in an abandoned store. In lieu of office furniture, which either hadn't been delivered yet or hadn't even been ordered, several long tables of the church basement variety were set up in the main room. The one along the windows served as a makeshift phone bank. Boxes were piled up on the wall to the right, and to the left were two doors, side by side, leading to inner offices for Clarke and Schuler.

The place was swarming with volunteers. The recent bombing seemed to have heightened interest rather than scaring people off. Some of them were manning the phones, which were already ringing at an alarming rate, while others were busy unpacking boxes.

"Where do we start?" said Peter.

"I don't know," I replied. "I don't know who the new office manager is."

"I am," said a voice just behind us. We turned around to find Shawn Stillman. Instead of the casual clothes he had formerly worn in common with the rest of us, he was now dressed in a new (but cheap) suit.

"You've been promoted," I said with a smile.

"Yeah. I think they asked Mary Linn-Hadden to do it first—just out of respect—but she didn't want to."

"You don't look too happy about it."

He grimaced comically. "The last office manager is dead."

"Point well taken. What do you want us to do?"

"You guys want to work together?"

"We don't need to," I said quickly, figuring that we'd be able to cover more ground separately.

"Okey dokey," Shawn replied. He turned to Peter. "Do you know how to do the phones?"

"You mean answer them? Yeah."

"Good then. There's one free over there." He pointed to the table by the windows. "Just sit and answer the phone for a while. We're kind of disorganized, this being the first day here and all. So I'll just leave you there for a while. If you get tired or run into any trouble, just yodel."

"All right," said Peter. He added, "See you later" to me as he went to the phones.

"Now you," Shawn said, putting an index finger to his chin and pursing his lips. "You work with those guys over there, would you?" He indicated a table by the wall where a couple of guys were unloading the contents of one of the boxes. My heart sank.

"Fliers."

"Yeah. Isn't it awful?" said Shawn. "All that work we did over at Lincoln, and the whole mailing—everything—was blown sky-high. We have to start all over again."

"Oh, Jesus!" I moaned.

"Yeah, but it can't be helped. That mailing is for the primary, so we've got to get it all out before next Tuesday. We had all the stuff sent up from Springfield."

I sighed heavily. "Are you sure we can't use a mailing service?"

He smiled. "After Clarke wins the primary, we'll have all the money we need. You know how the Democratic party is: They might not agree with everything Clarke stands for, and they might not exactly be supporting him now, but the minute he's the official candidate, that'll be all she wrote! They'd back an axe murderer if they thought he could win against a Republican."

I was momentarily taken aback by this. I hadn't gotten to talk to Shawn much during our mutual volunteering, but he'd always seemed very gung-ho for Clarke. Now he sounded almost mercenary. Although what he'd just said wasn't a direct aspersion on the candidate, it certainly could be construed as a very negative assessment of our party. And it was just the type of thing Agents Henry and Raymond had told us to listen for.

As I walked over to the work area I found myself shaking my head with disgust at my own thoughts. This was the very reason Peter hated this assignment so much: It was so insidious. What Shawn had said was no different from anything any of us—myself included—had said about both parties. I wondered how I was going to be able to report anything at all to our contacts.

Even though I might not have been happy to be stuffing envelopes again, it suited the needs of our investigation perfectly. I was joined at the table by Joe Gardner and Mickey Downs.

Joe was about as ordinary as his name. He had a sharply receding hairline, perpetually arched brows, and shoebutton eyes, all of which together gave him the appearance of a light bulb with pupils. He wore an old blue shirt and dull brown pants. If Peter was right and we were meant to find out who was gay and who wasn't, Joe's attire was one strike against him.

The only thing that would've made Mickey a candidate for the part of militia mole was his blond crewcut. It would've taken lead weights to get his feet to touch the ground. He was handsome in a seventies-disco-queen sort of way. His body was slight and taut and wrapped in a tight violet tank-top and even tighter denim jeans. On his feet were a pair of black sneakers with Winnie-the-Pooh laces.

"Honestly," said Mickey, once we'd settled into work. "I *thought* we'd finished this up at the old place."

He made it sound like it had been years since we were at the former office.

"I know what you mean," I said. "I have paper cuts all over my fingers."

"Ewww!" He pursed his entire face. "If I start getting paper cuts I'm going to have to take to my bed!"

Joe frowned and said nothing.

"I can't believe we have to do this thing all over again," I continued, angling to draw out my two companions. "God, and we were almost finished with it before the office blew up."

"Oh, well," Mickey said with a dramatic sigh, "a woman's work is never done."

Apparently he was already getting tired of the conversation.

"I supposed it's all worth it if we can get Clarke elected." I tried to sound naively enthusiastic. From the curious look I got from Joe, I had a feeling I sounded exactly like I was trying to pump them for the FBI.

"Do you really think he has a chance of winning?" Joe asked.

I blinked. "Sure. Why not?"

"Well, I got this the other day in the mail." He reached into his back pocket, pulled out a pamphlet that had been folded several times, and handed it over to me.

I opened it. Emblazoned across the top in red letters was: IS THIS WHO YOU WANT REPRESENTING YOU IN THE SENATE? Beneath the startling headline was a picture of a drag queen atop a float. He was in a sequined dress and feather boa, and leering directly at the camera with his tongue hanging way out. It looked like it had been taken at one of the pride parades.

"Oh, I know her!" said Mickey, glancing at the picture. "She's a tramp!"

"It's pretty effective, don't you think?" said Joe, ignoring him. "It makes gay people look like a bunch of freaks."

"Gay people"—not "us," I thought.

"It makes me so mad when I see stuff like this," he said as he took the pamphlet from me and stuck it back into his pocket. "It makes me think that gay people are their own worst enemies."

"You really think so?" I said with interest.

"I mean, normal people look at a picture like that and it makes them sick."

Normal people, I repeated silently.

"I've done drag," Mickey said. He made a little moue at Joe, and, imitating a hygiene commercial, said, "It made me feel soft and feminine."

Joe looked over at me and rolled his eyes.

"Anyway," he said, "I know gay people want to get Clarke

elected, but if they don't stay out of the limelight they're going to end up shooting themselves in the foot."

The way he put this pushed me past being suspicious. I was starting to get angry.

"Excuse me for asking this," I said, "but are you gay?"

Apparently I'd said this loudly enough for Peter to hear it over at the phone table. He looked up with amazement.

Joe's mouth dropped open and his skin grew white. "Of course I am. Why would you ask something like that?"

"Because you keep saying 'gay people do this' and 'gay people do that' as if you aren't one of us."

He looked down at the table and his face suddenly flushed bright crimson. "I'm sorry. No need to bite my head off. It's just a way of talking."

It was then that the door popped open, and John Schuler entered followed closely by Charles Clarke and his wife, Wendy.

"Hello, everybody!" called out the candidate with a wave. He turned to his wife with elaborate deference and said, "Wendy, this is the new office. What do you think?"

Wendy Clarke smiled and shook her head as if she were awestruck. She clapped her hands under her chin. "I think it's . . . it's . . . just *wonderful!*"

There was an audible sigh of relief among the workers, which made me wonder if someone had actually been worried about what the candidate's wife thought of the office.

John Schuler went back to his new private office, and Clarke moved to follow but paused just long enough to give Wendy a discreet peck on the forehead.

Wendy shrugged at the volunteers and said, "I'm going shopping. Keep up the good work, everyone! Goodbye!"

"Goodbye," we said in chorus. We sounded like the partygoers wishing a goodnight to the Von Trapp family children. Sure, that "So Long, Farewell" song of theirs was cute and all, but I always felt that the guests must've been awfully glad to see the retreating backsides of those insipid little brats.

Wendy Clarke left the office and everyone went back to what they'd been doing.

"Jesus Christ!" Mickey exclaimed in a delighted whisper as we resumed our envelope stuffing. "Isn't that Schuler guy a fox?"

"John Schuler?" I was a bit perplexed, mainly because Schuler seemed awfully straight-laced to be capturing Mickey's interest. "Is he gay?"

"Who cares? I like to look at him!"

"Schuler's not gay," Joe interjected with a force that was uncalled for. He glanced at Mickey with something bordering on contempt.

"How do you know?" I asked.

"He's just not," Joe said defensively.

"That's not what I hear," Mickey said with a gossipy little pucker of his lips. "I hear that our Johnnie has a past!"

"He's married!" Joe exclaimed.

"That doesn't mean he doesn't have a past!" Mickey needled.

"Why does everybody have to be gay?"

"As far as I know, they don't," I said.

"Don't you think he's handsome?" Mickey asked Joe.

"Not really."

I seized this as a golden opportunity to get some information.

"Oh, are you going with someone?" I asked, figuring I could use his lack of attraction to the campaign manager (who was pretty attractive) as an excuse.

"No. I don't have anyone right now," he replied sullenly.

I made a mental note of that and turned to Mickey. "What about you?"

"Always on the prowl," he said with a wicked smile.

I looked around the room for a moment. "What about Shawn Stillman?"

"What about him?"

"Do you think he's handsome?"

Shawn was across the room talking to one of the volunteers. Mickey peered over at him as if assessing him for the first time. "I wouldn't kick him out of my bed, as long as he kept his mouth shut—I mean, as long as he didn't talk. He's way too dull."

"What do you mean?"

"Haven't you talked to him since his promotion? He's way full of himself!"

"I only talked to him for a minute. He seemed all right, just a little frazzled."

"Don't let the frazzled bit fool you! Oh, yeah, he's pretending to be in over his head, but that's just an act. I knew Shawn from the clubs long before this, and he's so full of himself he would never ever say he was overwhelmed if he really meant it! He was probably angling for that job all along!"

"Why would he want a high-pressure volunteer job?" I asked.

"Volunteer job?" Mickey squinched his face up so tightly he looked like the butt end of a balloon. "What volunteer job? Office manager is one of the few paying positions here! Do you think the late and unlamented Jody Linn-Hadden was doing this out of the goodness of that lump of coal in the center of her chest?"

Now this was a wrinkle I hadn't thought of: that someone might've actually wanted Jody out of the way to get her job. I found myself mentally shaking my head. It couldn't pay that much. But I remembered the way Shawn had seemed to watch Jody at the old office.

"Did Shawn ever say anything about wanting this job?" I asked.

Mickey let out a bored sigh. "No, but you can bet he wanted it!"

"Humph!" Joe said. "Sounds like when you knew him at the clubs, he turned you down."

"I never asked," Mickey said, though he turned a bit pink. "Besides, Shawnie doesn't fool around. He's already taken."

"He is?" I said.

Mickey nodded. "He has a boyfriend. He's mentioned him from time to time."

"But you've never met him."

"Uh-uh." He smiled coyly. "Why? Are you interested?"

"Good grief, no!" I said, hoping to God that I hadn't appeared too nosey. "You see that guy over there? The one on the phone by the end of the table?"

"The guy you came in with?"

"That's my husband, Peter."

"Wow," Mickey said, echoing my sentiments exactly. "I can see why you wouldn't be looking."

Joe glanced over at Peter, then at me, as if he was trying to picture us together—I don't mean in the biblical sense—then lowered his eyes again.

"Peter and I are so happily married we even disgust ourselves. I was just asking about Shawn because I don't know anybody here very well. I mean, any of the people here today. Our friends Jo and Sheila volunteer when they can, but they're the only ones we're really close to."

"Oh," Mickey replied, barely listening. He had paused in his stuffing and was still looking over at Peter. "How long have the two of you been together?"

"About eight years now."

He sighed deeply and shoved a flier into an envelope. "I wish I could find something like that, but the only thing I meet at the bars are trogs, alcoholics, and assholes." He tossed the envelope into the "done" box, then leaned over to me and whispered, "If you want to know the truth, that's why I decided to volunteer."

I couldn't help smiling. "To meet guys?"

He shrugged. "Ann Landers says it's the best way!"

The two of us continued to chat as we worked, while Joe remained on the periphery of the conversation. He didn't seem overly fond of Mickey, which I chalked up to a general prejudice against the lighter of our brethren—although I hadn't made any points with Joe, either. If I'd wanted to draw him out I never should have been so direct, no matter how interesting I found the reaction.

Mickey went on at length about the other men who were working in the office. He was one of those guys who is overly well-versed in the sex lives of almost everyone around him. But I listened closely and didn't have to feign interest since all of it, assuming it was true, was useful to our purpose.

Although things were relatively peaceful at our table, the office itself was in a steady state of bustle. Delivery men were in and out, and new volunteers arrived as others left, and the phones rang constantly, which I imagined was keeping Peter from doing any sleuthing at all. Even with the number of volunteers there that day, I hardly recognized any from the old office. Most of them were new faces, presumably recruited by Shawn Stillman.

Shawn stopped by our table a couple of times to exhort us to work faster. He promised that some more help would be coming in the afternoon, but he didn't sound confident when he said it. He was so busy with his new job and trying to get the office together that it was impossible to get him to stay and talk, so I made another mental note that we'd have to try to discreetly tackle him some other time.

"Can I have your attention please?" John Schuler announced loudly. I hadn't noticed him coming out of his office. He seemed to suddenly materialize in the center of the room like a vampire congealing from vapor. I welcomed the chance to get to see in action the man whose only qualification for the job, in Jody's assessment, was that he was a leech. As he spoke he seemed confident enough, but he held a note pad in his palm and looked down at it repeatedly like a performer who hasn't quite mastered his lines yet.

"Charlie and I would like to thank you all for the hard and very necessary work you're doing. We realize that the place is a bit disorganized today . . ." Here he smiled like a politician. "And that's no reflection on Shawn Stillman, who's done a bang-up job of getting this place together in record time."

There was a smattering of applause for Shawn, who I swear to God was *trying* to blush. He wasn't successful.

Schuler continued. "Anyway, we know it's a bit disorganized right now, but Shawn and the rest of the staff are working very, very hard to get this place together as quickly as possible. We want you to know that we thank you for your patience, your hard work, and your support. Why don't you give yourselves a hand?"

He began clapping lightly, and there was another smattering of applause.

"Now, there're a few things we need to tell you about. First, of course you all know about the terrible tragedy that necessitated our move to these new 'digs,' and that there was a death involved. We need to remember Jody Linn-Hadden as a fine person, a woman of great conviction, and a tireless worker for our cause . . ."

He didn't mention her being liked by anyone.

"There will be a memorial service for her on Sunday at the Waverly Chapel. The address and time will be posted on the bulletin board. All are invited to attend. Now, because of the tragedy, the police will probably be in and out of here for a while, so I don't want any of you to be bothered by this." He manufactured another smile, this time to let us know that the matter wasn't something that needed to be taken seriously. "On a happier note, I'd like to remind you all that there will be a fund-raiser held on Friday night at the home of a gentleman named . . . um . . . Tony Milano."

I lowered my eyes and smiled. Peter and I knew Tony. It didn't surprise me that Schuler stumbled over his name.

"Mr. Milano has generously offered to sponsor this event to help raise money for this office, and we're very grateful. Unfortunately, Charlie and I will not be able to attend, but we'd like as many of you to be there as possible. I'm sure you'll all enjoy yourselves." It seemed to me that Clarke and Schuler were distancing themselves from the Milano event in the nicest possible way, but that didn't surprise me, either. There was a pause, then he thanked us all for listening and went back into his office.

My first impression of Schuler held through to the end of his presentation. He never ceased glancing at his notebook, and I got the feeling that even if he'd had his lines down cold, any interruption from the audience would have sent him spinning.

Peter and I had agreed beforehand that we would leave the office at two o'clock, which we did with great relief. After six hours of stuffing envelopes I was feeling sadly arthritic, and Peter said he'd developed a permanent crick in his neck from holding the phone between his ear and shoulder.

"Looks like it's time to hand out the rocking chairs," I said. "How were the phones?"

"It seems this open attack on Clarke has caused a groundswell of support."

"He was already popular."

"This goes beyond that. Most of the calls I took today were from people who said they'd been undecided on how to vote before, but after the bombing they'd decided to go for Clarke. If anything, the attack has helped his campaign."

"Makes you wonder if he did it himself."

Peter looked at me out of the corner of his eye. "Don't even say that."

"Just pointing out the obvious. Did you find out anything about anyone?"

He shook his head. "Not much. I didn't have much time in between calls. And the only people sitting close enough to me to talk to were Richard Birch and Annie Watson."

"But that's good," I said. "Both of them worked in the old office."

"Well, Richard kept talking about a guy named Jerry. I never did find out whether or not that was his boyfriend. He seems nice enough, but he never once said a word about politics unless he was answering the phone. Annie didn't talk about much of anything. She seemed distracted."

"Hmm."

"What?"

"Annie had a key to the old office. She was the one who opened up the day Jody and Mary were late—when they got that threatening phone call."

"So what?"

"So, she could easily have planted the bomb."

"Alex, anybody could've done that. Remember? Henry said they had no way of knowing whether or not the place was broken into."

I sighed. "I suppose. I guess it didn't matter if whoever it was broke a lock or a window to get in if the whole place was going to be rubble."

"Did you do any better than I did?" asked Peter.

"Shawn Stillman has a boyfriend, but I don't know who it is. Mickey Downs doesn't have a boyfriend but wants one. He's a barfly. He gets around quite a bit and knew a lot about the other guys in the office. He knows a lot less about the women for obvious reasons. Joe Gardner doesn't have a boyfriend and doesn't sound like he wants one, which is fortunate because he has the personality of a castrated rhino. But who knows? Maybe he could find another political fag with no taste in clothes." I gave him a rundown of everything else I'd heard, then ended with, "And by the way, that Jerry that Richard Birch mentioned *is* his boyfriend, but they have an open relationship so they sleep around with everyone they can find."

When I was finished I found Peter staring at me with his mouth hanging open.

"What?" I asked.

"In one morning you found out about the sex lives of almost everyone working there today!"

I shrugged. "I didn't have anything else to do, and Mickey likes to talk. I don't know if any of it is true."

"Did I hear you ask Joe Gardner point-blank if he was gay?"

"Yeah, but I had a good reason for it."

"You mean other than the obvious?"

I laughed. "No, I haven't lost my mind. He kept talking about gay people in the third person. It started to get on my nerves. I know we're supposed to be discreet, but it seemed like an appropriate question at the time."

"How did he react?"

"He went into a sulk, as Mother would say."

There was a beat, then Peter said, "So you think he's suspicious? You think he might be lying about who he is?"

I shrugged. "Either that or he hasn't gotten laid in a long time."

Our conversation was interrupted by the arrival of the Red

Line train, the noise of which would have drowned out the landing of a jumbo jet. The doors slid open and we got on.

Once we were seated, I heaved a frustrated sigh.

"What's wrong?" Peter asked.

"You're right about this case. What they've asked us to do is impossible. Only the FBI would think we could nose around and figure out if anyone is lying about who they are. I mean, of course Joe sounds suspicious when we're looking for something that sounds suspicious, but nothing he said was any different than anything half a dozen of our friends would have said. And Mickey sounds as gay as a floral arrangement, but if someone was trying to pass as a fag, isn't that exactly what they'd do?"

"That's what I've been saying from the start, honey."

"I mean, what do we have? We haven't found out anything concrete. All we've got is gossip."

I was silent for a moment, then added, "I really think we need to find out about that tape."

Out of the corner of my eye, I could see Peter's lips curl. "How exactly would we go about doing that?"

I thought about this for a minute. Then an idea hit me. "Maybe we can make gossip work to our advantage."

Peter rolled his eyes.

"What?"

"I know I'm in trouble when you get like this," he said. "And I haven't forgotten that Russian business. I don't want to end up stripped naked and strapped to a bed again."

I clucked my tongue. "There go my plans for the evening!"

We got home about three o'clock and found a note from Mother saying that she'd already left for the evening. The note assured us that she was busy trying to "find Simon out," and I shuddered to think what she meant by that. She was still in bed when we left for Clarke's office the next morning.

Thursday the activity at the office increased sharply. Apparently Shawn Stillman was quite serious about his job, and the fact that we needed to get the mailing out before Tuesday's primary. He'd managed to get even more volunteers in to help. This seriousness reminded me of what Mickey told me. I still found it difficult to believe that anyone would kill to get an office job, no matter whose office that might be in. And to try to get it by destroying the office where you want to work seemed . . . well . . . counterproductive. Anyway, several additional tables had been set up, and a dozen or more people were madly stuffing envelopes with unbridled exuberance.

The candidate and his campaign manager didn't appear that day. Clarke's schedule was filled with last minute baby-and buttkissing.

Peter was once again assigned to the phones—a testament to Shawn's having recognized my husband's undying patience—and I was once again relegated to stuffing. With the flurry of excitement and the elevated level of chatter going on, I figured it would be easy to put my plan into action. I found out very quickly that this new track was doomed to derail.

I decided to start with Mickey, who had proven a font of information, no matter how spurious it might be, the day before. I managed to wedge myself in between him and a young woman with black bobbed hair who looked like she had just stepped out of *Enchanted April.*

Mickey greeted me happily and then launched into a continuation of yesterday's topic: who was sleeping with whom. When he paused for a breath I seized the opportunity.

"You know what I heard?" I said.

Mickey eyed me attentively. He was very eager to add to his repertoire. "What?"

"You know Fritz Peterson? The Republican candidate?"

"Yeah?"

I leaned closer to him. "I heard that there's a *big* scandal involving him that the Republicans are desperate to keep silent!"

His eyes widened. "Really? What is it?"

I blinked. I'd been hoping he would wave me off and tell me it was old news—then tell me what it was.

"I don't know," I said, hoping I sounded believable, "but I hear whatever it is, it was caught on tape."

"Really?" Mickey replied with a wicked smile. "I can just imagine!"

"What?"

He suddenly looked confused. "Whatever it is . . . I can just imagine!"

I tried a different line. "Have you ever heard anything about Peterson?"

"Just that he's a big ol' phobe. And a Bible-thumper. Isn't that a funny expression? It always makes me think of *Bambi*. Anyway, you just know that whatever there is on Peterson *has* to be juicy, because when thumpers fall, they fall the hardest!"

I sighed inwardly. This wasn't going to get me anywhere.

Next I tried Joe Gardner. He had situated himself at one of the other tables, I imagined to try to be as far away from Mickey as he could. The day before Joe had struck me as the type of person who, although he might be gay, dislikes the more effeminate of our species. However, he could just as easily have been trying to avoid me, since I'd sounded so antagonistic toward him earlier. When I saw him go over to get a new box of fliers from the pile by the wall, I made my move.

"Here, I'll help you," I said.

"I don't need help," he replied.

I ignored him and carried the other side of the box anyway, which was unnecessary and made carrying it more awkward than if I'd just let him do it himself. He shot a glance at me over the top of the box as if he was thinking that very thing. We placed the box on the end of the table where he'd been working, and I broached the subject of Fritz Peterson's veracity.

Joe stopped in the act of pulling a handful of fliers from the box and said, "A scandal? Really? What?"

"I don't know exactly," I said more smoothly now that I was somewhat prepared for this response. "This is just something I've been hearing lately. And that whatever it is, it was caught on tape!"

He resumed unpacking with a shake of his head. "It doesn't surprise me. He's probably gay."

"Why do you say that? Because there's a question about his morals?" I wished I could take the indignation out of my tone, but the way this guy put things really ticked me off!

"No," Joe said without batting an eye, "because he's such an outrageous homophobe. You know as well as I do that gay people are the worst homophobes."

Even though what he was saying made me really angry, I couldn't disagree. Internalized homophobia is a big problem. But I still hated the way he said it, and the fact that he persisted in referring to us in the third person.

"You don't like gay people, do you?" I said.

He paused again with a handful of fliers. "No, I don't. They're irritating. They're either political and humorless, or they're so damn flighty they can't be serious about anything!"

After a beat, I said, "What was that you were saying about gay people being homophobic?"

He grunted. "You asked, and you know it's true."

"Well, if you feel that way, why the hell are you supporting Clarke?"

"Because I like his platform. I agree with him on the issues."

"You mean because he's pro-gay?"

He sighed with disgust. "Being pro-gay isn't *his* only issue. It's *our* only issue."

I smiled despite myself. "I'm glad to hear you say it."

He looked totally baffled. "What?"

"Our."

Work was interrupted at noon when the office received the first bomb threat since moving. Either the threateners were getting lax or the increased security was daunting them. Unlike at the old office, the minute this threat was received the building was evacuated. We were on the sidewalk on Wabash amid people from the other offices, all of whom seemed to appreciate the interruption. We were also surrounded by news crews.

Shawn spent his time making the rounds of the volunteers. When he got to us, he said, "Do not, under any circumstances, talk to anyone from the media."

"We weren't planning to," said Peter.

Shawn looked up at the building. "I think I managed that really well."

"Managed what?" I asked.

"The evacuation of our office. Everyone got down the stairs in an orderly fashion without a single hitch."

I was a bit surprised to hear him say this, since nothing had been required of him. When the threat was announced, we all just left the office. There might've been a bit more anxiety about it then there would've been a week ago, but it wasn't exactly a stampede.

"Jody couldn't have done it as well. She never evacuated the office," he added.

"The FBI told Jody that the bomb threats weren't serious," I said.

He snorted. "I'll bet they feel different now!"

He bustled away from us to cosset another group of volunteers.

"I didn't like the sound of that," I said to Peter.

"Neither did I," he replied, although he sounded as if his reasons were different from mine.

We were on the street for almost an hour while the bomb squad was called in and searched the building. When the place was pronounced clear, we went back up to our slightly shabby office with a profound sense of anticlimax. Not that anyone wanted the place to explode. At least, nobody that was in it.

Peter and I came away from the office that afternoon tired and frustrated. That is to say, he was tired and I was frustrated. When we got home, we found Mother doing the preliminary preparation for dinner.

"What are you doing here?" I asked unceremoniously.

"Darling, I live here," she replied with that Simon-induced lilt.

"I mean, aren't you going out tonight? Don't tell me you've finally broken little Simon's heart."

"Not at all," she said with a flip of her hand. "But tonight is one of the few classes he actually needs to attend, so you have me for the duration of the evening."

"I'm glad to hear it."

"It will give you a chance to fill me in on how the investigation is going."

I put a hand to my chest. "I didn't know you cared."

"Alex, you really are being tiresome."

I sighed heavily. "I know, I'm sorry. But while you've been doing Cinderella at an endless ball, our investigation has been going nowhere. I must've broached the subject of that videotape with a dozen people today, and all anyone had to say was 'I'm not surprised' at the idea of Peterson being involved in a scandal."

"The tape?" Mother said incredulously.

"The one Mary Linn-Hadden told us about—the one that was used to get Jody to the office when it blew up."

"I know *which* tape," she said with elaborate patience. "I thought you were supposed to be trying to find out if somebody's not on the up and up."

"We gave that up as a bad job. There's no way we can do that just by listening to people."

"*He* gave that up," Peter corrected. "I never thought it would work."

"You mean you've been asking about the *tape?* The one that got Jody killed? Have you gone completely mad?" She glanced over at Peter as if I'd been left in his care in her absence, and he'd been found wanting. "You see what happens when I leave you on your own!"

"I didn't cause any trouble," I said. "Nobody there knew anything about the tape. If somebody had heard of it, I'm sure they would've said something. God knows, the place is a hotbed of gossip."

"I know what you think you were thinking, darling, but you *weren't* thinking! If someone used that tape to lure Jody to her death, the last thing they'd do is volunteer any knowledge of it!"

"But it might not have been used as a lure. Someone might really have wanted to give some evidence to her. Suppose a third party found out about it and blew them both up? We still don't know if there was more than one person there at the time."

Mother stared at me for a moment, sucking in her lips. "The result is still the same. Whether Jody was lured there to be blown up, or she was meeting someone there and they were both blown up, the person who *did* it knows about the tape!"

"I think the two of you are missing something," Peter said after clearing his throat. "There may not be a tape at all."

"What?" Mother and I exclaimed in familial unison.

He shrugged. "The tape could've just been the lure."

I could feel myself deflating. I hadn't thought of that, and he was right. If Jody was the target, it would've been the easiest way to get her alone. There didn't really have to be a tape at all.

"If that's the case," said Mother, "it's even worse! If somebody made up the business about the tape, then it looks even worse if you know about it! Asking around about that tape has put you in a very dangerous position."

"I didn't ask around about it," I said nasally. "I only said I heard there was one."

"And everybody said they hadn't heard of such a thing," said Mother.

"Right."

"There you 'ave it!"

"What do I 'ave?"

"*Everyone* said they didn't know about it, but somebody must, don't you see?"

"Oh, God!" Peter groaned.

I was getting irritated, as I always do when it seems I'm the last to catch on.

Mother leveled her eyes at me. "If nobody else knows about the tape, that leaves only the person who planted the bomb. Then that person is now aware that *you* know something you shouldn't."

"Oh. But . . . it might not have been somebody from the office. Even Agents Henry and Raymond said they thought this was a long shot."

"They didn't know the real reason Jody was at the office, did they?" said Mother. "But who else would she have agreed to meet there at five in the morning? Surely not a complete stranger."

"That still doesn't have to have been someone from the office."

"Then why would he ask her to go there? Why not on neutral ground somewhere?"

I couldn't answer that.

"Alex, the most likely person to be claiming to have found dirt on Fritz Peterson would be someone connected to Mr. Clarke's campaign, don't you see? Nobody else would have a reason for it."

I sank onto one of the kitchen chairs. "But . . . whoever it is might not have been there today."

"It doesn't matter. You've started the ball rolling, and if the bomber really is in that office, he'll find out. People will natter about it. It's bound to get back to him. Honestly, Alex! Here I am in the midst of being courted, I only have just so much time with Simon as it is, and I'm going to 'ave to put everything aside and try to keep you from getting killed again!"

"You're being courted?"

She placed her hands firmly on her hips. "Is that *all* you got out of that sentence?" She shook her head briskly and made a *brrring* noise with her lips, then threw up her hands and left the room.

"I have to hand it to you, honey," Peter said. "It's been a hell of a long time since you got your mother so flummoxed she couldn't speak!"

After dinner I made my first report to Henry. That is to say, I reported that I had nothing to report. I wasn't about to tell him my suspicions of Joe Gardner—if you could even call them that—and Peter and I had already agreed that we wouldn't tell him about the tape. I thought that after what Mother had said Peter might be in favor of letting the FBI know about it, but he was still suffering an attack of conscience over the way we'd come by the information. And just for the record, so was I. So once I'd filtered out everything I couldn't tell Henry there was really nothing left. Then I asked him if they'd learned anything.

Henry said that they hadn't gotten any leads as to the bomber, and that they'd already checked all the threats, both those phoned into the office and the ones made to Jody's home, and without exception they'd been made from pay phones. As far as identifying the person who died in the bombing, they'd typed blood found at the scene and it matched Jody's.

"We haven't found evidence of anyone else being there," he added. "So it looks like we're safe in assuming it was Jody Linn-Hadden who was killed, and that she was alone."

"Isn't there any way to make sure it was her? How about DNA testing?"

He sighed. "There's nothing to test it against. It's not like she left children anywhere, did she?"

When Peter and I went to bed that night I lay awake for quite a while trying to convince myself that I'd taken the only road possible by pursuing the tape, but I had the disquieting feeling that Mother was right: I'd probably landed us in the soup again.

SEVEN

Friday we arrived at the Wabash headquarters to find that Clarke's offices had expanded into an additional suite. One full room was devoted to long folding tables at which the continuing preparations for the mailing were being boisterously performed. In the main room the bank of phones was still set up haphazardly on a row of tables, but the row had been lengthened and additional phones put in. Apparently Clarke's campaign was looking more viable by the minute as the primary approached. And that was partly due to the bombing.

Peter took his place at the phones, and I went into stuffing central. The number of volunteers had tripled in the past three days. Joe Gardner was at the center of a table by the windows, staring at the tabletop while he worked steadily. I had a feeling his dour expression was due to the fact that he'd had the misfortune to find himself seated directly across from Mickey Downs, who was chattering away at him, oblivious to his audience's reaction. Richard Birch and Annie Watson, the only two people Peter had been able to question at all, were both there, apparently taking a breather from the phones. At first those were the only four people I recognized, but then I saw Sheila of "Sheila and Jo," the friends who had gotten us involved in the campaign to begin with. She was working at the far end of one of the tables at the inner corner of the room. I went over to her.

"Hi," she said, flipping her bangs out of her eyes. She didn't miss a beat in stuffing, which she was doing with alarming alacrity. "Where's Peter?"

"In the other room on the phones. How about Jo?"

"She's at the shop. The place would fall apart without her. I thought I'd put in some time here this morning. Even if I was supposed to be at the restaurant, people can slop food on the tables without me."

She tossed a handful of stuffed envelopes into a box and pulled forward another pile of supplies. "Pretty scary about Jody, isn't it?"

"Yeah," I replied. I knelt beside her and said quietly, "Hey, Sheila, Jody was a friend of yours, wasn't she?"

"Yep."

"Did she ever say anything to you about Fritz Peterson?"

She stopped with a flier halfway into an envelope. "The Republican? Of course she did! I can't repeat what she said. I'm too much of a lady."

I smiled. "No, I'm not talking about name-calling, I'm talking about . . . oh, I'm not sure I know what I'm talking about. Did she ever say anything about Peterson being involved in some sort of scandal?"

She resumed her work with a laugh. "Of course not!"

I drew back slightly. "Why do you say that?"

"If Jody knew anything about a scandal, she wouldn't have told me, she would've told the whole world and you wouldn't have to ask. She hated Peterson, you know."

"I know."

"If she'd caught him up in anything, she would've gone straight to the media."

"Not if she didn't have anything solid yet," I said absently.

Sheila paused again and eyed me. "Say, what is this?"

"Huh? Oh, nothing!" I said quickly, trying to cover my lapse. "I

113

was just curious, what with her getting killed. It's the Jessica Fletcher in me. I don't like unsolved riddles."

She looked at me for a moment, then said in a pointed whisper, "Don't make waves, Alex."

"What?"

"Don't make waves. It's bad enough the police are doing it. Don't you do it, too."

"What are you saying? That you don't want anyone to find out who killed Jody?"

"Of course I do! But not at the expense of everything else."

I stared at her in disbelief. "I don't know what you mean."

She leaned in closer and whispered intensely, "Whoever bombed the office must have some pretty big grievances against Clarke. The primary's only a few days away. We don't need that getting aired right now. Clarke is the best candidate we've had in a long time. We need to get him elected."

"You don't think Clarke had anything to do with this?" I asked after a beat.

"Of course not! But no matter why that place was bombed, when the truth comes out it'll cast a pall over the election and hurt Clarke's chances. The public is full of morons. They won't know the facts, they'll just remember that something terrible happened in connection with Clarke and hold it against him."

"That's not the way it is now. People seem to be supporting him because of the attack."

Her lips tightened. "That'll change the minute they find out what the attack was about. Don't screw things up, Alex. We need to get Clarke elected."

"No matter what the cost?"

Sheila averted her eyes in a way that was uncharacteristically evasive. "Jody's dead. Nothing's going to bring her back."

I rose slowly. "I'd better get to work."

I walked away from her, still unable to believe what I'd been hearing. I knew that Clarke had generated an almost fanatical following in parts of the community, but I didn't know that it would translate into a callous disregard for the death of one of the community's own members. And at the same time, I couldn't entirely disagree with Sheila's assessment of the situation. Finding the killer might turn the bombing from an anonymous act of terrorism into a platform for airing grievances against Clarke, and at this stage of the game that would probably hurt his chances in the primary.

But unlike Sheila, I still thought the truth was more important than who got elected.

I was trying to find a place to work when John Schuler popped out of his office, once again carrying a note pad to which he referred continually as he spoke.

"People! People!" he announced. "Can I have your attention for a moment? First of all, I want to thank you all once again for all the hard work you're doing." He paused to smile. "Future Senator Charlie Clarke and I greatly appreciate your service. Now, as you know, the primary is on Tuesday. We're looking to have a great turnout, and a great day!"

He paused for applause, which he got once people realized why he had stopped.

"Now, we'll be holding a primary day rally. . . . I don't want to be premature by calling it a victory party . . ." He paused again and his smile became sly. "At the Grand Ballroom in the Piedmont Hotel."

There was a collective "Oooo" from the volunteers, as much for the semi-plush Piedmont as for the implied victory.

Schuler looked back down at his notes, then continued. "We would like each and every one of you to be there. A good showing is essential, because we're sure there will be lots of news cameras there to cover the big night. So let's have a great big turnout for them!"

I swear to God I heard a couple of people say "Yea!" as a healthier round of applause broke out.

"Thank you all again, and keep up the good work," Schuler said with a wave as he started back toward his office. He paused for just a second and added, "Oh, and don't forget the fundraiser tonight!"

With this he disappeared into his office. This time he hadn't even mentioned Tony Milano's name.

I gave another inward sigh, and was just about to get to work when an idea came to me. I went over to Peter, who was just finishing up with somebody on the phone.

"Yes," he said patiently, "I'll pass your recommendation along to Mr. Clarke." He replaced the receiver.

"You will?"

"Oh, of course I will," he said with a crooked smile. "That was a man who thought people should have their religious affiliation tattooed on their upper left arms."

I laughed as I crouched beside him for a whispered tête-à-tête. "Uh, honey . . . I have an idea, but I don't think you're going to like it."

His eyebrows went up. "*You* don't think I'm going to like it? Then I think I'm going to hate it."

"I think we should ask Schuler about the tape."

"What!" Peter exclaimed. We both glanced from side to side to see if we'd drawn anyone's attention. It didn't look like we had. "Your mother said—"

"I know what she said. And she's probably right. But if I've already gotten us in danger, then we might as well pursue it. It's not going to disappear on its own."

He eyed me warily. "It scares me that that makes sense to me. But why Schuler?"

"Because I don't think we're going to get anywhere just asking around about it. I think we should go to the source."

"The source?" Peter's voice raised for a second, but lowered quickly. "What makes you think he's the source?"

"Not the source of the tape," I said. "But if there really is dirt on Fritz Peterson, and someone in this organization was trying to get it, don't you think Schuler would know about it? Here's what I think we should do. . . ."

Peter pursed his lips while I explained. He didn't look pleased, but he didn't object.

"Let's go," he said, rising from the table as his phone started to ring.

We crossed the room and I was just about to knock on Schuler's door when Shawn Stillman appeared out of nowhere and interposed himself between us and our objective.

"What are you doing?" he exclaimed with an expression of utter astonishment on his face.

"We need to talk to Schuler," I said.

"You can't do that. He's very busy. Anything you think you need to talk to him about should go through me. If John really needs to know about it, I'll pass it on."

This was all we needed—to have our investigation sidelined by an office despot. I had a feeling I was getting a little taste of what it's like for agents when they have to go undercover as maids and waiters.

"Shawn, we really need to talk to him," I said again, unable to think of another way to put it.

"What's it about?" he asked. "I'll decide if it needs to get passed on."

I could feel myself going red in the face. Peter said quickly, "It's personal. And believe me, Schuler will be very upset with you if this is kept from him."

Shawn looked at him uncertainly. Peter always seems to know how to deal with people, and he shares my mother's propensity for coming up with a plausible lie on the spur of the moment. It appeared that the best way to get around Shawn was to make him believe he was going to get in trouble with his boss.

"Well, okay," he said reluctantly. "Wait. I'll see if he can see you."

He awkwardly twisted the doorknob without turning around, as if he was afraid we'd club him on the head and storm into the office over his prostrate body if he turned his back to us. Once he got the door open, he performed a palsied pirouette into the office, closing the door behind him.

Peter looked at me and said, "Petty Tyrant Syndrome. It can happen to the best of us."

"Hmm. It may be more than that. Maybe Mickey Downs was right about how badly he wanted the job."

In a matter of seconds Shawn reopened the door in a perfectly professional manner and said, "Mr. Schuler can see you now."

He stepped aside to let us through, then left, closing the door behind him.

The office was small but private. The walls were the same bilious color as the hallway, and there were cheap prints of wading storks hanging on the walls. The prints had to have come with the place.

Schuler was seated behind a desk that looked like it hadn't been moved for at least fifty years. The top was thick with varnish that accentuated the dints and scratches of all the previous owners. Schuler was busy listening to someone on the phone while tapping his teeth with the eraser of a pencil that had chew marks all over it.

It was a few moments before he acknowledged our presence. He waved the pencil like a magic wand at the two plastic chairs facing his desk. We took this as our cue to sit. He then reproduced the blank look people use when they're on the phone in front of guests and want to pretend they're alone.

"Uh-huh," he said into the receiver. He repeated this a few times, then said, "Yes, we'll see you there." He hung up the phone, laid the pencil down, and folded his hands atop the desk.

"Mr. Stillman said that you needed to see me on a *personal* matter. That's interesting. I don't know you, even though I've seen you in the office."

When he spoke, his head swiveled back and forth between us like an animatronic owl. He was trying so hard to appear competent that I almost regretted the fact that he wasn't pulling it off.

"Yes, well . . . there's a rumor going around the office, and it's something that Peter and I find really disturbing. Isn't that right, Peter?"

"That's right."

"A rumor?" said Schuler.

"You see, we decided to volunteer for the Clarke campaign

because we really, really believe in what he stands for. Especially because he isn't afraid to speak his mind and let the chips fall where they may."

"Uh-huh," said Schuler slowly, in a tone that implied I should get to the point. "What is the rumor?"

"That the Clarke camp is trying to dig up dirt on Fritz Peterson." I tried to sound as naive as possible. After all, so far as we knew, *I* was the one who had started the rumor. "You see, we got involved with this volunteering stuff because we believed that Clarke is running an honest campaign, and that there wasn't going to be any mudslinging."

Schuler continued to stare at me across the desk with his hands folded in front of him. When he didn't say anything immediately, I added, "It's . . . it's . . . the idea that Clarke might be looking for dirt that we find disturbing."

"It should be," he said, drawing back in his chair like a guest on a Barbara Walters special. "And let me set your mind at ease. There is absolutely no truth to the rumor. Charlie Clarke is running a clean campaign. No mud. We're not even interested in it. I'm sure that you've seen Charlie interviewed on television. He sticks to the issues. He rarely mentions his opponents at all. He wants people to know why he's the best man for the job of state senator, not why the other guys aren't."

Not only had we seen Clarke on television numerous times, we'd heard him use that very phrase almost every time. He presented it like a badge of honor, as well it might be. Except that every time he said it I pictured a group of crooked politicians in a smoke-filled room trying to come up with the perfect slogan.

"Isn't that position going to be a little hard to maintain?" said Peter. "If he wins the primary, his Republican opponent is bound to start slinging mud."

"First of all, there is no mud to sling at Charlie. He has a clean record."

"Nobody has a totally clean slate."

Schuler answered that with a smile. "Secondly, just because one candidate slings mud, that doesn't mean the other one has to."

"Tell that to Michael Dukakis," Peter said wryly.

"Will that be all, gentlemen?" Schuler said, attempting a professional smile as he half rose from his seat. "I hope I have allayed your fears."

Neither Peter nor I moved. "Are you sure nobody here's been trying to dig up dirt?" I asked.

"Of course I am. Why?"

"Because it's all over the place that somebody's been trying to find a tape."

Schuler lowered himself back onto his chair. Although he was making a good show of keeping himself composed, he couldn't stop some of the color from draining from his face.

"Tape? What tape?"

"A videotape, I think," I said innocently. "It has some sort of incriminating evidence on it."

"Where did you hear a thing like that?"

"Just around here," I said. "Some of the volunteers have been talking about it. They think that was why Jody Linn-Hadden was in the Lincoln office when it blew up."

"What?"

"They're saying she was trying to get some evidence."

There was a long silence during which Schuler stared me straight in the eye. Then suddenly he said, "Well, I suppose it's possible that Ms. Linn-Hadden was trying to do that. But if she was, she was acting alone. After all, we have no control over what a private citizen is doing on her own time. And if one of our people was trying to dig up dirt, that doesn't mean it was sanctioned by this office."

Maybe it was because I know that the campaign had answers prepared for every possible topic that I doubted his sincerity: His response was a little too "ready to his lips," as Mother would say. I had a feeling that he had known what Jody was doing, and would never admit it now for fear of being held culpable in her death.

"Okay, well, I feel much better about this all, then," I said as Peter and I rose.

"So do I," said Peter. He sounded awfully grave.

"Oh! One thing," I said. "*You* don't know anything about a tape, do you? I mean if it really exists?"

He narrowed his eyes at me. There was a very long pause. "As I just told you, we're not interested in dirt."

When we came out of the office we found Shawn waiting by the door.

"Well!" he said. "Was John as happy to see you as you thought he'd be?"

"Look, Shawn—" I started, but he cut me off.

"Forget it! Get back to work!" He marched away, but didn't completely forget himself. He added a weak "please" over his shoulder.

"Do you believe that guy?" I said.

Peter shrugged. "We all want to control our own little piece of the world."

"Huh? No, I mean Schuler," I said as we walked back to Peter's place at the phones.

He sighed. "I'd like to believe that Clarke isn't interested in dirt, but it's a little hard to buy. He can't be that naive. First of all, he can't be that clean. Everybody has something in their past that can be held against them."

"Really?" I said as he took his seat. "Do you?"

He gave me a coy smile. "Well, there was that six weeks with the dwarf. . . ."

"A dwarf, eh? Was everything in proportion?"

"The point is," he said as he laughed, "politicians can make even relatively innocent things look bad. Even trying marijuana once. And secondly, if Fritz Peterson starts hammering away at Clarke, Clarke is going to have to start swinging back sometime, or he's going to tank."

"I don't know about you, but I got the feeling that Schuler knew what Jody was doing."

He nodded. "Did you notice how quickly he pulled out the 'if she was doing it she was acting on her own' defense?"

"Yeah."

We heard a door open and looked up. Schuler emerged from

his office and made a beeline for Clarke's office. He opened the door without knocking and went in.

"I wonder what that's about," I said.

"It could be anything. He goes in there all the time," said Peter, once again being the voice of reason.

"Or it could be that we lit a fire under him!"

There was yet another note from Mother waiting for us when we got home late that afternoon. I was beginning to feel like her pen-pal. This one said that she was going shopping, then meeting Simon for dinner.

We decided to order in Chinese food, which we ate while watching the news on the tiny television on the kitchen counter. There were reports on all the senatorial candidates' activities as the primary approached, and another brief mention of the lack of developments in the bombing investigation.

"*She's* telling *us!*" I said with a nod at the female news anchor.

Peter popped a crispy won ton into his mouth, chewed on it for a little bit, then said, "We're still going to Tony's tonight, right?"

"Of course. It'll be a social situation—more social than at the office—and Tony knows a lot of people. Maybe we'll be able to pick up something there."

He grinned. "I wonder who'll be there."

My mouth dropped open slightly. "What do you mean? You don't think it'll be his clients, do you?"

He raised his eyebrows. "Who else does Tony know with money?"

EIGHT

Tony Milano owned a condo in one of the older, more elegant buildings on Lake Shore Drive just short of Lincoln Park. We took a cab through the park and were at the entrance to his building in a matter of minutes. Although we had a better than nodding acquaintance with Tony we'd never been to his place before, mainly because we didn't normally travel in the same circles—something for which I thanked God—and because Tony doesn't do much on a social basis unless he's getting paid for it.

A red-coated, brass-buttoned doorman directed us to the elevators, and we road up to the nineteenth floor in solemn silence in a walnut-panelled car. I leaned over to Peter and whispered, "I feel like I'm in a traveling confessional."

He laughed quietly. "It is kind of like a church, isn't it?"

The doors slid open and we stepped into an abbreviated hallway in which there were only four doors. Dignified party sounds emanated from the last one, accompanied by some stereotypical cocktail party piano music. I knocked lightly and the door was opened immediately by a fiftyish man in tails.

"Good evening, gentlemen," he said with a bow. "Welcome to the fund-raiser."

He smoothly extended an arm into the apartment.

"Thank you," said Peter as we crossed the threshold. We stopped abruptly.

"Wow!" I exclaimed gawkingly. I sounded like Julia Roberts when she first saw the lobby of the Regent Beverly Wilshire.

The apartment was like an art museum: bright white walls, polished hardwood floors, objects d'art on pedestals and in gilded frames. The furniture was minimalist, the largest piece being a plush mint-green couch facing a fireplace of silver marble. There was a white baby grand in one corner. The man playing it was smiling broadly and looked up only when one of the guests spoke to him.

As we'd feared, it was powder night at Tony's. The room was awash with rather hungry-looking gentlemen who were so old that if you tapped one of them on the cheek you would expect dust to fly off of them.

It wasn't hard to spot Tony: He was the one dark head standing encircled by a bunch of elderly men. He looked like a very healthy bloom surrounded by dandelions in the fluff stage.

Tony Milano was a sleekly handsome man. He had long black hair that he kept swept back off his broad forehead, flawless dark olive skin, and a butt so firm you could chew gum with it. He had bright brown eyes and a square, firmly set jaw. His statuesque features were mitigated somewhat by an endearing, slightly crooked smile that made him look as if he was aware of his beauty, and just a little embarrassed by it.

Tony had successfully managed to turn his looks into a career. He was a very highly paid, very high class, very selective escort in the truest sense of the term. From what I'd been told, sex wasn't involved. But beauty was. Men—usually older ones—were willing to put up a great deal of money just to be seen at important functions with Tony on their arms.

When he noticed us, he raised one perfectly groomed eyebrow and smiled. He disengaged himself from his admirers—I swear I saw little puffs of white powder poof off of a couple of them—and came across the room to us.

"Alex, Peter, how lovely to see you," he said, shaking our hands in turn. "I'm so glad you could make it."

"Thank you," I replied. "Tony, this place is breathtaking."

"Oh? The two of you have never been here before?"

"No, this is our first time," Peter answered.

Tony put a hand to his own chest. "That's purely negligence on my part." He said this with such sincere elegance it made my skin crackle.

"Where did you get all these beautiful things?" I asked.

He glanced around the room. "The art? Oh, they were gifts." The offhanded way he referred to the expensive items seemed completely sincere. He wasn't impressed by his own possessions, which to me was a point in his favor.

"Gifts?" I gaped.

Tony shrugged. "People give me things. I can't stop them. I wouldn't want to. Isn't that beautiful?"

He gestured toward a statue near the windows. It was pinkish marble, carved into a sort of twisted oval with a hole in the center, and polished to a shine.

"It's really impressive," said Peter. I couldn't tell whether or not he was being facetious. I was just mystified.

"My God, what's that?" I exclaimed, noticing the glint from one of Tony's manicured fingers.

He drew back his hand, looked down and smiled. "Oh. That's just a ring."

I reached out, drew his hand toward me and examined the ring. "It's a diamond-studded pinky ring. Was that a gift, too?"

"Yes," he replied with a tinge of sadness. "It was from Eustace. He was a very sweet man."

"Was?" said Peter.

Tony nodded. "He died last year. Such a waste. I think the expression is, 'he was one of the good ones.' "

"I'm so sorry," I said. "Was it . . . ?"

He looked at me questioningly for a moment, then realized what I meant. "Oh! No, no . . . It was heart failure. Eustace was eighty-seven."

I glanced at Peter, who was looking at Tony so incredulously I almost laughed. I cleared my throat. "I'm really glad that you're holding this fund-raiser. Clarke needs all the help he can get."

"Yes. It's nice to have a right-thinking candidate for once, so it's a pleasure to do it. And I figure I should do what I can since I have the resources." He extended his palm toward the coterie of old men.

"Uh . . . Tony," I said tentatively. "Those guys are all your clients?"

"Most of them."

"Isn't it dangerous to have them all here at once? Together, I mean. Aren't you afraid they'll be jealous of each other?"

"No. Why should they be?"

I glanced at Peter again.

"Well, they all date you, don't they?"

He shrugged. "They all pay me to escort them places. They know it's a business. Besides, they're all ardent supporters of Charles Clarke, and more than willing to donate to the cause. I think they were just waiting for a suitable occasion."

I couldn't help smiling. "Meaning they're all willing to give to the campaign just for the opportunity of being around you?"

He laughed. "We all have to do our own little bit."

He cast an affectionate gaze at his clients.

"Doesn't it bother you that the candidate himself isn't going to make an appearance?" Peter asked.

"Not at all," Tony replied. "It's enough that he supports gay rights. I'm a realist. He'd be taking a great risk in attending a party like this. I need him in office more than I need him here." He glanced over my shoulder and waved at someone just coming through the door. "Could you excuse me? More guests are arriving. Be sure to get something to drink. The bar is just over there."

He had started to move away from us, but I laid a hand on his arm and said, "Just a sec. Can I ask you something?"

He lowered his head a fraction and his face became a mask of concentration. Even when he was in a hurry he managed to look as if he was intensely interested in what I was about to say. It didn't surprise me that he was so successful.

"You get around a lot. We've been hearing lately that there's some really juicy dirt on Fritz Peterson. Have you heard anything about it?"

"I wouldn't wonder," he said with a shake of his head. "Everyone has a skeleton, don't they?"

Peter and I watched him as he walked away and greeted the newcomers: three men so old I was surprised they were able to stand up without assistance.

"From the look of his clients," I said, "some of us have more skeletons than others."

We made our way to the bar and requested a pair of rum and Cokes.

"Gladly, gentlemen," said the bartender as he slopped the liquid into the glasses. "It's nice to see you."

Peter and I glanced at each other. "Do we know you?" I asked.

He leaned toward us. "No, it's just nice to see anyone else under a hundred at this party!" He gave us a stage wink, and we laughed.

"Well! Did you find your tape?" a voice demanded from behind us.

I was glad I hadn't been taking a drink at the time, because this was hardly the place for a spit-take. Peter and I wheeled around simultaneously and found Shawn Stillman standing there with an angry smirk on his face.

"How did you know about that?" I asked.

"John Schuler told me, of course! I told you you could've come to me! I told you you didn't have to go bothering John!"

"Not that you're one to say I told you so," Peter muttered loud enough for Shawn to hear him.

Shawn glared at him and for a split second I thought he might cause a scene, but he controlled himself by spouting three little huffs in rapid succession.

"Look, Shawn," I said, "we weren't trying to go over your head.

This was just something that—well, we thought if it were true, that Schuler wouldn't have wanted anyone to know about it."

"Yeah, sure." He folded his arms over his chest.

"We were under the impression that the campaign was *secretly* trying to find out something on Peterson," I replied, trying not to sound as sarcastic as I was beginning to feel. "Secretly. That would imply that it wasn't supposed to be common knowledge." I was treading on thin ice here, because if anyone thought to trace the rumor they might find that it had originated with me.

"Why the hell do you care, anyway? If they're trying to get something on Peterson, who cares? All the candidates do that!"

"We wouldn't be working for one that did," said Peter.

"Oh, come on! Nobody's that honest!"

There was a beat before Peter said, "Our candidate is supposed to be that honest, remember?"

Shawn was stumped by this, and he clearly didn't like the feeling. He looked as if he would've liked to argue the point, but arguing against the honesty of his own candidate wouldn't be very wise.

"You still should've told me about it first. At least then I would've been prepared."

"For what?" I asked.

"For when John called me into his office and asked me if I knew about this tape. How in the hell should I know anything? Jody didn't talk to men! It made me look like an idiot! I'm supposed to be running the office. It made me look like I don't know what's going on right under my nose!"

I didn't think it advisable to point out that, in all probability, he *didn't* know what was going on right under his nose. "Shawn, we really weren't trying to bypass you. We honestly didn't think Schuler would want us to discuss the tape business with anyone else. I'm sorry we hurt your feelings."

He pursed his lips for a few seconds and seemed to deflate a little. "It's all right. I was overreacting. I'm sorry about how I was at the office . . . and here. The pressure's getting to me. There's just a . . . This job is a lot more than I bargained for, you know."

He sounded sincere, but he kept looking at us as if he wanted to make sure we were buying it.

"It doesn't surprise me," I said. "Things are picking up fast with the primary so near."

He bridled. Apparently he didn't want anyone to agree with him. "Well, I think I can handle it."

"I'm sure you can," I replied.

We fell silent and I finally got to take a swig of my rum and Coke. It had gotten a bit diluted from the melting ice, but it was still so rum-heavy that if I'd been there on my own I would've thought the bartender was trying to get me drunk.

Shawn shifted from one foot to the other. Now that he'd spoken his piece, there wasn't anything else for him to say and he didn't know how to gracefully excuse himself. After a few minutes of this, he suddenly heaved a sigh and said, "Well, I suppose I should mingle—try to sell everyone on Clarke. Get those donations."

"I don't think you'll have to sell them on Clarke," Peter said. "They're sold on Tony. They'll give."

He creased his forehead, not knowing exactly how to take this, as he walked away from us.

"My, my," I said, "Shawn has certainly gotten into the inner sanctum very quickly."

"What do you mean?"

"Schuler called him in and told him all about our conversation."

"He asked him about it, honey. He was just trying to find out if Shawn had heard anything. He's the office manager, after all. I don't think there's anything sinister about that."

I curled my lip at him. "You know, sometimes you're just no fun!"

The number of guests had doubled in the time we'd spent talking to Shawn, and the noise level increased accordingly. Hors d'oeuvres were being propelled through the room on silver platters by a handful of gorgeous young men in black vests, black slacks, and white shirts. I assume the waiters and their edibles were meant to whet all kinds of appetites.

"Look at that guy," I said as a shortish one with a perfect, inverted, heart-shaped ass glided away from us. "Tony must be planning on getting some serious money tonight."

"I don't even want to know how you mean that," Peter replied.

Although John Schuler needn't have worried about what the turnout for this event would be, his repeated (though unenthusiastic) announcements had brought out many of the volunteers. Then again, the prospect of free food and drink was probably enticing enough. As the pace of the party picked up, I began noticing some of our fellow office workers milling amongst the elderly. It was beginning to look like visiting day at a very upscale nursing home.

Mickey Downs was there flitting from guest to guest like a busy little bee who was finding that each of the flowers on which he landed had died. He was dressed in pants so tight he was running the risk of castration, and an equally tight knit shirt that showed off his taut torso. I watched him for a while, then noticed Joe Gardner sitting on the ledge of one of the windows overlooking the lake. He was alone and staring dejectedly into the crowd. Peter and I decided to join him.

"What are you doing all by yourself?" I asked cheerfully.

"Sitting," he said unceremoniously. "I'm not any good at this stuff."

"What stuff?" said Peter.

He flapped his hand at the crowd. "This kind of party."

I could feel myself going red in the face again, and fought hard to control it. I don't know how one person could so consistently sound like he hated his own people, but Joe certainly managed it.

"Look at all these guys," he continued. "There's no reason for me to be here at all."

"Then why did you come?" I asked, trying to moderate my voice so that it sounded like a question rather than an challenge.

He looked up at me with his eyebrows closely knit. "Because Schuler asked me to."

"He did?"

"He asked us all to. You heard him."

"Oh, that. Yeah."

"But look at all these guys. There was no reason to come. This kind of thing is never fun. Except for somebody like Mickey."

We all looked into the crowd and there was Mickey, chatting animatedly with a man who looked a little too much like Max Schreck in *Nosferatu*.

"By the way, did you ever find out about that tape?" Joe asked out of the blue.

"What?" I exclaimed.

"The tape. The one you were talking about the other day. You ever find out what it was?"

I glanced at Peter. "Oh. No. That was just a rumor I heard." It didn't sound convincing, even to me. "Why do you ask?"

He gave me a bored shrug. "I just wondered. It's always nice to know I'm working for the right candidate."

"Yeah," I said slowly. I didn't know what the hell to make of that.

"Gentlemen and gentlemen," Tony Milano announced, clapping his hands together several times as he climbed onto the rise at the foot of the fireplace. "Thank you all very much for coming. We all know why we're here. I can't say anything about Charles Clarke that hasn't already been said. But I'm sure you all know how important it is that we get him elected." He reached down and picked up an enormous, ornate glass bowl. "For this evening we'll be referring to this Freidrichstein original—a gift from my dear Walter—as 'the donation bowl.' I expect each and every one of you to contribute. Nothing, *nothing* would please me more than to see your names on some healthy checks made out to the Charles Clarke Campaign Fund."

There was an expectant murmur among the old men. The wording Tony had used wasn't lost on them. Apparently pleasing him was something for which to strive. When he bent down to replace the bowl, every wrinkled neck craned like a sea of aging turkeys.

"Now," he said as he righted himself, "I'd like to provide you with some entertainment. Tonight we have a lovely young singer with whom many of you are already familiar. So without further ado, I'd like to introduce Miss Phnom Pehn."

There was enthusiastic applause as the singer appeared in the archway that led to the hall. She had a long braid of jet-black hair coiled into a bun atop her head, and wore a long white satin dress slit on both sides all the way to her hips, giving teasing peeks at her shapely legs. Her long black fingernails clutched a tiny white fan, which she used to hide the lower half of her face.

"Oh, Christ, just what we need! A drag queen!" said Joe a little too loudly. A couple of the old gentlemen nearby looked down at him—literally—but nobody else seemed to have heard him.

"Really?" I said in disbelief. If this was a drag queen, it was an awfully convincing one.

"Of course it is!"

Phnom Phen got to the piano in a series of very quick baby steps, bowed to the pianist who bowed back, then closed her fan and faced the audience. The pianist played a brief intro, at the end of which the singer opened her mouth and began croaking "La Vie en Rose" in a raspy baritone.

"I wonder if she knows that Phnom Phen is in Cambodia," I whispered to Peter.

"I wonder if she knows that geishas aren't," he replied with a sideways nod. We moved away from Joe and over to the pink marble statue. "Jeez, I see what you mean about him."

"Who?"

"Joe Gardner. I've seen internalized homophobia before, but he really seems to hate all things gay, doesn't he?"

I nodded. "Especially guys that aren't particularly masculine. Did you catch the tone in his voice when he talked about the drag queen? And Mickey?"

He folded his arms and puckered his lips. "So what are you saying?"

"What am *I* saying? What are *you* saying?"

He rolled his eyes. "Are we saying that *we* think Joe might be the mole?"

I thought for a minute, then released a disgusted sigh. "You know, I really hate it when you're right!"

"Right? About what?"

"This is just impossible! Speculating like this!"

"Keep your voice down," Peter said softly.

"Sorry. But you were right. We're never going to figure out who the bomber is this way. It's like you said. Joe could be acting obnoxious because of internalized homophobia or anything from self-loathing to bad digestion. Or he could be just plain obnoxious. And hell, half of the people we know hate drag queens. None of it means anything."

There was a slight pause, then Peter said, "He did mention the tape."

"Because I asked him about it before. That doesn't prove anything, either. Except that he was interested in whether or not I found out anything about it."

We both looked over at Joe, who was still sitting on the window seat and staring at the singer with barely masked contempt.

"Look," I said, "he's the only one of the volunteers from the old office that looks at all suspicious to me. At least sexually."

"So do you want to tell Henry and Raymond about him?" He sounded disapproving.

I thought for a moment, then smiled. "No. I think we should perform a test."

Peter raised his right eyebrow. "I don't like the sound of that!"

"Don't be silly!" I said. "Come with me."

I headed straight for Tony, who was standing beside the fireplace, gently shaking the hand of a stooped gentleman who had just placed a check in the bowl.

"Thank you, Jonathan, so very much."

"Tony? Can we talk to you for a minute?" I said.

"Excuse me, Jonathan," he said, releasing the withered hand. He then came over to us. "Certainly. What can I do for you?"

"Well, this is going to sound really strange, but . . ." I glanced at Peter who stared back at me defiantly, making it clear he wasn't going to help.

"Yes?" said Tony.

"You see that guy over there? Sitting by the window?"

Tony carefully looked over my shoulder. "The one with the curly hair. He looks like he's been sucking lemons. Who is he?"

"His name's Joe Gardner. He's one of the volunteers at campaign headquarters."

"Yes?" Tony said again when I didn't go on immediately.

"Well, Peter and I have been trying to figure out if he's gay. I mean, not everybody at the office is, of course. I suppose most of them are . . . but not everyone."

Tony didn't take his eyes off of me. "Yes?"

I looked at Peter again. He looked away. "So . . . well . . . we've made a little bet. Peter says he's gay and I say he's not."

Tony raised an eyebrow until it formed a point at the center. "Why on earth do you care?"

"I . . . we . . . we just do . . ." I sputtered.

"Alex, tell him the truth," Peter said with a sigh.

"Huh?" I was dumbfounded. Peter knew that we were never supposed to tell anyone about our working for the government.

He turned to Tony. "Alex has an overactive imagination."

"I do not!"

"Yes you do!" He eyed me as if he were trying to convey something that I wasn't getting, then turned back to Tony. "He's been worried ever since the bombing."

"I can understand that," said Tony.

"Anyway, he thinks that Joe has been acting suspiciously. Joe says that he's gay, but he also says all these anti-gay things, so Alex thinks he's some sort of . . . some sort of . . ." He made a show of not wanting to say the word.

"Spy?" Tony offered, thoroughly amused.

Peter flashed his most indulgent smile and made a quick eye movement in my direction. "He's just not going to sleep until he gets proof that Joe is what he says he is."

I would have found this offensive if I hadn't been so busy trying to keep my mouth from dropping open.

"But I don't know how anyone could find out if he is what he says he is," Peter concluded.

Tony had been looking intently at Joe. A smile spread across his face. "And you want me to find out?"

"I couldn't ask you to do something like that. It would put Alex's mind at ease, though."

In an effort to include myself in this, I said, "The one thing we know, at least from what he's said, is that he doesn't like sissies, and you're the most masculine man we know."

Tony moved his lips to one side. "There's no need for flattery, Alex." He looked at Peter. "So, he says he's gay and you think he's straight, and you want me to find out if it's true? This sounds like fun. I love a challenge!"

He glided away from us and went to Joe, who looked up with interest as Tony introduced himself, then sat beside him.

I turned to Peter. "I see you in a lime green fedora with a little yellow feather sticking out of the band."

"Shut up. It was your idea."

Phnom Phen finished her song with a flourish and gave a humble bow in response to the applause. She then went into a stirring rendition of "Our Love Is Here to Stay."

"Well, look who's here!"

I almost gave myself whiplash when I spun around at the sound of the all-too-familiar voice. Some of my drink sloshed out of the glass and dappled my shoe.

"Mother!" I exclaimed. "What are you doing here?"

"It's a fund-raiser," she said. "I have funds."

Simon was standing beside her. He appeared to be having difficulty taking in the surroundings: or at least, the people in them. Perhaps he was just worried. With his stately good looks he probably didn't feel quite safe in the middle of a flock of faggots.

"There's a great turnout, isn't there?" Mother continued.

"Bigger than we were expecting," I intoned.

She turned to her date. "Simon, would you mind getting me a drink? The bar's right over there."

He glanced at it uncertainly, then said, "Of course. Martini?"

"Why not?" she said grandly. He went to the bar.

"Ten bucks says he orders it shaken, not stirred," I said to Peter. I then turned to Mother. "Now, what are you really doing here?"

"I've had an idea."

"Oh, Christ!" I said, rolling my eyes.

"I told you that it's time for me to take things in hand and try to keep you from getting killed. If there's a tape involved, we'd better find it. Assuming it really does exist."

"I thought you thought it was dangerous to do that," I said.

"I think it's dangerous for you to do it, not for me."

"What?"

She gently laid a palm against my cheek. "Darling, I love you with all my heart, but you're not a very good liar. I think I'm much more suited to this sort of thing. I can go around saying I've heard a rumor about a tape without arousing suspicions. It's the accent, you know. People go all credulous over it."

"But we've already done that," Peter said. "Or at least, *he* has."

Mother's expression grew sober. "Yes, well, I'm not quite so interested in actually finding the tape as I am in creating the impression that someone other than Alex knows about it."

"But you're my mother!" I said, always ready to point out the obvious.

"That's just the thing. If you were the only one talking about the tape, then you might look unduly curious to whoever is involved. But if I'm talking about it . . . well, there you have it!"

"I never do when you say that."

Peter laughed. "I think she means that nobody would believe your mother was sleuthing. They'll be more likely to think the tape is common knowledge."

"Exactly!" she exclaimed.

"What about Simon?" I asked.

"Oh, he doesn't know anything about the tape," she replied with a wave of her hand.

"No, I mean you're going to do all this with Simon in tow?"

"Well, of course!" she said, surprised that I would ask such a thing. "He won't suspect a thing! He'll just think I'm gossiping!"

"Oh. Hey, wait a minute! How do you know he doesn't know anything about the tape?"

"I tried it on him first," she said proudly. "He hadn't heard a thing about it. Seemed quite surprised."

"He hadn't heard about what?" Simon appeared at Mother's side and proffered her a drink.

"Oooo, about that nasty videotape there's supposed to be of that Fritz Peterson person," she said as she took the glass from him.

Simon laughed. "Oh, yes. You Americans get much more in a dither about sex scandals than we do."

"Really?" I said. "Who said anything about a sex scandal? We don't know what's on the tape."

He faltered in the act of taking a sip of his drink, and his face reddened. "Oh. I'm sorry, I guess I was just assuming, what with talk of a video and all."

"It could be of a payoff or something like that."

"Or a drug deal," said Peter. "Of course, Clarke isn't running for mayor of D.C."

"Of course it could. Where is my mind?" Simon said self-effacingly. He had recovered his poise and took a drink. "You know, I really admire your Mr. Clarke."

"Why's that?" Peter asked.

"He must be very brave. I read in your papers about his office being blown up, and of course Jean has told me some about it. It seems he has people who are quite serious about keeping him out of office. If I were him, I don't think I'd be brave enough to stay in the race. I think I would drop out. Surely if these people were bold enough to blow up the office, they won't be stopped. They'll most likely try again."

"Really?" said Peter.

"I would drop out," Simon continued. "After all, what's more important? Your life or being a bleedin' senator?"

Peter folded his arms across his chest, a sure sign that he was unhappy with what he was hearing. "Some people believe that serving in public office is important and worth the risk."

Simon shrugged. "There's always someone else to do it, isn't there?"

"It might not be someone who feels the same way you do, or would vote the way you would."

"Well, it all comes out in the wash, doesn't it?"

"Not necessarily. There are some people who will risk their lives for what they believe in."

"Fancy that!" said Simon. He took another sip of his drink, then cleared his throat. "You know, there's something I've been meaning to say to you. I don't like the idea of the two of you working in a place that someone is willing to bomb. I don't think you should work there."

He sounded so imperious that neither Peter nor I spoke for a few seconds. There was something in Simon's tone that implied we should accept his suggestion without question.

"Oh, you don't?" was the best I could manage.

"Alex and I happen to be two of those people who think what we're doing is important."

Simon smacked his lips. For the first time in our acquaintance, he looked displeased. "I was merely expressing concern," he said smoothly. "If for no other reason than I know how important you are to your mother."

"There, now, isn't that nice?" Mother said in a tone that gave me the weird feeling she was mocking everyone at once, which is entirely within her capabilities.

Simon completed his thought without noticing Mother or taking his eyes off me. "Take it for what it's worth."

"Oh, my boys don't need any protecting," Mother said with a sidelong glance at me. "Usually."

Simon shrugged again and downed the remainder of his drink.

"Oh, look!" Mother exclaimed. "There's Dickie Stevenson! I wonder what he's doing in town! Simon, I have to introduce you to Dickie. He's an old friend of mine!"

She led him away.

"Did that sound like a threat to you?" I said.

"Which part?" Peter replied.

"That business about how Clarke should drop out of the race. That sounded like a veiled warning."

"Why tell us?"

I looked at Simon's retreating back. "Maybe he's onto us."

"How?"

"Mother asked him about the tape. Maybe he figured it out. Or maybe he's always known."

"What?" Peter said incredulously.

"Say he's the bomber. It's beyond the realm of coincidence to me that he would choose Mother as an avenue to infiltrate Clarke's headquarters by accident—I mean, without knowing that we work for the government."

Peter sighed. "Sweetheart, you're going off the deep end again. If all he wanted to do was blow up the office, then why go through this elaborate ruse of striking up a relationship with Jean at all? Why not just break into the place and plant the bomb? It's not like anybody would ever know."

"I don't know, I don't know. Why in the hell does the FBI think someone might've infiltrated the office?"

"They were just being thorough, Alex. I don't think either of them seriously believe one of the office workers is involved."

"Yeah, I know," I said with frustration. "Henry said they were just covering all the bases. It doesn't make any sense."

"Well, there's one thing I'll give you about Simon," Peter said. "I didn't like the way he said we shouldn't be working there. He made it sound like he expected us to quit on the spot."

I shook my head slowly. "I think we're going to have to find out about him."

"Alex, you can't turn your mother's boyfriend over to the FBI."

"I know, I know. . . ."

"Especially since—" He stopped abruptly, not wanting to go on.

"You might as well say it."

At least he looked apologetic. "All right. Especially since I have a feeling you're suspicious of Simon for reasons that have nothing to do with the bombing."

I sucked in my lips. "You're right," I said with a disgusted sigh.

We were interrupted at that point when Mickey fluttered up to us.

"Isn't this a wonderful party?" he gushed.

"You're enjoying yourself?" I said with a smile. I couldn't help it. Mickey's enthusiasm could be infectious.

"I realize most of the guys here were personally involved in building the Sphinx, but I don't think I've ever been in such demand before!" His mouth suddenly dropped open. "Oh, my God! Look at that!"

We followed his gaze and were just as astonished as he was by what we saw. Tony Milano and Joe Gardner were still seated by the window, but were now engaged in a very deep kiss.

"Now, *that's* interesting!" Mickey said nasally. "I have to go tell Richard about this! He'll just die!" He whisked away into the crowd.

I was about to say "well, that answers that" when I saw something very unnerving. Joe's eye opened just a slit and looked in our direction. Then he gently pushed Tony away, got up made his way through the throng of guests and out the door.

Tony sat staring after him, his expression totally perplexed. He rose slowly and came over to us.

"That is one very peculiar young man," he said.

"What happened?"

"I can't say I know. We were sitting there exchanging pleasantries—if you can call his insistence on discussing politics pleasant—when he suddenly took me by the collar, pulled me to him and gave me the most probing kiss I've had in weeks. I've had prostate exams that were less intrusive."

"You didn't do anything to . . . ?" I let my voice trail off suggestively.

"Good heavens, no! I couldn't have been more surprised." He shook his head. "Very odd."

"But gay?" I asked.

Tony drew his lips to one side as he had earlier. "If not, he's willing to go much farther to keep up a front than most people I know. But still, he does carry that angry young man thing to the extreme. Young people are far too intense. That's what I like about my clients. They're all so laid back."

"They're practically laid out," I said.

"I beg your pardon?"

"I'm sorry, Tony," I said sincerely. "I'm just more confused than ever. I didn't mean for that to happen."

"It's quite all right," he replied with professional aplomb. "It may be hard to believe, but this sort of thing has happened to me before."

I smiled. "I don't find that hard to believe."

"Now, if you'll excuse me, I think I'll go brush my tongue."

Once Tony was out of earshot, I said to Peter, "Did you notice anything strange when the two of them kissed?"

"You mean that Joe looked over here?"

"Yeah. Like he wanted to make sure we were watching!"

We didn't stay much longer after that. When Phnom Phen launched into her medley from *The Flower Drum Song*, something that the crowd seemed to have been anxiously anticipating, I felt it was time to go.

We tracked Mother down to a small circle of geezers who were hanging on her every word, and pulled her aside just long enough to tell her we were leaving and ask if she wanted to go with us. She declined and went back to her admirers.

We didn't mean to snub Simon, but neither of us remembered him until we started to walk away and I found myself caught by the elbow.

"Alex? Peter? You're leaving?" said Simon.

"Oh, I'm sorry. Yes, we are."

"I . . . I just wanted to say that I'm sorry if I sounded . . . full of myself earlier. I mean, when I said I was worried about you working in that office. I really was only worried."

"Yes," I said, staring at him quizzically. "Thank you. I appreciate that. But we'll be all right."

He flashed that broad, ingratiating smile of his. "I'm sure you will." Without another word he went back to Mother.

We said goodbye to Tony, then left while the party carried on.

NINE

We were in bed long before Mother got home. I wasn't exactly happy with the meager progress we'd made, but it was certainly a lot better than feeling worthless, as I had before being given this assignment. Any frustration over the work was better than the frustration of not having any. I was out like a light almost the minute my head hit the pillow.

I found myself in a dream version of the party we'd just attended. It was one of those unnerving dreams where everything is perfectly normal, exactly as it was when the real event actually took place, only everything has taken on a menacing edge. Most of the guests were a ghostly white, their faces long and cadaverous. Occasionally they would bump into each other, and disintegrate in a puff of dusty powder.

Joe was sitting on the window seat, a set of plans sticking out of his breast pocket. Somehow I knew they were the plans for a bomb. Tony, looking positively vampirish and swathed in a sort of white silk toga, assured me he'd be able to get the plans away from Joe. Before he'd even finished his sentence he was spirited to Joe's side where, in a soft-core-porn haze, his toga fell away as he sank his fangs into Joe's neck.

I was about to scream when my attention was diverted by a drag queen who looked exactly like Ethel Mertz wearing a geisha wig with chopsticks poking out of it, and the dress of an American Indian. She glared at me as she sang "I'm just a girl who can't say no . . ." She made it sound like a threat.

I put my hands to my ears and cried out, but the sound of my voice was blocked by the shriek of an alarm bell. All movement stopped at the sound of the bell, and all of the guests looked toward the sky in uniform amazement. The alarm bell rang again and again.

The scene suddenly melted away, and I realized through my grogginess that the phone was ringing. Peter mumbled something in his sleep, and I fumbled for the luminous clock on the nightstand. It was two thirty. I picked up the receiver and rested it against my ear.

In my half-sleeping haze I managed to say something like "Yalloo."

"I understand you're looking for a tape."

"Huh?" I said, coming full awake in a rush.

"I understand you're looking for a tape." The voice was very strange. It sounded as if it was hitting two pitches simultaneously.

"What tape?"

"You know what tape. You want it and I have it."

"I don't know what you're talking about. I'm not looking for anything." I was lying to draw him out, but he wasn't falling for it.

"Are we going to play games, or am I going to give you the tape?"

I poked Peter's side to wake him up. "If you have something incriminating, you should bring it to the police."

"I can't do that!" said the voice. "If I give it to them, they'll want to know how I got it and that would get me thrown in jail. If I give it to you, you can use it however you want, and if the cops want to know where it's from, you don't know."

"Whaaa . . . ?" Peter said as he turned over.

"Now one more time: Do you want the tape?"

"Yes."

"Then be at Clarke's office in half an hour."

"You've got to be kidding!" I said sharply. "Do you think I'm nuts?"

"I'm not the one who blew up the other place. If you want the tape, be there in half an hour. I'm going to the office. I'll leave the tape in the top right hand drawer of Clarke's desk."

"But—"

The line went dead.

"What the hell was that all about?" said Peter. He'd managed to wake himself.

"It was somebody who said he has the tape."

"A man?"

"Really hard to tell. The voice was very strange." I pushed back the covers and rolled out of bed. "Come on, get dressed."

"What?"

"He wants me to meet him at Clarke's office."

"Alex, no! You can't be that stupid! That's exactly what Jody did!"

"It's not like the old office," I said as I picked up the pair of briefs I'd tossed on the floor when we undressed. I slipped them on. "There's security in the new building. You have to go through a metal detector and past a guard."

"A guard who's half asleep!"

"I assume the alarm from the metal detector will wake him up."

"Alex, this is insane! In all likelihood this person has already blown up one office! He could find a way to blow up this one."

"He said he wasn't the one who planted the bomb," I said as I pushed my arms through the sleeves of a shirt.

"Oh, that's all right, then!" Peter replied, his voice dripping with sarcasm. "Why was I worried? Alex, we should call the police! Or the FBI! The last thing we should do is go there!"

"Then nobody will get the tape."

"If there is one."

"If there is one," I conceded. "He said he's going to leave the tape in the top right hand drawer of Clarke's office."

"So what?"

"Don't you see? He said he's *going to* leave it. That means he hasn't been there yet. If we hurry, we might catch him before he plants . . . the tape, the bomb, whatever!" I paused in the middle of buttoning my shirt. "Are you getting dressed or what?"

He rolled his eyes and climbed out of bed. "I should have my head examined."

He threw on some clothes and we were off. On our way out I stopped and looked in Mother's room to make sure she was home. If she was still out I would've left her a note so she wouldn't worry when she came home and found us gone. But she was in bed and sound asleep. Duffy, who was lying on the foot of the bed, raised his head when he heard the door and cocked it in that quizzical way peculiar to Westies. When he saw it was me he rested his chin back down on his forepaws. I closed the door and we headed down the stairs. It wasn't until we were halfway to the back door that I thought to be relieved that she was alone.

We raced back to our rickety garage and in a couple of minutes were on our way to Lake Shore Drive.

"I can see it now. We go in there, you open that drawer and we end up sprayed all over the Loop!" said Peter.

"Don't be so melodramatic!"

"Melodramatic! This is probably the craziest thing we've ever done, and we've done a lot of really crazy things," he said as I turned onto the Drive. "If this person has the evidence, why doesn't he just go to the police?"

"Because he's afraid," I said. "He doesn't want anybody to know he's connected with the tape. He said something about the way he got the tape would land him in jail." We picked up speed as we came off the short ramp and onto the Drive.

He heaved a frustrated sigh. "That's really convenient! He *can't* go to the police! That's probably the very same thing he said to Jody. Alex, I want to know, for my own peace of mind, that you realize how incredibly insane what we're doing is."

"Come on, Peter! This guy can't possibly get a bomb into this building! There's a twenty-four-hour guard."

Peter was silent for a moment, then I heard a sharp intake of breath. "What a minute! Wait a minute! There's a twenty-four-hour guard? Honey . . . honey . . . don't you have to sign in after hours?"

"Yeah, I think so." I couldn't understand why he was breathing so heavily.

145

He turned his face to me and it had gone whiter than the ghosts in my dream. "This guy that called, he doesn't want anybody to know who he is?"

"Yeah?"

"And if he goes to that building, he'll be seen by a guard and he has to sign in?"

"Uh-huh. I can understand why he doesn't—" My mouth dropped open. "Oh, Jesus!" I yelled as I slammed on the brakes.

We swerved about halfway into the lane to our left and sent a blue Pontiac that had been running alongside us careening to the next lane over. Then we veered toward the right and ran up onto the shoulder. The car scraped along the guardrail for about fifty feet before coming to a halt.

"Get out!" I yelled as I opened my door.

"This side's stuck!" said Peter.

"Come this way!"

He scooted across the seat and out of the driver's door just as a van rode by with its horn blaring. It barely missed taking off our door, not to mention us.

"Come on! We've got to get out of here!" I cried.

We ran around the front of the car, jumped the short guardrail, and scrambled down the lawn toward one of the baseball fields at the far south end of Lincoln Park. When we felt we were a safe enough distance from the car, we stopped, turned, and looked back. Both of us were out of breath from fear and exertion.

But the car just sat there.

The sense of relief and anticlimax was overwhelming. It had seemed so clear to me only a few seconds ago that if somebody wanted to get rid of us, the best way to do it was to put explosives in our car and make sure we were in it when they went off. And what better way of doing that than promising to give us the elusive evidence we wanted if we got to a specific place by a specific time. The same idea seemed to have flashed through Peter's mind as well, which just goes to show that two minds, great or not, can have the same lunatic thought at the same time.

We looked at each other and burst out laughing.

146

"I can't believe we've gotten so paranoid!" Peter managed to choke out.

"I can't either," I replied, gasping for breath. "Mother's going to kill me when she sees—"

The end of my sentence was cut off by a blast so powerful that the roof of our car shot straight up in the air and hung suspended for a moment before crashing down onto the burning interior. The hood flapped backward and sparks flew off the engine. The initial blast was followed by a second, stronger, flame-laden explosion as the gas tank blew.

Although the traffic wasn't terribly heavy at that time of night, cars went careening wildly across the lanes to get out of the way, or maybe just out of surprise, and smashed against each other like some wild, out-of-control bumper car ride. Other cars on both sides of the Drive screeched to a halt.

Even as far away as we were standing we could feel the heat from the burning wreckage.

Peter looked at me. "You were saying . . . ?"

I stared open-mouthed at the inferno. "What do we do now?"

He shrugged. "I could stand by the side of the road, show a little leg, and see if I can get us a ride."

I stayed with the bonfire while Peter ran to find a phone to call for help. He needn't have bothered. Before much time had passed, a patrol car spotted the mess, stopped, and radioed for help. The fire department made it to the scene before Peter got back, and more patrols arrived shortly after the fire trucks.

In the meantime, one of the cops from the first patrol car on the scene questioned me about what had happened, while the other was busy directing traffic around the wreck. I couldn't tell him much more than the fact that the car had exploded. I didn't think it would be wise to mention a bomb, since that would've tied us up with the police for hours (if not days) to come.

"You say the car just blew up with no warning?" Office Barton asked me for the third time.

"That's right."

"Hmm," he said with a sidelong glance at the burning car. "It's really amazing that you got out of it alive. I mean, if it blew with no warning."

"Yeah, it is," I replied, finding it very hard to look him in the eyes.

"Hmm. I've never seen a car go up like that, outside of the movies."

The implication was pretty obvious. I was trying to think of an answer when Peter finally returned. He came up beside me and put his arm over my shoulder. "You all right?"

"Yeah."

"Who is this?" Barton asked.

"This is my husband, Peter Livesay."

"Your husband," Barton said slowly.

I turned to Peter. "I was just telling Officer Barton that the car blew up without any warning."

"Oh," said Peter, who then looked at Barton. "That's right."

Barton frowned at him. "You were in the car?"

"Yes, I was."

"And you left the scene?"

"I went to call 911."

"You've been gone a long time."

Peter sighed. "We're not exactly close to a phone here. I had to go all the way over to Clark Street."

"Officer!" One of the firemen, who was standing about twenty feet from the back of our former car, waved to Barton.

"Excuse me a minute," he said as he walked away from us. "Don't leave."

"God! I thought you'd never get back," I said as we watched Barton join the fireman.

"I couldn't find a phone."

"As it turned out we didn't need to call them. The police showed up and they called the fire department."

"I wasn't worried about them. I called Agent Henry. He and his partner are on their way. I also called your mother."

"What?" I said.

"On the off chance that she would wake up and hear about this on the news before we got home. You can't be too careful."

"Obviously *we* can't be! I never thought I'd say this about calling the FBI, but thank God! Officer Barton is pretty sharp. He already thinks there's something fishy about the way the car exploded."

"That's probably because you told him it blew up without any warning. If that were true, we'd be dead."

I put my hands on my hips. "You know, that's the second time in the past twenty-four hours that I've been accused of not being a good liar as if there's something wrong with that! What was I supposed to tell him? That we jumped out of the car because I had a premonition it was going to blow?"

He slipped his arm around my waist. "I'm sorry, honey."

Even hearing that irritated me, because there was something about the way he said it that seemed to imply that one had to make allowances for me. I was tempted to step out of his embrace, but I reminded myself that I was overtired and scared, and that when you've been married as long as we have you do have to make allowances for each other.

Barton and the fireman finished their conference, then Barton motioned to his partner to give up the traffic directing and come with him.

"Mr. Reynolds, Mr. Livesay," he said as they reached us. "That fireman over there, he seems to think there was a bomb in your car, and I have to say I agree with him. You have any idea why anyone would want to do something like that to you?"

"I don't . . ." I glanced at Peter helplessly. He didn't offer any assistance.

"But what's even more . . . confusing," Barton continued, "is that it looks like you knew there was a bomb in your car, 'cause you managed to get it parked and get out before it blew."

"I'd hardly call what I did parking the car!" I snapped.

"You had to make it look good," he replied with a superior smile.

"What are you talking about?"

"Well, if you knew the car was gonna blow, and you don't know anybody that'd want to put a bomb there, then I'd say . . . maybe we got a case of somebody looking after some insurance money here."

I couldn't believe what I was hearing. "You think we blew up our own car?"

He shrugged. "We think it's a possibility, don't we, Jim?"

His partner nodded. I half expected him to say "yup."

"You got a better explanation?"

"There is one," I said, "but I really can't give it."

"Uh-huh. I think you'd better come with us."

"Really!" I looked to Peter again, but he just shook his head as if he was finding it difficult to believe that we'd gotten into this situation. I heaved a sigh, then said, "All right. Look, nobody's supposed to know this, but we're working for the FBI."

"Uh-huh," Barton said after a beat. "You got some identification?"

"Well . . . no." I already knew how the next part was going to sound. "We're working undercover."

"Uh-huh," he replied again after a longer pause.

"It's true!" I said with the profound sense that I was sounding nuttier by the minute.

The two cops looked at each other and laughed.

I raised my eyebrows at Peter. "Apparently I can't even tell the truth convincingly."

Peter formed his lips into an O, and looked exactly like he would have liked to disavow any relationship to me.

"I think you guys better come along with us," Barton said when he'd recovered himself.

"We can't leave here," I said. "The men we report to are on their way."

"Come on, come on," Barton said, growing impatient. His partner moved to Peter's side.

"Believe it or not, officer, he's telling the truth," Peter said. "We are working with the FBI."

"Yeah," Barton said, gently but firmly taking hold of my arm, "and we're working with the little green men. We want you back at the spaceship."

150

He tried to move me forward but I stood fast. I slipped my arm from his grasp. "You're Area Three, right?"

This stopped him dead. His face went blank. "Yeah? I don't work out of there, but that's my area."

"Why don't you radio in and see if you can get hold of Commander Frank O'Neill. He knows who we are and what we do."

He stared at me for a long time trying to figure out whether or not I was insane. Then he reached down slowly and pulled the radio off his belt. "Frank O'Neill, huh? This is a joke, I'm not gonna laugh."

He'd barely gotten the thing to his lips when Agents Henry and Raymond arrived. They pulled up onto the shoulder of Lake Shore Drive and stopped a safe distance from the smoldering remains of our car, then climbed out and headed across the lawn to us.

"Officer," Henry called as they approached. "What's going on here?"

"Who are you?" Barton asked.

Both of the agents showed him their identification while Henry gave their names. Barton looked from the IDs to Peter and me as if he thought this might be part of an elaborate hoax, but couldn't fathom how we could have done it.

"Officer . . . ?" Henry said.

Barton came to attention. "Yeah, sorry. These guys say that they're working for you. You know them?"

Henry looked so displeased that I was relieved when he didn't deny knowing us. He asked Barton again what had happened, and the officer explained what we had said, and what he and the fireman believed to be true.

Henry gave a nod in our direction. "Well, we'll take over with them from here. Here's my card. You can reach me there anytime if you need to know anything further about this incident."

As the agents led us away from the befuddled and obviously unhappy Barton, I said to Peter, "What do you want to bet that if that cop calls that number he's going to find out that he doesn't need to know anything?"

When we got to their car, Raymond held open the back door

and we climbed in. Then Henry got behind the wheel and Raymond joined him in the front seat.

"What? Are we under arrest?" I said.

"We need to have a talk," Henry replied as he started the engine. "We'll go to your house."

Since the explosion had occurred just short of the North Avenue exit, Henry pulled around the wreckage and exited the Drive, then headed back to Fullerton through the park. Not another word was said on the way home, but we hadn't gone far before my hand stole into Peter's. I was much more shaken up by what had happened than I thought.

Mother was waiting at the door for us.

"Are you all right?" she demanded, her face fraught with concern.

"We're fine," I said. "Not a scratch on us."

She narrowed her eyes at me. "We'll talk about this later."

"Mrs. Reynolds," Agent Henry interrupted, "I'm afraid we're going to have to talk about it now. May we?" He gestured into the living room.

"Of course."

The agents came in and sat down on the couch, and the three of us pulled up chairs on the opposite side of the coffee table from them. Somehow I found a little solace in the fact that we had them outnumbered.

"Now," said Henry, staring directly at me, "tell us what happened."

"Our car was bombed," said Peter. "I'd think that was obvious."

"It is. What we want to know is, why?"

"How in the hell would I know?" I said.

"If somebody tried to kill you," said Raymond, "it means there's been a breech."

When he said the word *breech*, I could see a row of cartoon arrows appear over my head, flashing wildly and pointing at me as alarm bells rang.

"I don't know what you mean," I said.

Henry sighed impatiently. "If the bomber targeted you it

means that he knows you're working for us—or at least that you're working for the authorities. How did he know that?"

"That doesn't necessarily follow," Peter said. "He killed Jody. Does that mean he thought she was working for the FBI? I doubt it."

"He must've known you were a threat. Now, how could he have known that?"

Peter and I looked at each other, then over to Mother, who also (for once) seemed to be at a loss for an explanation.

"I don't—" I started slowly, but Henry cut me off.

"You want to tell us what you were doing out in the middle of the night? Why you happened to be in the car when it was set to explode?"

I stared at him dumbly. It had never been our style to tell the Feds any more than we had to, because it was often difficult to know whose side they were on, regardless of the fact that they were employing us. The only one I trusted implicitly was Agent Lawrence Nelson, our boss at the CIA. And I even had some reservations about him. But in this case we were supposed to be reporting to these guys. I just wished I didn't feel so backed into a corner.

Mother suddenly broke the short silence.

"Now, Alex! I really don't hold with this business of someone trying to blow you up. You tell these agents about the tape!"

I was so flabbergasted when she let this out that my mouth fell open. When I didn't respond right away, she added, "Tell them the truth."

She made it sound like she was trying to get me to 'fess up to breaking a window. However, there was a slight glint in her eye that seemed to add, "Or at least as much of the truth as you deem right and proper."

I turned to Henry. "Have you heard about the videotape?"

"What?"

"It seems that there is a videotape somewhere of Fritz Peterson, the Republican candidate for senator. It supposedly shows him being involved in some scandal."

"How do you know that?" Raymond asked.

I silently gulped. "It's going all around the office."

"And what's supposed to be on this tape?"

"We don't know. But it occurred to us that if somebody wanted to get Jody to the office to kill her, the tape might've been good bait. She was rabidly anti-Peterson. She would've done anything to get evidence on him."

"What does any of this have to do with the attempt on you?" Henry asked.

"Somebody called us at about two-thirty and said that they had the tape. We thought it might be a trap, but we decided to risk it."

There was a long pause during which both agents gazed at me without flinching. Finally, Henry said, "You thought it might be a trap. That brings us back to, how did they know to call you?"

There was that corner again. All I could think to do was plead ignorance.

"I have no idea."

Peter said, "We've been asking around about the tape since we first heard of it. We tried to be discreet, but maybe somebody thought we were being too nosey."

"Why didn't you tell us about this tape business before?" said Raymond.

"We just found out about it ourselves," I replied. "And so far as we knew, it was just a rumor."

Mother and Peter simultaneously did a slow take in my direction. I beamed triumphantly. After thirty-some-odd years at my Mother's knee, I was finally learning to lie off the cuff. She must've been proud.

"Well, this changes things," said Henry.

"You're bloody well right it does!" Mother said indignantly. "You people always assure us that there's no danger involved in your silly cases, and then we always end up being blown up, or shot, or burned to death."

"I think you mean 'almost,' " I said.

"Quite right!"

"Mrs. Reynolds," said Henry, "we were proceeding on the assumption that it was unlikely the bomber had infiltrated the office. Unlikely, but possible. According to Alex's report . . ." Here he paused and shot a look at me that was designed to remind me that I'd left a few things out of my report. ". . . you haven't seen or heard anything suspicious. The only person we knew of connected to the office who was at all suspect was David Leech, the young man who had a fight with Jody Linn-Hadden before she was killed. We've done extensive research into his background and have come up with no evidence that would connect him with any group that has threatened Charles Clarke."

"But he might have been working alone," Raymond chimed in.

"David's not a bomber, he's an angry little queen!" I snapped.

Henry blinked at me. "We'll take your word for that. Anyway, we thought there was a slim chance that *if* it had been someone in the office, they might keep working there after the bombing. That's why we asked you to keep your eyes and ears open. But now that's changed. Now it looks like the bomber really was part of the office, and must still be working there. And somehow he got tipped off that your boys were working for the authorities."

"We're not her boys," Peter said testily. He wouldn't have objected if Mother had referred to us that way, which she often does, but it sounded condescending coming from Henry.

"Sorry," he said without sounding it.

"What you're saying about this person, whoever it is, being in the office, that's not necessarily true," said Mother. "There was a fund-raiser tonight. There were hundreds of guests there, and only a few were from the campaign headquarters. We asked all around about the tape at the party."

"That's right," I said. "And the attack on us happened pretty much right after the fund-raiser."

"Well, either way, you're out of it now," Raymond said with finality. "If somebody's made you a target, we're pulling you off the case."

"Well, that's really nice of you," I said wryly, "but pulling us out of that office isn't going to stop us from being targets. Somebody might think we were looking for that tape, but they don't know we were doing it officially. For all they know, we're still looking for it. I mean, why would they think we were professionals? God knows Jody wasn't . . . was she?"

"She didn't have anything to do with us," Henry replied stiffly.

Mother laughed derisively. "Now doesn't that inspire confidence! That could mean anything from 'she didn't know you personally,' to 'she wasn't working for your department.' Your lot never gives us the whole truth."

The amazing thing was that she managed to sound so indignant when we never give them the whole truth, either.

"Mrs. Reynolds, I assure you that Jody Linn-Hadden was not working for the government." There was a pause, then he added with some obvious discomfort, "At least to my knowledge."

"Hmm. Just like you assured us that the case wouldn't be dangerous?"

"It doesn't matter anymore, because you're out of it!"

"The hell we are!" said Peter. "In the first place, we were working in that office because we support Charles Clarke's campaign long before you came along and asked us to spy. In the second place, as long as somebody's trying to kill us, you're going to be damn sure we're in it!"

"And we're going to stay in it until we find out who killed Jody and who tried to kill us!" I added.

"Not officially, you're not!"

I squinted at him. "When you checked our backgrounds, you didn't spend very much time talking to Lawrence Nelson, did you?"

"Why?"

"Because he would've warned you that we're much, *much* more trouble when we're left to ourselves!"

The agents tried to convince us that without any official standing it would be lunacy for us to continue investigating, but they had no way of knowing how lovingly we embrace lunacy. They warned us that we would get no assistance from them whatsoever, and that if we got in the way of an official investigation, we would be dealt with accordingly. However, it was difficult for them to make much of an impression on us while Mother was giving them the bum's rush out the door.

"Well, that was fun!" I said as she closed the door after them. "We haven't thrown federal agents out of the house for ages!"

Mother wheeled around and faced me, her expression anything but amused. "What on earth do you mean going sleuthing in the middle of the night! Didn't I bring you up better than this?"

"We didn't have much of a choice. The caller said now or never."

"Honestly, Alex, you *knew* that was exactly how Jody was lured to her death, and yet the minute you get a call, off you go like a rabbit after the hounds!"

"Like a . . . huh?"

She turned to Peter. "And I would've thought that you'd have had a little more sense!"

"I don't suppose it would help to say that I objected at the time," he replied.

"But you went along with him anyway!"

"Will you please stop acting like he's my keeper!" I said in a very unlovely tone.

"The moment you stop behaving as if you need one!" she replied grandly.

"Look, we figured it might be a trap, but we thought if it was, it would be at the office, and as long as we knew where it was, we could try to avoid it. We had no idea the *car* would be the trap!"

"Forgive me for pointing this out, darling, but I believe it's the element of surprise that makes it a trap!"

"She has you there, honey," said Peter.

"The point is," I said testily, "that we had to take the chance. It might've meant getting the tape."

"Bugger the tape!" said Mother, giving way to a rare bit of profanity, albeit British profanity, which just sounds quaint. "How could we ever have been so foolish as to ask about that tape the way we did!"

I said, "What I don't understand is why you wanted me to tell the FBI about it. I thought our policy was don't tell even when asked."

"Because I want them to find the bloody thing!" she exclaimed. "If somebody's trying to kill you because you know about it, then the authorities bloody well better find it and make sure *everybody* knows about it!"

"That's just the trouble," said Peter. "According to Mary Linn-Hadden, Jody was afraid that if it fell into the hands of the FBI, they wouldn't make it public."

"Did you learn anything at all at the party?" I asked Mother.

"Only that Tony knows some rather salacious old men," she replied through her aquiline nose. "I introduced the subject of the videotape to several little cadres of them, and rather than giving me information, they seemed desperate to hear the details of the tape from me. Some of them fairly slathered. It was quite unattractive."

"You didn't get anything at all?"

She sighed heavily. "Nothing that was any help, I'm afraid. Most people were more than willing to speculate about what was on the tape, but even that was rather one-note."

"Let me guess," said Peter. "Popular opinion is that if the tape exists, it's of Fritz Peterson caught in a homosexual tryst."

"Exactly."

I snorted with disgust. "Sometimes I wonder if Joe Gardner is right. Maybe we are our own worst enemies."

"So what are we going to do?" said Peter. "Do we proceed on the assumption that there is a tape, or that there isn't?"

"Oh, I think we can be fairly certain that the tape exists now," said Mother.

"Why?" I asked.

She smiled in response, waiting for me to get it. But I didn't.

"Because somebody tried to kill us," said Peter.

"I might be willing to believe it didn't have to exist in order to get Jody to that office, but if somebody is willing to kill two more people merely out of fear that they know about it, then I have to believe it's real." She shook her head. "I still can't believe the two of you were willing to rush into a trap knowing what had happened to Jody!"

"You know, there's something that puzzles me about that," I said. "I mean, when the call came, we took it seriously because we *knew* what had happened to Jody. But I wonder why *she* took it so seriously."

"What do you mean?" Peter asked.

"Well, if we'd gotten a call like that out of the blue before any of this other stuff happened, I would've just thought it was a crank, wouldn't you? I don't think I would've gone running out after it."

"But didn't Mary tell you that Jody was daft on the subject of getting evidence against Fritz Peterson?" Mother asked.

"Daft, maybe. But wouldn't you still be wary of going to meet someone at five in the morning in a deserted place on the strength of an anonymous call?"

"Oh, yes!" Mother said, nodding. "I see. She must've had a reason for believing there was a tape."

"And she must've known the caller," I added.

"Not necessarily. *You* didn't know him, and you went."

"That's true. But that just proves what I was saying. She must've already known there was a tape.

Peter said, "We need to talk to Mary again."

"I don't think Mary could know anything."

"Why not?"

"Because if she did, she'd be dead. Hell, somebody tried to kill us just for mentioning the tape."

"I don't think it was just for that," said Peter. "I think it was because we asked about it in such a way that it made the killer think we were looking for it."

At least he was gracious enough to say "we."

"But I still think we need to talk to Mary as soon as we can," he continued, "because even though she might not know anything about the tape itself, she might know what Jody was doing to try to get evidence on Peterson."

"You're right," I said. "Because that led to her death."

"Just see to it that it doesn't lead you down the same path!" Mother said soberly.

TEN

I had a very difficult time getting to sleep. Our brush with death left me hyped up, but at the same time I had a strange feeling of emptiness. It was like being an electrified corn husk. I tossed and turned for close to an hour, then tried to get myself under control without much success. I lay on my back for a while, then on my side with my butt touching Peter's thigh. Finally I turned over on my other side, slipped my arms around him and spooned him so hard you would've thought I was on a toboggan run. It was in that attitude that I finally fell asleep.

I woke up around ten o'clock Saturday morning. The digital clock was giving its usual precise reading but there didn't seem any point in that kind of accuracy just then.

I climbed out of bed slowly, weighed down by residual drowsiness, and went into the bathroom. When I came back out I stood in the doorway and watched Peter sleep. He was on his back, his left leg straight and his right bent with the sole of the foot against his left calf. He has beautiful legs: slender and muscular with a dusting of dark brown hair. His right arm was stretched across his forehead, and his left hand rested on his stomach. Eight years together and the mere sight of him still excites me.

I stepped out of my briefs and got back into bed, snuggling up next to him. I laid my hand over his and gently kissed his nipple. He stirred, and although he didn't open his eyes, he smiled.

"What are you doing?" he said, his voice husky with sleep.

"Just glad you're alive," I said, kissing his chest. "Every time somebody tries to kill us, I'm just glad to be alive."

His eyes fluttered open and he looked at the ceiling. "You know, before I met you I never imagined that I would ever be thinking in terms like 'every time somebody tries to kill me.'"

I pursed my lips. "Shut up and make love to me!"

It was another hour before we got down stairs. Mother had left a note that she was out looking at cars and had taken Duffy with her. Apparently she had to make sure the car had dog appeal before making a purchase.

We tuned into the local news while having a bite to eat before setting out. Charles Clarke and his dutiful wife Wendy were shown smiling and waving at a rally attended by an incredibly broad range of people, at least as far as I could tell from the five-second sweep the camera took of the crowd. Clarke fairly oozed sincerity as he addressed the people—even though he was my candidate I still couldn't help but think of him in terms of oozing—and Wendy managed to look as if her only regret was that the rally was keeping her from baking cookies for all the low-income children of Chicago.

Shorter shrift was given to the two other democratic candidates, William Lederer and Melvin Colton, since they were no longer considered serious challenges to Clarke. Their coverage pretty much consisted of having their pictures flashed on the screen while the talking head said something that amounted to, "Oh, they had rallies, too."

Much fuller coverage was given to the Republican candidate. Fritz Peterson was accompanied by his wife, Tippy, as they visited a hospital and then appeared at their own rally. Unlike the Clarke affair, the revelers at the Peterson rally were all wearing straw hats, and there was a whole lot of red, white, and blue in evidence. It was the usual, noisy, "the only true Americans are Republicans" affair.

Fritz Peterson was a tall, husky man with premature gray on both his head and his mustache, which made him look much older than he really was. His wife was a bit shorter than him and had a habit of standing with her fingers pressed together beneath her nose as if she were constantly praying for guidance.

"Why are you looking like that?" Peter asked just before taking a bite of his sandwich.

"Like what?"

"Your face is all scrunched up."

"Oh. I was just wondering what on earth they have on Peterson. I hope to God he's not gay. I mean, look at him! He looks like he's taking a break from selling chicken! I don't want to see a tape of Colonel Sanders boinking another guy!"

We finished eating and quickly washed up after ourselves. We were in a hurry to leave, but I needed to make a call first. I picked up the receiver of our kitchen phone, dialed, and waited. It rang three times before being answered by Agent Lawrence Nelson.

"Yes?"

"Hello, Larry. It's Alex Reynolds."

"What are you calling him for?" asked Peter.

I shushed him.

"Yes, Alex?"

I had to hand it to Nelson. He never sounded surprised to hear from me even though he almost never had reason to expect a call. And he never let on that it irritated him when I called him Larry, although I liked to think it did.

"I think you know we've been asked to do a little job of work for the FBI," I said.

"I also know that you've been relieved of duty," he replied without emotion.

"Already?" My heart sank. I'd thought it would take Henry at least a little while to let Nelson know what happened. Then again, it was almost noon.

"I was told very, very early this morning."

"He didn't waste any time, did he?" I said flatly.

"We usually don't in cases such as this."

"You mean when two of your people are almost blown to bits?" I was starting to get angry, even though I knew it was important to hold my temper if I was going to get him to cooperate.

"Is there something I can do for you, Alex?"

"Yes. I have a favor to ask you, and I want to know if I can ask it of you in confidence."

"That depends on what it is. You do understand that you are no longer under any authority to work on this case?"

I could've sworn there was a smile in his tone, were it within Nelson's nature to smile.

"Of course I understand that."

"And you know that even though you're not on the case, if you have any information bearing on it, you are obliged to turn it over."

"Yes," I said reluctantly.

"All right, then ask your favor."

I took a deep breath. "I want you to find all the information you can on someone named Simon Tivoli."

"What?!" Peter exclaimed loudly. "Alex, you can't!"

I put my hand over the mouthpiece and whispered. "We'll talk about it in a minute."

"Simon Tivoli?" Nelson repeated, ignoring Peter's outburst which I felt sure he'd been able to hear over the phone.

I uncovered the mouthpiece. "Yes, that's right. He's from London, England. He came here about a week ago. He says he works for a computer company called Cyberdyne. I want to know if he's legit."

There was a short silence. "*Does* this have something to do with the bombing of Charles Clarke's office?"

"I don't know. I don't think so. I hope not."

"Um-hm. It would be easier to run him if I had his fingerprints."

"I could lift them from my mother, but that hardly seems practical."

There was a longer pause. "Oh. I see."

"It may not have anything to do with Clarke, Larry. It's a long shot. I just want to make sure."

"Yes, well, it's better to be safe than sorry, isn't it?" Nelson replied.

Once again I had the annoying feeling I was being made fun of. "And do me another favor, will you? When you call back with the information, if you get Mother or the answering machine, please don't leave a message. Only talk to me."

"All right."

We both said goodbye and hung up.

Peter was beside himself. "Alex, I can't believe you! You can't check up on your own mother!"

"I'm not checking up on her," I countered, "I'm checking up on her boyfriend, just as any dutiful son who had the resources of the CIA at his disposal would do!"

"Honey, you really have lost your mind! We already discussed—"

"I know what we discussed!" I said loudly. Then I took a couple of seconds to calm myself. "Look, believe it or not I'm not any happier about doing this than you are, but we have to be thorough, and we have to face facts."

"What facts?"

"The tape, Peter, the tape! Simon was with Mother last night at the party when she asked about the tape. And the attempt on us wasn't made until after the party."

"Well . . . well, so Simon heard your mother ask about it. Nobody tried to kill her."

I sighed. "I know you don't agree with me, just for a minute pretend that he might be a suspect."

"Okay," he said with a smile.

"You and I started asking about the tape the day before the party and nothing happened to us. When Mother was at the party, that was the first time she asked about the tape, and it was right after that the attempt was made on us."

"That's true," Peter said skeptically.

"If Simon's the bomber, he couldn't very well have killed Mother last night because he would've been the last person to be seen with her. We were a different story. Mother was in bed, alone, when we got the call, so Simon could easily have been the one that did it."

"All right," Peter conceded, "so we'll consider him a suspect. For the time being. Even though I still find it hard to believe."

"Well, in all likelihood you're right and I'm wrong. But Nelson should be able to settle it once and for all. If Simon isn't what he says he is, Nelson will find it out."

We took the El down to North and Clybourn and walked back up to the Linn-Hadden home. I half expected to find Mary still standing there, staring out through the picture window like a sunken-eyed waif, but the curtains were drawn against the glaring early afternoon sunlight. We knocked and waited.

After a minute the locks snapped and the door was opened by Annie Watson.

"Oh, hello," she said, apparently as surprised to see us as we were to see her.

"Hi, Annie. Is Mary here?" I asked.

"Uh, yeah. Come in, I guess."

She stepped aside to let us in and closed the door behind us.

"Who is it?" Mary called from the back of the house. She sounded as if her spirits had done a complete about face since we'd last seen her.

"A couple of guys from the office," Annie said loudly.

"Who?"

"Alex Reynolds and Peter Livesay."

"Oh. Just a minute."

She emerged from the kitchen, drying her hands with a limp dishtowel. Some of the color had come back into her cheeks since last Sunday, although that could've been makeup. She had obviously taken more pains over her face, and since she hadn't known we were coming, I could assume the effort hadn't been for us. She looked positively debutantelike in her pale blue knee-length skirt, white knee-high socks, and starched white blouse. A pink bow loosely tied her neatly combed hair.

"I didn't think I'd see you again," she said hesitantly.

"We need to talk to you," I said.

"Right now?" said Annie. "You have to talk to her now? She needs to rest. She's in mourning, you know."

I glanced at Mary. "I can see that."

"Annie came over to bring me a casserole," Mary said quickly.

"It's one of those traditions I've never understood. Baking casseroles. Nobody likes them, but that's what you're supposed to do when somebody dies," Annie added.

"I like them," Mary said with sincerity.

A looked passed between them that I can only describe as something I wish I hadn't seen, given that it was the day before Jody's memorial service.

"We really do need to talk to you," said Peter.

"Alone," I added.

I had the satisfaction of seeing Annie's face turn beet root. "I'll go finish up in the kitchen."

She marched very deliberately to the back of the house and disappeared through the swinging door that separated the dining room from the kitchen.

"She brought over a casserole," Mary repeated with a reticent smile.

"So you said."

"It was very nice of her. It was so near noon I asked her to stay for lunch."

I didn't know what to say, so I just nodded and smiled, hoping that I looked like I believed her and that she would stop explaining, which was getting more embarrassing by the minute.

"We were just cleaning up when you rang the bell. She's going to stay and help me sort through the bills." She put her hands to her cheeks fretfully. "I don't know anything about paying the bills. Jody always took care of everything. I couldn't even . . . I had to search the whole house just to find the checkbook. Annie said she'll show me how to do them."

"We need to talk to you about Jody," said Peter, thankfully bringing the matter of Annie's visit to a close.

She lowered her hands. "What about her?"

166

"The other day you told us that Jody was trying to get dirt on Fritz Peterson. We need to know how she was going about it," I explained.

"I . . . I don't know how," she said unconvincingly. "Why do you want to know?"

"Because last night somebody tried to kill us."

Peter said, "They tried to blow us up just the way they did Jody."

Mary's doelike eyes grew wider and her jaw dropped, but not so much as to be unladylike. "That's . . . that's awful! Why would somebody try to kill you?"

"We think it's because we were asking about the tape."

She gasped. "You what?"

"Don't worry," I said. "We were just trying to find out what was on it or if anyone knew about it. We didn't tell anyone how we knew about it."

"Oh God, oh God!" she exclaimed, her palms going back up to her cheeks. The color drained from her face, bearing evidence that the rosiness hadn't been cosmetics. "What have I done? I never should've told you about it!"

"It's all right, it's all right," I said. "We'll be fine. But we have to find out who tried to kill us, and in order to do that, we have to try to trace what Jody was doing. You told us that somebody called Jody and said they had a tape of Peterson?"

"That's true," she said plaintively, as if she suspected she was being accused of lying.

"We know that, but what we wanted to know is why Jody believed it so readily."

She blinked at me. "I don't understand. . . . I told you, she got this call. . . ."

"She'd never heard about the existence of a tape at all before that?"

"I . . . no." Mary was having a very difficult time looking either me or Peter in the eye.

"So before she got that phone call," I pressed, "she'd never heard about the tape. Then she gets this call and that was all it took to get her to go out and meet this person? I don't believe it. I don't believe Jody was that stupid."

"No, *we're* the only ones that're that stupid," said Peter.

"I don't know anything," Mary said desperately. "I don't . . . I don't . . ." She started to cry, but from the look on her face it was from fear rather than sorrow.

"Hey, what are you doing to her?" Annie had come in from the kitchen without our noticing her. Her neatly plucked brows were knit together, and her small mouth formed a frown.

"We didn't mean to upset her," Peter replied. Then he turned to Mary. "We really didn't. But Mary, this is very important. Jody's been killed and our lives are in danger. We have to find out who's doing this."

Mary looked up, her watery eyes wide with terror. "Because of the tape? But then . . . then I'm in danger!"

"Maybe, but I don't think so. The killer had to know that Jody would tell you what was going on, and he hasn't hurt you yet."

"Nobody's going to hurt you," Annie said, laying a soothing hand on Mary's shoulder. "Maybe we should go away for a while."

I was too stunned to say anything. Peter said, "That might not be a bad idea. But first we need to know what Jody was doing. I don't think you're in any danger, but if you are, telling us isn't going to make that any worse, and it may help. Are you sure she never said anything about that tape to you before she got that call?"

She nodded meekly.

"Then please, how was she trying to dig up the dirt?"

Mary looked for guidance to Annie, who stared back at her stoically. If there was anything to be read there, I couldn't see it. Mary turned back to us and said, "She was just . . . she asked around. She talked to everybody."

"At the office?" I asked.

Mary nodded.

"She didn't talk to us."

"She didn't think you knew anything."

I gritted my teeth and glanced at Peter.

Peter said, "It's hard to believe that she did much asking around the office and we didn't hear about it."

"Well, actually, I don't think she talked much to the volunteers, but I know she talked to Mr. Schuler about the possibility of finding stuff on Peterson. I don't know if she talked to Mr. Clarke, because he wasn't as accessible."

So Schuler did know Jody was looking for dirt.

"Who else?"

Mary shook her head slowly and shrugged. "I told you, she talked to a lot of people. People at the office, and Jo and Sheila because they're friends of ours. . . ."

"She even talked to me," said Annie.

"But who told her about the tape? You must know," I asked Mary.

She didn't answer. She just looked at me with those wide wet eyes and continued to shake her head.

"Mary," Peter said gently, "I know how close you and Jody were. I can't believe she came across an important piece of information and didn't tell you about it."

Tears began to course down her cheeks again. She nervously wiped them away. "She didn't. I swear it!"

I heaved a frustrated sigh. "Who else did she talk to? I mean, outside of the office?"

"She went everywhere. She asked at the bars, because she thought if there was anything going around she could probably find out about it there. She even went to Ned Turner."

"Ned Turner?" I said. "The gossip columnist? She knew him?"

"She didn't, but she tried everybody she could think of, and couldn't find *anything!* And all anybody ever said was that they heard Mr. Peterson was gay. But then she thought of asking Mr. Turner. She figured if anybody knew anything dirty on anybody, especially about sex, it would be him."

That made sense. Turner wasn't just a gossip columnist, he was a bitchy gay gossip columnist. He worked for *Chicago Lite,* one of the seedier of the local rags. Ned specialized in very thinly veiled blind items that virtually outed famous people as well as items that weren't blind at all. Turner's columns had been the beginning of the end for more than one politician, as well as fanning the flames beneath the dubious sexuality of many movie and television stars. It made perfect sense that she would go to him, since he would be likely to know all the rumors, and which were true and which weren't. I silently kicked myself for not having thought of this on my own, although since we didn't know him personally (and rarely read his column), there was no reason why we should have.

"She didn't tell you what Turner told her?" I asked.

"No . . ." Mary replied vacantly. "No, she didn't say anything about it."

"Wasn't that unusual?"

She looked up at me, and the tears suddenly stopped in midstream. It was apparent that she had just realized something that hadn't occurred to her before. "Yes . . . yes, it was!"

"Mary," I said as sincerely as I knew how, "we're going to try to find out what happened to Jody and see that something's done about it."

"Thank you," she said softly without looking me in the eye.

Peter added, "But in the meantime, taking a vacation really might not be a bad idea."

On our way back to the El, I said, "Annie certainly has moved in fast, hasn't she?"

Peter sighed. "Well, they were friends before, weren't they? Didn't you tell me that she was the only other one that Jody and Mary trusted with a key to the office?"

"Yeah, but still! I was getting sort of a lioness-protecting-her-cub feeling from her that made me awfully uncomfortable. It made me feel like she'd been waiting in the wings for something to happen to Jody." I was silent for a moment, then added, "Would you do me a favor?"

"What?"

"If something ever happens to me would you at least wait a week before taking up with somebody else?"

He smiled. "Sweetheart, if anything ever happened to you I would throw myself on your pyre!"

I laughed. "I still find it hard to believe that Jody didn't tell Mary about the tape before."

"If she knew about it before."

"Granted."

"But I don't find it that hard to believe. It looks like Jody protected her from everything. Maybe she wouldn't tell her something if she thought it would upset her."

"You're probably right. I think it's really significant that Jody didn't talk about whatever Ned Turner had to say."

"I think so, too."

"Well, at least Mary confirmed one thing," I said. "Schuler knew what Jody was doing."

"Yes, but so what? It doesn't give him a reason to kill her. Despite what he says, I would think he'd be glad to get the skinny on Peterson."

We walked along in silence for a few moments, then I said, "Oh! I just thought of something! We were probably there when she talked to him."

"Who? Schuler? We were?" Peter scrunched his face into an attractive puzzle.

"Remember last Saturday when she came out of Schuler's office and was so disgusted with him? I'll bet that's when she talked to him about the tape."

"You're probably right."

"You know, there's one thing that bothers me about what Mary said. I don't understand why she hasn't been killed, either. It seems like everybody else who knows about the tape has had an attempt made on them."

"Not everybody. No one's tried to kill your mother."

"That's right."

"You sound disappointed!"

I gave his shoulder a playful slap. "No, I just don't understand it! You know what I mean!"

"Yeah, I do. And you're right. It doesn't make sense."

I thought about this for a moment. "Unless . . . unless it's like you said earlier: because you and me and Jody were the ones that gave the impression we were pursuing the tape."

"Yeah, but your mother asked about it, too. The same way we did. I mean, if the killer was assuming we were trying to find it, wouldn't he assume the same thing about her?"

"Probably, but not Mary. He must know that Mary didn't tell the authorities about the tape, because they would have been on the trail of it right away."

"That's true."

We fell into a frustrated silence as we reached the El station. We zipped our fare cards through the turnstile machines and went down to the platform.

"Wait a minute," said Peter. "Where are we going?"

"I thought we were going to the office."

"Shouldn't we talk to Ned Turner first?"

"You're right."

Since neither of us knew where the *Chicago Lite* office was located, let alone whether or not Turner would be there on a Saturday, we went to the pay phone on the platform and called directory assistance. They gave us the number, but didn't have the address.

The phone at the paper was answered by a perky near-falsetto voice that swung upward as it said, *"Chicago Lite,"* as if the air was rapidly escaping from it.

After explaining in the vaguest possible terms that I needed to talk to Ned Turner I managed to elicit the fact that he normally stopped in at five to drop off his column and pick up his correspondence, but that he was difficult to catch.

It was a bit harder to get the guy to give me their address, something they were reluctant to do for fear of being targeted by various nut cases. It wasn't until I explained that the matter I needed to see Turner about concerned Jody that he relented and gave it to me.

With over three hours to spare before being able to see Turner, we decided to go on to the office. I would've loved to have challenged Schuler again on whether or not he'd known about Jody's quest for the tape, but there was no reason to think he'd do anything but continue to deny it. But we figured that if nothing else, we could get a couple of hours of volunteering in before going to see Turner.

When we walked into the office we were stopped by the guard, who signaled to Shawn Stillman. He frowned and came over to us.

"You finally got here! I was beginning to wonder."

"What's going on?" I asked.

"I told Jerry to stop you when you came in because the big man himself asked to see you the minute you got here."

It took me a minute to realize that Jerry must be the name of the guard. "Oh. Okay."

Shawn led us to Clarke's office and rapped lightly on the door.

"Come in," Clarke called out in his pleasing baritone.

Shawn opened the door, popped his head in and said, "Sir, they're here."

"Bring them in."

As we entered, Clarke rose from behind his desk and greeted us with the smile that had won the hearts of his followers. He shook hands with both of us in turn and said, "Thank you, Shawn," then went back behind his desk and sat.

Shawn departed without a word after a slight hesitation that showed his disappointment at not being included in the meeting. Apparently he thought that since it involved members of his staff, he would be allowed to sit in. He closed the door with a sharp click.

"Be seated, gentleman," said Clarke. I sat in the chair across from him, and Peter pulled another one over from the conference table by the windows and sat beside me.

"Well!" Clarke said expansively as he sat back in his chair. "We've had a lot of excitement here today!"

"We have?" said Peter.

"Yes. Some gentlemen from the FBI were here this morning questioning everyone. First, let me say that they told me that the two of you were involved in some sort of accident yesterday."

"If you can call having your car blown up an accident," Peter replied.

"I know, I know," he said ruefully. "I couldn't be more shocked by this. Are the two of you all right?"

"Uh, yeah," I said. "We weren't in the car at the time."

"Of course. The agents did explain that this was a deliberate action. It's just so hard to believe that anybody would do something like that."

"It's not the first time it's happened," I said. "It's just the first time they missed."

Clarke shook his head in apparent disbelief. "It's so hard to understand people who would kill someone just because they were working for me."

I glanced at Peter. "Mr. Clarke, I don't think that's the reason. It seems Jody was killed because she was trying to get a videotape containing evidence that involves Fritz Peterson in a scandal."

Clarke's eyes glazed over at the mention of the tape. "Yes. That's one of the things the FBI agents were asking about. I'll tell you the same thing I told them: The Charles Clarke Campaign isn't interested in dirt on any of the other candidates. If Jody Linn-Hadden was looking for scandal, she was doing it entirely on her own accord and if I'd known about it, I would've put an end to it."

"You mean you didn't know?" Peter asked.

There was a beat before Clarke said, "No. Why would I?"

"Because we were told that your campaign manager knew."

This was the good thing about the fact that Mary had told us things that she wouldn't tell Agents Henry and Raymond. It gave us the chance to be the ones to surprise him with the information.

Clarke went saucer-eyed and he dropped the pencil he'd been toying with. "What? John knew?"

"That's what we heard."

Clarke stammered for a moment, then pressed a button on top of his desk. We heard a buzzer sound in the next room. He then raised a palm. "Just . . . just a minute."

After a brief wait Schuler came into the office. "Yeah, Charlie?" He spotted us and added, "Oh. Hello."

"John, I want to know something. Did you know beforehand that Jody Linn-Hadden was looking for this . . . this tape that the FBI was asking about?"

Since he'd positioned himself a few feet behind us, both Peter and I had to twist around in our seats to see his reaction. He eyed us with contempt, then looked up at his boss.

"As a matter of fact, I did."

"Why didn't you tell me about it?"

"I didn't want to bother you with it. I told Jody in no uncertain terms that we would have nothing to do with it, and that she was to stop it immediately. I sent her away very unhappy, but I thought that was the end of it."

"You should have told me."

"I'm sorry, sir," Schuler replied.

Clarke then turned to us. "I want it to be clear that whatever Jody was doing, she was doing it on her own. It had nothing to do with this office. You don't realize how damaging something like this could be if it got out. No matter how much I disavowed my involvement, people would still think I was planning to run a smear campaign, and nothing could be further from the truth. I also want it to be clear that under no circumstances do I want anyone to keep looking for that tape."

"Mr. Clarke, you don't seem to understand," I said. "This is no longer a matter of politics. That tape may be evidence in a murder. It has to be found."

"So you're going to continue to try to find it?"

"We have to, if for no other reason than someone has tried to kill us over it!"

He sat back in his chair and sighed deeply. "Then I'm going to have to relieve you of your duties."

"What?" I said in disbelief.

"And ask that you not concern yourself in my campaign anymore."

"You're kicking us out?" Peter asked incredulously. "But we're volunteers!"

"I'm sorry, but I can't have anyone even remotely connected

with my campaign running the risk of making it look like I'm involved in trying to smear another candidate."

"But Mr. Clarke—"

"Gentlemen!" Schuler interrupted loudly. "You heard the man. Now, we're very busy and the office has already been disrupted enough because of you."

"John . . ." Clarke said warningly.

"Because of us!" I exclaimed indignantly. "You mean because of a murder!"

"So, I'm going to have to ask you to leave," he said, completely ignoring me. "Or am I going to have to call the guard and have you removed?"

Both Peter and I were struck speechless. When I regained the used of my vocal chords, I said, "That won't be necessary."

We got up and exited the office without another word.

All eyes were on us as left the headquarters. I suppose it had gotten around that we were the cause of the FBI presence at the office that day. I'm not sure I could blame them for their attitude. Most of these people believed wholeheartedly in Clarke, and the thought that we'd somehow been connected with a potentially volatile incident probably didn't set well with people who didn't have all the facts. Then again, we didn't have all the facts, either.

"Well," I said as we rode down in the elevator, "we've been fired twice in the same day. That's a record, even for us."

"Yeah," said Peter. "And one of them was a volunteer job. I don't think we can get much lower than that."

With a couple of hours left before we could try to catch Ned Turner, we went home. I almost let out a yelp when we walked in the door and found Mother seated on the couch beside Commander Frank O'Neill.

"Frank!" I exclaimed, "What a pleasant surprise!"

He stared at me blankly for a moment. "Alex, Peter."

Perhaps it was his close proximity to my mother, or my concern about her current love life, but I found myself assessing Frank anew. He was still ruggedly handsome—the type of man I'd probably find myself attracted to if he wasn't twenty years older than me and interested in my mother. Oh yes, and if I wasn't married. And his good looks were only nominally marred by the slightly hangdog quality that develops in most of Mother's former suitors. And he's nice enough. I don't know exactly why their romance didn't work out, and I never asked, figuring that it was one of those chemical things that is best left undiscussed between Mother and son.

"Frank stopped by when he heard about our car trouble," said Mother.

"You make it sound like the engine's developed a rattle," I said. "The engine is splayed all over Lake Shore Drive."

"So I heard," said Frank. "I was just telling your mother that we don't have a clue yet as to who tried to kill you. Neither does the FBI. All we know so far is that the call to your house came from a pay phone just south of the Loop."

"Has there been any progress on the first bombing? The headquarters one?" Peter asked.

Frank let out a muffled grunt. "I'm sure I don't know anything you don't already know." His tone once again implied that he believed we'd lied to him about working with the FBI on this case.

If the conversation had taken place a few hours earlier, we would've had to backpedal like mad to try to explain that we were working for them, but hadn't been when he accused us of it. However, at that point the truth seemed much easier.

I said, "Frank, I can honestly say that we're not working for the FBI."

"Hmm. That's funny. Because when your car was bombed last night you told two of my men that you *were* working for the FBI, and Agent Henry and Agent Raymond showed up and took you away. You know, I don't so much mind you working for them—except for the fact that you keep endangering your lives"—he glanced at Mother out of the corner of his eye—"as much as I mind you lying about it."

"Well, we *were* working for them last night, but we're not now!" I said pleadingly.

"And when I first asked you if you were working for them?"

"We weren't then."

"So you weren't, then you were, now you're not?"

I threw up my hands. "You see! This is why we lie! The truth always sounds so crazy!"

"Alex, please!" said Mother. She then turned to Frank. "Henry and Raymond asked us to do a little job of work for them. But that's over. Unfortunately, it looks as though this little job may have caused us a spot of trouble."

Frank raised his eyebrows. "Somebody blew up your car!"

Mother blinked. "Yes, well, p'raps that was a bit of an under-statement. Anyway, of course I'm worried, so I wondered if you could fill us in on what's being done." He looked at her so long and so hard she was compelled to add, "I'm not asking you any more than anyone would under the circumstances."

Frank shifted in his seat, then said, "Yeah, well, my people have been cooperating with the FBI. I don't know very much. I do know that from what they've been able to piece together, the bomb that destroyed Clarke's office wasn't exactly sophisticated. . . ."

"It got the job done," said Peter.

"Right. What I mean is, there was nothing to tell them whether or not it was done by a pro. According to Henry, technically they believe the bomb could've been built by an amateur. They don't have anything yet about the one in your car. They've been follow-ing up leads on the first bombing—mostly the threats—and get-ting nowhere."

"I know how they feel," I said.

"Then this morning they brought up the subject of a video-tape." He looked at me pointedly. "Which apparently they hadn't known about."

"We hadn't gotten a chance to make a report about it yet," I said lamely.

He turned back to Mother. "I believe they're over at Fritz Peter-son's headquarters right now questioning him about the tape."

"As if that would do any good," said Peter. "He certainly wouldn't admit to it."

"Well, we'll see. Maybe they can get something out of him. I'm assuming you've told Henry everything you know."

"Of course we did." I was startled by the question, and I'm afraid I faltered enough to make myself look guilty.

Frank rolled his eyes, then he said his goodbyes and left. As usual, he looked at lot less happy on his way out than he did when he arrived.

"Did you find out anything?" Mother asked.

"Yeah," said Peter with a laugh. "We found out nobody wants us. Clarke has informed us that since we won't stop our investigation, we are relieved of our volunteer duties. It seems word of that tape has spread very quickly, and he doesn't want anything to do with it."

Mother knit her brows. "It sounds like he doesn't want it found."

"He doesn't," I said. "He's afraid it will look like his campaign has been trying to smear Peterson. And he's right. Jody was the manager of his headquarters, so if it comes out that she was digging for dirt, no matter what Clarke says people will believe that he was behind it. But he's managed to cover his ass. If the tape comes out, now all he has to do is say he dismissed the people who were looking for it the minute he heard about it."

"It still seems odd to me," said Mother. "Because even if it would look as if Clarke was involved in getting dirt, once it comes out—even though people might not like it—the scandal would probably hurt Peterson more than it would Clarke."

"Depending on what it is," Peter pointed out.

I sighed. "I just hope it's not what everybody says it is. I really hate it when homosexuality is used as a scandal."

"That's just chat, though," said Mother. "There's no telling what's really on the tape until we see it. But I did learn something rather interesting about that this afternoon."

"What's that?"

"I had a chat on the phone with Larry Nelson."

"You did?" I said warily.

She looked surprised. "Yes. Shouldn't I 'ave?"

"Of course, of course," I said quickly. "I was just . . . I don't know what I was thinking."

She laughed. "You made it sound odd that I would talk to him! Anyway, since he's been on to those FBI fellows, I thought I'd ask him if he knew how they were getting on, and he said the same thing that Frank did: They're trying to trace the tape, but he added something very interesting."

She paused dramatically.

"Out with it!" I said irritably.

"He said that the FBI doesn't believe there is such a tape, and that he doesn't either!"

"What?" Peter and I exclaimed in unison.

"And after talking to him, I'm inclined to agree."

"You've got to be kidding!" I said.

"It's as Larry put it to me: If there was a scandal so big as to be caught on videotape, it's sure to have come out before now. The way Larry explained it, political candidates have become so fearful of something that can be used against them being discovered that they hire detectives to look into their own pasts to see if anything can be found! You'd think something as dire as a videotape would've surfaced, wouldn't you?"

"Not if nobody knew about at the time," I said, "but we know the tape exists now."

"No, we know somebody *told* Jody that it did."

"Yes, and now we think we know who," said Peter. He then filled her in about Ned Turner.

"But you see, that's still just a lot of chat," Mother countered. "If Ned had any proof, he'd have printed it, wouldn't he? And if the proof was tangible enough to get around to him, then it would've been found before, don't you think?"

My mind was spinning. What she said made perfect sense, but there was something wrong with it that I couldn't put my finger on. I had that sick feeling in my stomach that you get when you sense that the answer to something important is just out of your reach.

"No, no, no," I said finally, slowly shaking my head. "It won't do. Jody must've been told about the tape *before* the night she was killed. And something had to have happened between the time she first learned of the possibility of its existence, and the phone call she got in the middle of the night."

Peter said, "Obviously she tried to find it."

"But who would she have been asking about it?" said Mother. "Nobody in Peterson's camp would've admitted knowing, and you proved for yourself that nobody in Clarke's camp did, either."

"Maybe she tried to blackmail somebody with it," I said.

"No, she was much too straight an arrow for something like that," said Peter.

"That's not the kind of blackmail I mean. She could've called Peterson and told him that she knew about it to try to get him to drop out of the race. I wouldn't put that past her."

"It doesn't work," Mother said with a cluck of her tongue. "Whoever killed her knew that she didn't have the tape, because he lured her to her death with it." She heaved a disgusted sigh. "Honestly, I wish that silly girl had kept to herself!"

"Well, maybe Ned Turner will be able to give us some help. If he knows about the tape, he might have given Jody a lead for how to find it," said Peter.

I turned to Mother. "Do you want to come with us?"

"No. I'd love to, but I have a date."

"With Simon?" I replied, trying not to sound too displeased.

"Of course."

"I'm surprised he hasn't been scampering after your heels today."

"This is the last day but one for his seminars, so he couldn't take me around today. But we are having dinner."

"And then what?" I asked. "I mean, after his seminars are all over."

She gave me her most enigmatic smile. "Then . . . we shall see what we shall see!"

ELEVEN

The office of *Chicago Lite* was located in a converted factory about a block off Wells just north of Goethe. The outside of the building was dirty, dull white stone with rows of small windows so rigidly spaced they resembled a line of sinister exclamation points. The place looked like headquarters for the Third Reich.

The front door was locked. To the left of it, exposed to the elements, was a rusty intercom and a row of buttons, beside which were tiny rectangular cards that held rain-smeared names. We pressed the button beside CHICAGO LITE, and almost immediately the intercom crackled.

"Yes?" said a rather high-pitched male voice.

I said, "It's Alex Reynolds and Peter Livesay. We phoned earlier. We're here to see Ned Turner."

The intercom crackled again, and I was afraid that the response had been lost in the static when suddenly the voice said with alarming clarity. "Oh yeah. Come on up!"

The door buzzed and we went in.

A makeshift directory on the wall by a wooden staircase listed *Chicago Lite* as occupying suite 4C. Of course, there was no elevator, so we mounted the stairs as quickly as my out-of-shape legs could carry me. Peter sprinted like a gazelle up the steps beside me, his progress only hampered by mine. *Chicago Lite* was in an office at the end of the hall behind a door of frosted glass.

The reception area was pretty much what we expected: the obligatory cheap halogen lamp, potted palms, uncomfortable chairs, and a side table on which were piles of back issues of the paper. Seated behind the reception desk was a young blond man in a pink shirt and jeans.

"You're Alex and Peter, right?" He blinked his baby-blue eyes at us. I had a feeling he was more dimly lit than the room was.

"Yes," I said. "Remember, we called earlier. Is Ned Turner here?"

"You're in luck. I told you he'd be here around five, and he is! It's hard to know with him, you know, because there's real time and then there's Neddy time, and Neddy time doesn't really have anything to do with real time. Usually, he's later than he's supposed to be. I think he's really supposed to drop off his column by four, and that's why he's usually here at five, so that's why when you called I told you five instead of four, even though four is when he's supposed to be here. It's funny, you know, 'cause there's almost always an hour difference. It's like Neddy's on New York time instead of Chicago time, or like he just never turns his clock back when the rest of us do."

Peter and I looked at each other, then back at the receptionist.

"So he's here?" I asked again.

He looked confused for a moment, then said, "Oh, yes! Yes, he is. Didn't I say?"

I was tempted to say, "I don't know," but I was afraid that would complicate matters.

"Could we see him?" asked Peter.

"Sure, sure! I told him you might be coming, so you're sort of expected."

He didn't make any further comment or move to call Turner, so I said. "Should you let him know we're here?"

"Oh, there's no need for that! Just go down to his office. It's the last one on the right."

He made a fleeting gesture toward the doorway opposite his desk, beyond which was a hallway.

"Thank you," Peter said kindly. As we proceeded down the hall, he whispered to me, "I think we can assume he wasn't hired for his office skills."

The door to Turner's office stood open, and the man himself was seated at an antique desk sorting through the mail. Turner appeared to be approximately the same age as the desk. He was painfully thin, immaculately dressed, and had dark gray hair that he wore slicked back. There were huge jewelled rings on three of his slender fingers. He had small round glasses perched on the bridge of his excessively angular nose, and he kept his lips in a disapproving pucker. He looked like a bird that might peck at someone without provocation.

When we stopped in his doorway, he looked up and said, "Yes?"

"Mr. Turner? I'm Alex Reynolds and this is Peter Livesay. We'd like to talk to you."

"So I hear. Come in." He waved his elegantly manicured hand at the two soft chairs in opposite corners of the room, far away from his desk. Peter and I sat down.

"What can I do for you? Steven, our twink-on-guard, was rather vague, which is his natural condition. He was able to tell me that he thought you might be coming, but I'm afraid the purpose of your visit was beyond his meager capabilities."

"It's about Jody Linn-Hadden," I said.

He sat back in his chair. "Ah yes, dear, dead Jody. I heard someone blew her up. I was surprised. She was so intense when she visited me I expected her to explode on her own."

"Uh . . . Mr. Turner . . ." I began.

"Ned."

"Ned. We understood that Jody came here to talk to you."

His eyes narrowed, which made him look even more like a predatory bird. "Oh you do, do you?"

"Her partner told us that," said Peter.

"Did she. How interesting."

Peter and I glanced at each other over the abyss across which we'd been seated.

"Yes. Didn't she come and talk to you?"

"Now, that is a question," he replied smoothly. "It requires another question. Who wants to know?"

"Well . . . we do," I answered blankly.

"Yes, but then the question becomes, who are you, my dears?"

"Two people who are fighting for their lives," Peter replied pointedly. "Whoever killed Jody tried to kill us last night."

Turner's eyes flexed slightly. He opened his center drawer and pulled out a pad and pencil. "Now that *is* interesting. Do tell." He poised the pencil over the pad.

Peter leaned forward. "Because our lives are in danger we've been trying to find out what happened to Jody, and the trail led us to you. So we want to talk to you off the record."

"On something as juicy as this? You must be joking!"

"No, we're not," I said. "We've stumbled into the same mess that Jody did, and that may have started with you. So we need to know what you talked to her about. Don't you see that?"

"Why, of course I do, young man!" he replied with a ravenous smile. "But what I'm talking about now is tit for tat. I would love to be the first to have the inside story on the murder of one of our own, and you sound like you can help me in that area."

I looked over at Peter who was staring at Turner as if he were an insect.

"I can give you the inside scoop," I said evenly. "Something you told Jody may have led to her death."

Turner looked singularly unimpressed by this statement.

Peter said, "I can tell you something else. Both the police and the FBI have been pressing us for information since the attempt was made on us. We've been reluctant to share anything with them, but maybe it's time we changed our tune and told them that the trail leads here."

"Do you think we should?" I said to Peter with mock surprise, taking up the thread. "I mean, it would take the pressure off of us, but wouldn't that put Neddy here in the middle of a really, really difficult situation?"

Turner puckered his lips so tightly he looked as if he was sucking in a worm. He laid his pencil atop the pad and sat back again.

"The two of you are quite amusing. I would suggest your act would be more appropriate to the theater rather than the office.

"It's not an act, Ned," said Peter. "We'll tell the authorities what we suspect."

Turner eyed Peter for a long while. "Do you think for a moment that that prospect frightens me? Do you think I haven't had the authorities down my throat, so to speak, before? Trying to find out where I've gotten my information? This paper may be the rectum of the popular press, but it's still journalism, and subject to all of the same protections afforded the more prestigious periodicals." He fairly sneered the word "prestigious." "Still and all, I suppose I should do my little bit when called upon in a matter such as this. So let me propose a little exchange."

"What kind?" I asked warily.

He made a temple of his fingers and held them to his chest. "I will answer your questions about Jody, inasmuch as I deem suitable, in exchange for an exclusive with you once the matter's settled. Is that agreed?"

Peter and I glanced at each other again. He gave a nod, and although I had a feeling I was making a deal with the devil, I said, "Agreed."

"Good!" He rested his elbows on his desk and propped his chin on the temple. "I'll accept that as the word of a gentleman. Now ask away!"

"Well," I said slowly, not at all happy about the arrangement or the relish with which he approached his job. "We understood that Jody came to you looking for dirt on Fritz Peterson."

"Naturally."

"Naturally what?"

"Naturally she came to me. Who better?"

"What did you tell her?" Peter asked.

He spread his palms broadly and smiled. "Absolutely nothing."

"Nothing?" I was truly shocked. I had been so certain—without any real evidence—that Turner was the source of Jody's information.

"I have absolutely nothing on Peterson other than idle gossip, and I certainly don't report that in my column. It's called a 'gossip' column, but believe it or not, I don't print anything I can't prove."

"What's the gossip on Peterson?" asked Peter.

He shrugged. "Just the usual rampant rumors about Peterson's possible proclivities." He rolled his tongue around the alliteration as if he was savoring it for future use. "Surely you've heard it all: that although he's the image of a God-fearing family man, and he's staunchly against homosexuality, that he's really a closet queen. The more colorful stories involve the police smuggling young— very young—hustlers in to him when he was maintaining a place on Fullerton."

"On Fullerton?" I shuddered at the thought of Peterson having lived so close to us.

"But if it were true, where's the proof?" Turner said expansively. "The way the tales are told, there should be a veritable parade of lusty young men waiting in line to sell their stories to the newspapers, but none have come forward. And in addition to that, I can't believe that in this day and age his party would have backed him if there was a breath of truth to the rumors. And then there's Clarke. Everyone says he's a homosexual. The stories are the same with only small variations. I'm sure you've heard the rumors about The Man of the People."

"Yes," I said, "and the whole thing makes me sick! They say Peterson is gay because he's against us, and they say Clarke's gay because he's for us. Nobody can win. And the worst part is that the rumors are spread by gay people without realizing that we make it sound as if being gay is the worst thing we can say about someone else!" I turned to Peter and said, "Pardon me for borrowing your soapbox."

"Anytime," he said with a proud smile.

"Be that as it may," Turner said with exaggerated patience. I suddenly had the embarrassing thought that I'd become one of those political fags I dislike. "I have nothing on either candidate."

I was dumbfounded by this pronouncement, and from the expression on Peter's face, he was, too. Although we had only gotten the vague impression from Mary that Turner had been the source, I thought that maybe sounding more definite about it might make him a bit more forthcoming. "But we were told that you did."

"You were told wrong. I fear your source is mistaken."

"You didn't tell Jody anything about a tape of Peterson?"

It was Turner's turn to look perplexed. "A tape of him? Good God, no! I don't know anything about that. And I don't believe for a minute that there is such a thing! Good heavens, if there were, the whole world would know about it! If a tape was discovered of either candidate at this stage of the game, I would retire to a cottage in Michigan and raise sheep!" He paused and repuckered his lips, eyeing us shrewdly. "However, if you do find something of that sort, I'll consider it part of our agreement that I am the first one you let know."

"Now I'm really confused," I said. "We thought that you talked to Jody about a tape."

He stared at me for a full minute before his face suddenly brightened with understanding. "Oh, no no no no no! That wasn't anything about the candidates. That was about Miss Schuler."

"Miss Schuler?" I parroted, so startled I could barely move my mouth. "You mean John Schuler? What about him?"

Turner leaned forward, his face sharpening so much it looked like a wedge. "Rumor has it that our little John was quite randy with the boys back when he was in college."

"But he's married, isn't he?" I said stupidly.

Turner *tsk*ed with distaste. "Don't be so naive! So is Peterson! So is Clarke!"

Peter said, "Is the Schuler thing just another rumor, or is there proof of it?"

"He was frisky enough that there's proof. *Rumor* has it . . ."—

188

his emphasis on the word belied it—"that Miss Schuler liked to videotape herself."

"You're kidding!" I exclaimed.

He shook his head. "I haven't actually seen any tapes, but I have it from more than one reliable source. And I believe I could lay my hands on one if I wanted."

"If you can prove it," said Peter, "why haven't you printed something about it?"

Turner sighed wearily. "This will, no doubt, come as a shock to you, but I do have ethics . . . of sorts. If I published now, it wouldn't just ruin Schuler, it might very well ruin Clarke. And like any good little homosexual, I want Clarke in office. In November, after the election, you can be sure that I'll pry little Miss Schuler out of her closet in a minute! It won't make any difference to Clarke. He'll be in office and will live or die on his record. By the time he's up for reelection, everyone will have forgotten his *former* campaign manager."

"Well, you're right," I said after a pause. "Those are ethics of sorts."

"I don't believe it," I said as we came out onto the street. "Jody was trying to get evidence on Schuler?"

"No," said Peter. "She was trying to get it on Peterson; what she found was dirt on Schuler."

We walked back to Wells and headed north. We were both so keyed up by this bit of unexpected information that by tacit agreement we walked rather than hailing a cab.

"Do you realize what this means? This is the first direct link we have to Jody's death!"

"Direct link?" Peter said doubtfully.

"Yes! She talked to Turner on Friday. We saw her go in and talk to Schuler on Saturday. She was angry when she came out. On Sunday she was dead."

"Jody was born angry. I don't think we can make a case out of that. Besides, all she said about her talk with Schuler is that he wasn't qualified for his job."

"But don't you see? We've finally found one person who isn't what he says he is! That's what the FBI wanted us to look for to begin with! I think we should call them and pass it on."

Peter stopped so abruptly that I'd gone several feet before I realized he was no longer by my side. "Wait a minute! Do you know what you're saying?"

"What?" I said, turning around. I was caught off guard by his tone. He looked like it was taking a great effort to control his temper.

"Alex, the FBI asked us to look for someone who might have infiltrated the campaign: someone from a militia group or some other organization. We thought that was like asking us to find out if a straight person was masquerading as gay. But we're not talking about a masquerade any more, we're talking about somebody who may or may not be in the closet."

I swallowed hard. "I thought we were talking about a murderer."

"There's no proof of anything yet! Only the unsubstantiated claim of a gossip columnist! He says he can get proof, but he didn't produce it!" There was a long silence. He took several deep breaths to compose himself. When he looked back into my eyes, his love for me had overcome most of his anger. "Honey, Ned Turner considers it his job to out people. Do you consider it ours?"

"Well . . . no."

"Are you willing to out someone just so you can prove to the FBI that you can do the job?"

"No," I repeated softly. There was a huge lump in my throat. I was ashamed of myself for not having realized the ramifications of what I was contemplating doing.

Peter noticed how upset I was, and as if he'd read my mind, he whispered in my ear, "It's all right. I just got there before you did."

We started walking again, and were silent for quite some time. Then I said, "But if what Turner said is true, there's a possibility that Schuler is the one who killed Jody. We can't let that go."

"That's right," he said, slipping his arm around my waist. "But we have to find proof."

190

We went on in silence for a while, then it was my turn to stop. "Oh, God!"

"What is it?"

"I just thought of something. So what if there's a tape of Schuler? What does it matter? Jody never would've pursued it."

"What do you mean?"

"She wouldn't have jeopardized Clarke. Turner was right. Exposing him now would've hurt Clarke. Jody would've realized that."

We resumed walking again as Peter replied, "I don't know. I can't imagine she would've put up with anyone being in the closet."

"Even so, and even though she didn't like Schuler, she wouldn't have done anything to cost Clarke the election."

"There's one thing she might have done. She might've confronted him, told him he was a danger to Clarke and threatened him with exposure if he didn't step down voluntarily."

I shook my head. "It wouldn't work. He would know she couldn't do it."

By the time we reached North Avenue, I was almost ready to scream with frustration.

"Peter, we've got to find that tape!"

TWELVE

It was after seven when we got home, and Mother was gone for the evening. Peter and I threw together some leftovers for dinner, and after finishing them off and cleaning up, we were just about to settle in to watch a movie when the phone rang. I reached over and grabbed the receiver from the phone on the end table by the couch.

"Hello?"

"Alex? Nelson."

"Larry? I wasn't expecting to hear back from you today. Oh, by the way, thanks for not telling Mother that I'd called you when you talked to her."

"You asked me to keep it confidential." His tone implied that there was never a question as to whether or not he would keep his word.

"What's going on?" I asked.

"Alex, you asked me to check out a person named Simon Tivoli. Are you sure he lives in London?"

"Yes," I said, my heart speeding up. "What's wrong?"

Peter shut off the television set and sat looking at me with concern.

"I've been in contact with my British counterpart. He's checked for me and found nobody by that name living in London."

I could feel myself trying not to panic. "Well . . . well, there can be any number of reasons for that. He could've just recently moved there. Our maybe he lives in a suburb?"

"My contact did all of the necessary checking," Nelson said with that same eerie lack of emotion.

"But . . . but . . ." I sputtered.

"That's not all. You say he told you he works for a company named Cyberdyne?"

"Yes."

"That's another thing. There's no business by that name operating in England."

"What?!" I sat bolt upright.

"What is it? What's wrong?" Peter asked.

"Are you sure?" I said into the phone. "The name sounds so familiar! I'm positive I've heard of it before!"

"We're quite sure. Neither in England, nor here."

My mind reeled. We had narrowed our investigation down to a search for a tape that Jody had been trying to get when she was killed, culminating in the information we'd just gleaned that pointed the finger at John Schuler. All the while Peter had dismissed my suspicions about Simon as paranoid fantasies. In fact, inwardly I had done that, too. And now, here I was, being told that my suspicions of Simon were justified. Mother was dating an imposter.

Nelson called me back to the present. "Now, there is the possibility that we're not coming up with his name for some perfectly innocent reason, or perhaps you misunderstood the name of his company. But Alex, I think you know what this means. Confidentiality aside, I have to turn this matter over to the agents on the Clarke bombing."

"No!"

"Alex, this man came onto the scene just before the office of a political candidate was bombed. He connected himself to you in a way that gave him access to that office. It may be entirely innocent, but under the circumstances, it doesn't look very good."

"But he's still here," I said. "Would he stay here after bombing the place?"

"Possibly. If he didn't get his target."

"But why the attempt on Peter and me? It doesn't make any sense! I mean, if Simon is some sort of hit man, then he'd be here to kill Charlie Clarke, wouldn't he?" It didn't escape me that I was now arguing the opposite side of my former position.

"Again, possibly. It's also possible that the office was the target, and the purpose was to frighten Clarke out of the race."

My mind flew back to what Simon had said at the party: that if he were Clarke, he would have dropped out after the bombing. Even at the time it had sounded to me like a veiled threat that he'd hoped we would pass on to Clarke. But that was another thing that I'd written off as paranoia.

But something still bothered me.

"Then the attempt on us still doesn't make any sense."

"Alex, you're missing the point. Whatever his motives, he's traveling this country under an assumed name and was in the area during a political bombing. That has to be investigated. And since you've been removed from the case, it's not your problem."

"The hell it's not!" I exclaimed. "This guy is out with my mother right now!"

There was a beat, then Nelson replied, "All the more reason that this should be put in the proper hands as soon as possible. We need to turn this over to the FBI."

"No, wait!" I said quickly. "Please . . . let me look into it first."

"I can't do that."

"This involves my mother, and I want to make sure we're on the right track before it goes to Agent Henry."

"Alex, if Tivoli's involved in this, we can't afford to give him the opportunity to get away."

"The office was bombed a week ago and he's still here!"

"Your car was bombed last night," Nelson countered.

"And he's still here! Obviously he's not in any hurry to go anywhere! Please, Nelson. If Mother is linked to a suspect, she'll get dragged through the mud. Publicly. I want to make sure he really is a suspect before that happens."

I was counting on the prospect that our emotionless superior had at least to some extent fallen under my mother's spell. After the longest pause yet, he said, "I can't hold off forever."

"Give us twenty-four hours. We'll see if we can find out anything definite." I could sense that he was about to turn me down, so I quickly added, "Come on, Nelson. Twenty-four hours. What could happen in twenty-four hours?"

He emitted a slight "Hmph," but had the decency not to point out that I'd caused much more trouble than this in much less time.

In the end, he relented, albeit reticently.

Throughout my conversation with Nelson, Peter had continued to ask what was wrong with increasing anxiety. When I finally hung up the phone, I explained it to him.

"You're kidding!" he exclaimed once I was finished.

"I wish I was."

"But I still think that's crazy!" said Peter. "Why go to all the trouble to get to know Jean and everything just to blow up a building?"

"It's just not possible," I said, shaking my head. "I don't believe it."

"I thought he was your favorite suspect."

"That was before I knew how suspicious he really was!" I said, then added with great reluctance, "And that was only jealousy and you know it!"

"And Nelson said there was no Cyberdyne company?"

"No, and I really don't get that because it sounds so familiar!"

"To me, too."

"Why would he give us the name of a company when that's so easy to check?"

"I don't know. You were questioning him as if you were suspicious of him. Maybe he felt cornered into coming up with a name."

"Cyberdyne . . . Cyberdyne . . . Cyberdyne . . ." I repeated aloud, pounding my fist limply into the seat cushion beside me as I tried to remember. "Why does that sound so . . ." Then it came to me. I dropped my head into my hands. "Oh, Christ! Cyberdyne!"

"What is it?"

"We don't deserve to be called movie buffs!"

"What?"

I turned to him. "Cyberdyne! That's the name of the evil corporation in the *Terminator* movies!"

He went a bit pale. "Oh, Alex, that's nuts! Why would he use the name of a company we might recognize?"

"Who the hell knows!" I said. "Maybe he was toying with us! Maybe he's been toying with Mother! Maybe he's the type of person who likes to do that when he's going to blow things up, like Jeremy Irons in that *Die Hard* movie!"

"We've got to tell your mother," Peter said.

I jumped up from the couch. "We've got to do more than that! Come on!"

"Where are we going?" he asked as he got up.

"To the River Edge Motel!" I replied, heading for the door. "That's where he said he's staying, isn't it?"

"Alex, we can't!"

"We have to. We can at least check it out. We've got to find out what this guy's up to." When Peter still hesitated, I added, "Besides, we haven't burgled anything in a long, long time! It'll be fun!"

I ran upstairs to grab a couple of things I thought we might need, then checked the phone book for the address of the motel. I let out an audible gasp when I saw it.

"What's the matter now?" Peter asked.

"The River Edge Motel is at six hundred south Mersey."

"So?"

"That's just south of the Loop, Peter! Remember what Henry told us? The call that we got about the tape came from a pay phone just south of the Loop."

"Oh, God!" he said.

As the name would imply, the River Edge Motel was situated on the bank of the Chicago River. It was a two-story, rectangular cracker box with a balcony providing access to the second level. All of the windows overlooked the river, which might have been romantic had not that particular area of the water looked so much like a sewage canal.

As we emerged from the cab whose driver had only reluctantly driven us to that address, I said, "Oh, my God! An outhouse with a view. I can't believe Mother's beloved Simon is staying in this dump. You would think a hit man could afford a better hideout."

"Maybe he's trying to keep a low profile," said Peter as the cab drove away. From the look on his face he was having difficulty picturing Simon there, too. "We don't know what room he's staying in. How are we going to find it?"

I shrugged. "The easy way. We'll ask."

The motel's office extended off the far end of the building like a puss-swollen blister. A mountainous man in a faded red plaid shirt and blue jeans that could barely contain him was perched on a stool behind the desk. His dull eyes were glued to a tiny black and white television that had a bent coat hanger for an antenna. He didn't look up when we came through the door, despite the incongruous "Avon calling" doorbell that rang out to announce us. We went up to the counter and I cleared my throat.

"Yeah?" the mound of flesh said without taking his eyes off the set. The picture was so fuzzy I couldn't tell what he was watching.

"We're here to see Simon Tivoli."

"So?"

He was so abrupt and disinterested that, despite the fact that we didn't particularly want to attract his interest, I was tempted to grab the front of his shirt and shake him to get his attention. However, with his layers of fat I had a feeling it would take too long for the ripples to get to his core. And besides, there was an aroma—something resembling burned beans—emanating from him. I wouldn't have touched him with a pair of sterilized tongs.

"We don't know what room he's in," I said evenly.

"Eleven. Second floor."

I thanked him with an ironic perkiness that I'm sure was lost on him, and Peter and I left the office. As we went up the stairs to the second level, Peter said, "Have you given any thought to how we're going to break into this place?

"Yeah. Here." I reached into my pocket, pulled out the contents and showed them to him.

He stared down at my hand incredulously. "Bobby pins?"

I nodded. "To pick the lock. They always use a bit of stiff wire to do it in the movies. I got them from Mother's room."

"I didn't know she had bobby pins."

"And I brought a nail file. I don't know why, but it seemed like a good thing to have."

"You actually think we'll be able to pick the lock?"

"Look at this place! I can't imagine it being very hard to get in."

The right edge of his lip curled. "I can't imagine anybody wanting to get into this place."

The only sign of life on the second level was the room at the end of the balcony. A table lamp illuminated the badly stained curtains which were drawn against prying eyes. From inside a recording of The Carpenters crooning "Top of the World" was blaring at top volume, as if the occupant had mistaken them for a heavy metal band.

Room number eleven was the next-to-last room. We could tell it was the right place only because of the barely visible shadows of the numbers that had once been nailed to the door.

"Should we knock first?" Peter asked quietly.

"I don't see why. There's no light on, and we know he's out with Mother."

He pointed at the doorknob. "Look. There's a lock there, but no deadbolt."

"Isn't that against the law?" I said.

He put his hands on his hips. "When we're done breaking and entering do you want to turn them in?"

"Oh, shut up," I said, lightly thumping his shoulder. I crouched down in front of the door and scrutinized the keyhole. "So how do we do this?"

"Wait a minute. Why don't you try a credit card?"

I looked up at him. "What?"

"A credit card. Sometimes you can run a piece of plastic in there and slip the lock open." He paused to smile. "Like in the movies."

I smiled back. "Are you making fun of me?"

"Whatever you're going to do, would you do it fast? We're not exactly hidden here."

"I don't think the rats will call the police," I said.

I pulled my wallet out of my back pocket and extracted my Visa. With one hand on the doorknob, I slid the card in between the door and the jamb. When the card was about halfway in, it struck something and would go no further. I moved it up and down, then flexed it back and forth, but the lock refused to pop. With one last effort, I bent the card outward and pushed at the same time, hoping this would wedge it through the catch. The result: my Visa snapped in half.

"Oh, great!" I said, falling from my crouch to a sitting position. I tried to pull the card out using the half that was dangling from the door, but it peeled off leaving the other half behind with only one jagged edge exposed.

"How the hell am I going to get that out?"

"Didn't you bring a pair of tweezers?" said Peter.

I pursed my lips at him. "You're not helping."

I gripped the corner of the now defunct credit card between my thumb and forefinger, pressed as hard as I could and pulled. After three or four attempts, I was finally able to work the card out of the door. I looked down at the two twisted pieces of plastic in my palm.

"We had a lot of happy times together."

"Here," Peter said with a sigh, "let me try."

He crouched down beside me and pulled a small plastic library card from his wallet. With his left hand gently pulling the door-knob, he stuck the card into the space that had signaled the demise of my Visa. He worked at it silently for a few moments, then we heard a click and he slid the door open.

"There!"

"Oh, sure, after I loosened it up for you," I said as he helped me to my feet.

We stepped inside the door and quietly closed it.

"Do we dare turn on the lights?" said Peter.

"I don't see why not. The only two people who would know it wasn't Simon in the room are out dancing right now."

I flipped the wall switch and a lamp on the small table by the window came only dimly to life. The room was a horror: There was an orange shag rug, dotted with cigarette burns and stains I didn't even want to think about, and on the bed was a dark green spread that looked as if at one time it might have borne a pattern. A television set rested on a battered chest of drawers across from the foot of the bed. Two wooden chairs with olive-green vinyl cushions were on either side of the table.

"Jesus!" I exclaimed softly. "You'd think even lying low he'd do better than this!"

"Let's search the place and get out of here."

It didn't take long. There was nothing in the chest, and not even a Bible in the night stand. I looked in the bathroom and found an array of toiletries in a small zipper bag, but the only thing in the medicine chest was alive, so I closed the door as fast as I'd opened it.

Peter looked in the closet and found four very nice suits hanging on the rod, and a suitcase on the one shelf. He took down the suitcase and placed it on the bed. I sat beside it and gingerly pressed the latches. I half expected it to explode, but all it did was pop open.

"Wow!" I said as I rifled through the contents.

"What?"

"He has beautiful underwear."

Peter rolled his eyes. "You're not shopping, Alex. Hurry up!"

I pushed aside the shorts and socks and caught my breath when I saw the manilla folder beneath them. I took it out of the suitcase and opened it.

"Oh, my God!" I said when I saw the contents.

Up until that point I had been hoping that the paranoid fantasies I'd developed about this guy were wrong, and that Nelson had been mistaken when they couldn't identify him. But what I found in that folder took away any doubts.

"What is it?" Peter asked anxiously.

"It's about Mother. It's everything about her: her address, her likes, her dislikes, everything! Even the kind of car she drives!"

I took the sheet of paper from the folder and handed it to Peter. As he scanned it, he sank onto one of the chairs.

"I don't believe it!" he said.

I was getting angrier by the minute. "He studied her. He studied her so that he could ingratiate himself into her life! Oh, my God! I mean, I know I had my suspicions about him before, but still I didn't believe he really used her to get to Clarke. It's just crazy!"

"I know," said Peter, placing the paper on his lap. "We've been involved in some weird things, but this is incredible. You wouldn't think something like this could happen."

"How could he have found out about her in the first place? How could he know we worked for the government? We never tell anybody! And especially Mother! She would never have told anyone! How could he know about her?"

We were silent for a time. Peter looked down at the list while I just steamed.

"So, what do we do now?" Peter asked.

I looked him in the eye. "Wait for him!"

"You're joking!" he exclaimed. "You want to confront a bomber?"

"I want to confront the bastard that's been using my mother, yes!"

"Are you out of your mind? We need to call the police or the FBI!"

"Not without any proof of anything!"

"Alex, he's staying in a strange city under an assumed name! He's gathered all this information about someone whose life he's entered!"

"Hell, my mother's done that much! Or have you forgotten her little escapade in Los Angeles? That doesn't give us any proof he's the bomber!"

"Keep your voice down!" Peter said in an apprehensive whisper.

I lowered my voice in kind. "Look, that stuff may be suspicious, but we need something to tie him directly to the bombings. We didn't find any trace of explosives in this room, or anything to make a bomb with."

"Of course not! He wouldn't keep them here! He probably has them stashed in a locker somewhere!"

"The only thing we know for sure is that he isn't who he says he is, and I'm going to stay here and find out who he really is!"

"What if he has a gun?" Peter asked, still trying to be the voice of reason.

"Where would he have it? There's no gun here, and he can't be carrying it with him. He and Mother were going dancing. Surely she'd feel it." I stopped and shuddered as I realized the implication of what I'd said.

"Who knows where he might have it hidden?" said Peter.

"I don't care!" I exclaimed, raising my voice again and then lowering it quickly. "I don't care. Look, you can stay or go but I'm not leaving. I'm going to confront his ass when he gets here! Even if he has a gun somewhere, we have the element of surprise on our side. He won't be expecting us here. We'll have the jump on him."

"And how do you expect to get any proof from him?"

"If he's been using my mother, I'll beat the truth out of him!"

I switched off the light and sat in the chair opposite Peter. We had a long, boring wait in the dark during which my resolve alternately flagged and flared up.

I found myself softly singing along with the string of The Carpenters' greatest hits which continued to blare through the wall for the next half hour or so. I was relieved when it stopped, not because I had anything against the duo but because I was afraid we wouldn't hear Simon's approach.

We intermittently engaged in whispered conversation, which

usually revolved around how we were going to explain this turn of events to Mother. I'd found the girlish lilt she'd been projecting for the past week while she dated this monster irritating, but now that I was put in the position of stopping it I didn't want to. In his usual, practical way, Peter kept reminding me of the fact that it would be difficult, but it was something we had to do. That is, of course, if we lived past the encounter with Simon.

It was after eleven and I was beginning to think that if our vigil went on much longer I was going to have a hard time staying awake, let alone staying angry, when we heard footsteps approaching on the balcony outside.

We hurriedly got up and I stood beside the door with my back to the window. My body was tensed but I made sure not to jostle the curtains. Peter stayed next to me. There was such a sense of unreality about what we were doing that for a moment I felt like I was outside myself, watching a movie of someone who looked exactly like me about to do something that was dangerous in the extreme. I wanted to cry out to tell him to stop.

For a split second I was overwhelmed with the feeling that what we were doing was totally irrational. I almost hoped the footsteps would reach the room and keep going, but they stopped directly outside the door, and without a pause a key was slipped into the lock.

The door opened and Simon's vaguely backlit form stepped through. When he reached for the light switch, I leapt at him. He gave a choked cry as I grabbed his neck, spun him around and slammed his back against the wall, pinning him there. I was amazed at my own dexterity, but in retrospect it wasn't exactly surprising that I could do this given the alarming regularity with which it's been done to me.

I kept a grip on his neck with my right hand and held his left shoulder firmly against the wall with my left. All the while he struggled in vain to pull my hand away from his neck.

Peter swiftly closed the door and turned on the light. When Simon saw who his assailant was, he stopped struggling and his eyes practically goggled out of his head.

"Alex! What . . . what are you doing?" He managed to choke the words out of his throat.

"Who are you!" I demanded.

"You . . . you know who I am. What are you doing in my room?"

"I'll ask the questions! We know your name isn't Simon Tivoli, which I might add is the most ridiculously British alias I've ever heard! Now, who are you?"

"I'm . . . just . . . Simon . . ."

I turned to Peter. "Will you look?"

He stepped forward and reached behind my prisoner's back, fished around for a moment, then pulled out his wallet. He flipped it open.

"Simon Collingsworth," he read.

"God, that's not much better!" I turned back to Simon. "What are you doing with my mother?!"

He managed to look confused and frightened. It was a very convincing act, but I had no doubt that if I eased my lock on him, Peter and I would most likely end up dead.

"I'm dating her," he stammered.

"Very funny!" I shot back. "You know what I'm talking about!"

"I haven't laid a hand on her!"

"Laid a hand on her!" My face was so hot now that I thought I might spontaneously combust. "You're using her, you bastard!"

"I don't know what you're talking about!"

"We searched the room, Simon," said Peter.

I added, "We found the dossier on my mother."

"Dossier?" he said, trying to appear completely perplexed.

"Likes the color blue, likes to dance, her favorite perfume, her favorite chocolates, the kind of car she drives! Everything!" On the last word I pulled him forward and slammed him back against the wall. "I know why you chose her! I know what you've been doing! But what I want to know now is *how* you knew about her?! How did you find out?!"

"Well, of course I knew about her," he croaked through his constricted throat.

"How?"

"I live in London, don't I? Of course I've heard about her!"

"That's not possible!" I said loudly. "How could anyone know?"

"Well your mother has family there, doesn't she? *They* know!"

"You're lying! We've never told anyone about it! Nobody! Not even family! How could they know?"

Simon looked at me as if I were completely insane. "They're your relatives, aren't they? Of course they knew about your father dying."

"My father—" I stopped cold. I could feel my mind turning to putty. "*My father dying?* What does that have to do with anything?"

He blinked. "Well, that's when she inherited all her money, in't?"

For a moment I had the uncanny feeling that I'd just been dropped into an alternate universe, where everything from the world as I know it was reversed. I stood holding this man's neck and staring into his eyes. He appeared to believe that what he was saying made perfect sense, and yet it sounded like the bleatings of an alien species to me.

After a long pause, the light started to dawn.

"The money . . . ?" I said slowly.

"You see, not long past I was introduced to your Aunt Ida one day—your father's sister—by a mutual friend. She's a very nice woman and fair talkative. She told me all about your mother."

"You're after my mother's money?"

"It's not quite as pat as all that. It's not just the money," he said as if a bit offended. "After all, she's an attractive woman, and very nice to boot. I was perfectly willing to marry her."

I couldn't believe what I was hearing. "You're a gigolo."

"What a terrible word. Makes it sound so tawdry. It's not as if your mother doesn't like me! I say, Alex, do you think you could let go of me? I'm not as young as I used to be and I'm having a bit of a bother breathing at the moment."

I looked at Peter, whose face had fallen open like a trap door. The sense of relief and the magnitude of how far off we'd been struck us both at the same time. We burst out laughing and I released my grasp on Simon's neck.

As he tried to pull himself back together, he appeared to be even more baffled by this reaction than he'd been by the attack. He tucked the tails of his shirt in, straightened his tie, and adjusted his jacket with wounded dignity.

"I know you must not think me much of a gentleman," he said as we laughed. "But I really do think your mother is smashing. At least, I do now. I wouldn't have you think I'm entirely mercenary."

"Oh, that's all right," I said. Then without preamble I drew back my right fist and punched him in the face with the full force of a son defending his mother's tarnished honor. Never have I felt anything as soul-satisfying as when my knuckles connected with his beautiful nose. His head snapped back, hitting the wall. He slid down into a crumpled mess on the floor. Blood flowed freely from both nostrils.

"Gawd!" he said with a newly acquired twang. "I think you've broken my nose!"

"How fortunate that you have National Health Insurance," I said, standing over him. "They can take care of that when you get back to England. Now, I suggest that you call my mother as soon as you can pull yourself together and explain to her that you've been unexpectedly called back there. Then I suggest that you never, ever come near my mother again . . . or I'll break your other nose!"

THIRTEEN

We left the broken and bruised bastard still slumped on the floor. It was a healthy walk back to the south end of the Loop, the nearest place we could get a cab.

"You know what this leaves us with? Nothing!" I said, stumbling as I stepped on a beer can I hadn't noticed.

Peter caught me up. "Nothing that we didn't have before. With Simon out of the picture, the only person we have anything against is Schuler. And we don't know anything about him for a fact."

"That's not exactly true," I countered. "Ned Turner said he knows there're tapes of Schuler. If he's to be believed, then there's a lot of proof out there."

"Yes, but even if that's true, everything else is just conjecture: the idea that Jody confronted him, that he killed her, everything! And it certainly doesn't give him a reason for wanting to kill us. We told him we thought Jody was looking for dirt on Peterson, not him!"

I had another one of those moments where I thought the frustration was going make the top of my head blow off. That, coupled with the fact that my adrenaline level was taking a nosedive now that the matter of Simon had been settled, suddenly made me bone-weary.

"I can't think anymore," I said. "I need to go home, lie down, and sleep for a year!"

Peter sighed. "I know what you mean."

We crossed over the river at Harrison and then continued north to Congress where we finally found a cab. Although it was only a twenty-minute ride back to our house, I found myself dozing off. In fact, I actually must've fallen asleep at some point because it seemed we were pulling up in front of our house without my being able to recall how we got there. After paying the driver, we got out of the cab and it pulled away.

As we mounted the stairs to our front door I said, "I have a feeling I'm going to be dead to the world the minute my head hits the pillow."

I unlocked the door and we went in. Mother was in the living room, sitting at the far end of the couch, brightly lit by the lamp on the end table. Her hands were folded neatly in her lap, and her features were frozen in a half-frown.

"Jean, you're still up," said Peter as I locked the door.

"You have the funniest look on your face I've ever seen," I added. I was beginning to fear that she somehow knew what we'd been up to.

"We have company," she said.

"What?"

"Hello!" came a voice from behind us.

Peter and I both turned around. John Schuler was pressed up against the wall so that we couldn't see him before coming into the room. He was wearing a long black coat over his usual blue suit, but most importantly, in his right hand he clutched a gun which he raised and pointed at us. Beads of sweat broke out on his forehead.

"He was waiting outside when I got home," said Mother. "He had that gun. There was nothing I could do."

"There was nothing *you* could do? We're in trouble," I replied.

"Shut up!" Schuler snapped. He stepped away from the wall and waved the gun at us, motioning us further into the room. "Get in here. Get in here and shut up!"

For the first time I noticed the wildness in his eyes. He looked like someone who knew he had nothing to lose. Peter and I slowly moved to the center of the room.

Schuler stammered, "I think you should . . . yeah, you should sit down there."

He indicated the couch. We complied.

"John, what are you doing?" I asked quietly. "I mean, this is nuts!"

"You don't have any idea what you've done, do you?" he said in a low rumble. "You have no idea how much trouble you've caused! You've ruined everything, because you couldn't keep your god-damn noses out of my business! You had to go blabbing to the police! Now everybody knows about the tape! Everything will come out! They're going to look into everybody's past and they're going to find them!" He stopped and a wave of grief washed over his face. "Today . . . today . . . everything went to hell! First those FBI agents showed up, and they asked about the tape!" The grief passed quickly and the anger returned. "I know they heard it about it from you! Jody didn't tell anybody!"

"How do you know?" said Peter.

Schuler looked down at him. "I *know!*"

I tried to sound calm and rational, which I certainly didn't feel at that moment. "John, it was all going to come out anyway. You taped yourself having sex when you were in college. Did you think that wouldn't get around? Once your name started getting in the papers, somebody was bound to come forward."

"Who told you about it?" he demanded wildly. "I know it wasn't Charlie!"

Oh, God, I thought, my heart sinking, *Clarke knew about the tapes!*

Given the fact that Schuler had already killed one person, had tried to kill us once before, and was now apparently planning to finish the deed, I wasn't about to implicate Ned Turner or Mary Linn-Hadden. When I didn't answer, he advanced, kicked the cof-fee table out of the way and shook the gun in my face.

"I said who told you about it!"

"Jody did," I said after a beat.

He recoiled as if he'd just been slapped. "That can't be! That can't be! She wouldn't!"

"But she did. It's because of her that we know about the tape," Peter verified.

The corner of Schuler's mouth drooped, and his lower lip began to tremble. "Then I was done for from the start."

I nodded. "John, you were going to be exposed after the election, when it was too late for your scandal to hurt Charlie Clarke. He would've been forced to get rid of you."

He scowled and shook his head. "He never would've done that! He would've stood by me!"

"He wouldn't have been able to," said Peter.

"That's what that bitch dyke said!" He ground his teeth together as if he had Jody between them.

"So she did confront you about the tape," I said.

"You know she did! She told me I should step down before it came out and I took Charlie down with me. But I told her to fuck herself! She might hate me, but I knew she wouldn't do anything to hurt Charlie! But I couldn't let her live! Once she knew about the tape, I couldn't be sure she wouldn't blow the whistle, even if it meant destroying everything! I had to do something about her. So I called her and got her to come to the office to meet me. I told her I'd give her the tape. All those bomb threats that kept coming into the office, that's what gave me the idea!"

I still didn't understand why Jody would go out in answer to his call to see a tape she already knew about, particularly since he'd already admitted to its existence. But I wasn't about to ask him about it at that particular moment. There was something else I wanted to know.

"Where in the hell did you learn how to make a bomb?"

"Off the Internet, stupid! It's the easiest thing in the world! Hell, I could've made a bomb big enough to take out the whole damn block! But that wouldn't have been as good. People might've suspected it was meant for Charlie's office, but they wouldn't have been sure. By just blowing up his headquarters, I could get rid of Jody and make Charlie look like a hero for staying in the race at the same time! And it worked! His approval rating went up! Can you believe it?" He beamed proudly. "And they say I can't manage a campaign!"

"You're insane," I said quietly.

"Honey, I don't think this is the best time to point that out!" said Peter.

"And then the two of you came along," Schuler continued, his voice seething with contempt. "You with your subtle threats about the tape! I knew what you were talking about!"

"What?" I said in utter disbelief. "We didn't know that the tape was of *you!* We thought it was of Fritz Peterson! All we knew was that Jody was looking for dirt on Fritz Peterson!"

"Cut the crap! What do you think, I'm stupid? Sure, you used that Peterson line at first, to get me off my guard, but then you started asking about the tape and I knew what you were up to! Do you think I'm a fucking idiot? I knew what you were talking about!"

I frantically searched my memory, sure that I must've said we were looking for a tape of Peterson. But now that he'd said this, for the life of me I couldn't recall having mentioned Peterson's name in relation to the video. I had the unpleasant realization that we were about to be murdered over a simple misunderstanding.

"I was asking about Peterson!" I exclaimed, not that convincing him of it at that point was going to help anything.

"Stop lying!" he yelled. "I know what you were doing!"

If I hadn't been so dire at that moment I would have taken the time to point out to Peter that this was yet another example of someone not believing me. Instead, I said, "What are you going to do then, John? Kill three more people? How do you expect to get away with that?"

He smiled venomously. "If I take care of you now, I can still save Charlie. And maybe even myself. You've been fired. You don't work for him anymore. There won't be anything to connect your deaths to me. Who's going to miss you?"

I swallowed hard. "The FBI, for one."

His smile flickered, then disappeared. "What?"

"We were working for the FBI while we were in Clarke's office. They already think the reason our car was blown up was because someone—you—found out about us."

His mouth hardened. "You're Feds? Prove it!"

I looked at Peter and said disgustedly, "Oh, I give up!"

"Alex," Mother said sharply, "Enough." She had been silent through all of this, and still sat with her hands folded in her lap. She looked up at our captor and spoke quietly but firmly. "Mr. Schuler, don't you think you should stop this now? One person is dead, and you know yourself that no matter what you do now, you're going to be found out. I really don't think you should make things worse for yourself or for Mr. Clarke by killing more people, do you? What good would that do? The authorities already know about the tapes."

He looked at her while she spoke, and for a time he almost looked rational. But that passed quickly. He shifted the gun from his right hand to his left, then reached down into the pocket of his long black coat. He pulled out a videocassette which he held up in front of us.

"They don't know about this one. I think this is what you've been looking for."

Neither Peter, Mother, nor I knew what to say. The tape itself didn't seem important at that point. He shoved it at me.

"Put it in the machine! I know you want to see it!"

"I'm afraid you're mistaken," I said. "I don't want to see you having sex."

Schuler huffed. "That's what you think this is all about? You're dumber than I thought! Put this in the fucking machine!"

"Not in front of my mother."

"Alex, I hardly think protecting my tender sensibilities is our most pressing problem at the moment," Mother said witheringly.

"Do it!" Schuler yelled, waving the tape in my face. "It's okay that you see it now, since you're not going to live to tell anybody about it!"

After a pause I took the tape from his hand and rose from the couch. The entertainment center was on the opposite wall. Schuler stepped back so that he could keep all three of us in range while my loved ones and I were on opposite sides of the room. I switched on the TV, which was already set to video, and popped the tape into the VCR, then stepped back from the set.

The picture sprang to life. It was black and white and not of great quality, but clear enough that there would be no doubt of anything—like clips I'd seen on talk shows of household crimes shot with nanny-cams.

A man stepped into the picture, close enough to the camera that he was visible only from the neck to the knees. He was naked and turned sideways so his erection was very prominent.

"That's me," Schuler said. He sounded proud.

Another naked torso came onto the screen and pressed up against him. Apparently they were kissing. The new arrival then slowly slid down Schuler's body until his face came into view. There he was: The Great One: The Man of the People; The Hope for the Future; Charles "Charlie" Clarke. He paused for just a moment when he got to his knees, took one tentative lick, then began vigorously performing oral sex.

Of course, I thought, mentally slapping myself on the forehead, *they'd gone to college together.*

Peter said quietly, "I don't think it's going to help him to say he didn't inhale."

I switched off the set and turned to Schuler, who wore an expression so triumphant it turned my stomach.

"You see?" he said. "When that Jody bitch told me to step down, I told her I had her hero, Charlie Clarke, on one of the tapes. I told her if she didn't fuck off, she'd see it on the news."

"But she didn't believe you," I said.

He frowned. "She said she'd have to see it to believe it. And I told her it would take me a while to dig it out. It was a lie. I just needed time to think about what to do."

"But if you had this tape and there was nothing Jody could do to hurt you without bringing Clarke down, why did you have to kill her?" I said.

He produced a malevolent smile. "Because I couldn't be sure of her. You never can be sure of a political queer!"

The irony of this statement seemed to elude him.

"She would overlook almost anything, but you know how fast one of them can turn on you when they're scorned! I couldn't trust her not to turn on Clarke once she knew about this, even if it meant flushing him down the toilet!"

"So that's it? All this time you haven't been protecting yourself, you've been protecting Clarke?"

He looked at me with astonishment. "Protecting Charlie? You really don't get it, do you!" He leaned in toward me as if intent on getting me to understand, and said, "I was in a crummy auditing job! A fag auditor, if you can believe that! Charlie was on his way up! I wanted to get out! I wanted to get ahead! He was going to mount this run for senator, just like he always wanted!"

"So?"

He features hardened. "I knew he was looking for a campaign manager. I came to him and told him I wanted a job. I asked for it, just like anyone else applying for a job! I was willing to play the game. But even though we were old friends, very old friends, he told me no! He said I wasn't qualified! Friendship didn't count for anything! But he didn't know about the tape!"

I stared at him, dumbfounded. "Are you telling me that this really has all been about getting a job? You used this to blackmail him for a job?"

"You should've seen him! I thought he was going to die right there! Right when he saw himself on the screen! He didn't. But he knew it was all over. I told him nobody would ever know about it if he kept me with him!"

It was then that I became aware of a very faint sound. I glanced at Mother. She was looking me directly in the eye and drumming her fingers on the arm of the couch. She raised her eyebrows and cocked her head ever so slightly in Schuler's direction.

I turned back to him. "So you're telling me that this whole thing, blowing up the office, killing Jody, trying to kill us, was all over a goddamn job?"

"Not just any job!" he said loudly. "Charlie's going to be state senator! And I'm going to be right there with him, helping him shape the state! Hell, helping him shape the damn country!"

"Shaping the country into what?" I said, edging slightly to my right. "The disturbed mess that goes on in your head?"

"Shut up!" His eyes followed me.

"You didn't have a single thing going for you. You didn't have the wherewithal to get the job on merit," I continued, moving a bit more to the right which forced his eyes to keep on me. "So you had to resort to blackmail, like the shit-slime loser you are!"

"Shut up!"

I moved a little more and rested my hand on the television set. "So you proved you were worthy of a job in the government by showing Clarke that you were a sleazy enough fuck to be a politician?"

"You shut your mouth!" he yelled, focusing his full attention—and the gun—on me. He had now had to turn far enough that Mother was out of his line of sight.

"I don't believe it!" I said. "One woman is dead and the three of us are going to be killed, and for what? So some half-assed little closet-case CPA can blackmail his way out of a low-level accounting job and into the government?"

"I'm not—!"

I don't know what he was going to say, because he was cut off abruptly. I saw Mother's hand jerk forward as she yanked the lamp cord, pulling the plug and plunging us into darkness. The last thing I saw as the light disappeared was Schuler wheeling around, his notice having been attracted either by the noise or having sensed the movement.

I dove in the direction of his arm, hoping that it would still be where I'd last seen it, and thanked God when I caught it. I swung it upward just as he fired.

"Hit the lights!" I cried as I wrestled with him, desperately struggling to keep the gun pointed upward. When it went off a second time, I yelled out "Hit the lights!" again.

The whole scene sprang into view when Peter managed to locate the switch on the lamp on his side of the couch and turned it on. Light flooded the room just in time for me to see Mother wielding the other lamp—the one she'd unplugged—at Schuler's head. He saw her out of the corner of his eye at the last minute and dodged, but didn't get fully out of the way. The base of lamp clipped his skull, and he was hurt enough that it distracted him for just a moment: all the time I needed to bring his wrist down as I brought my knee up sharply. When they came in contact, the gun flew out of his hand, hit the wall, and fell behind the couch.

But he didn't stay distracted for long. He realized immediately that he'd lost the gun. He reared back and threw a punch into the center of my stomach while I was still off balance from my move. The impact doubled me over and sent me reeling backward into Peter, who was just turning around from switching on the lights. When I knocked into him, he fell onto the couch.

With us disabled for a second, Schuler let out an animal-like scream and ran toward the back of the house. I righted myself with an effort, and helped Peter up. "Call the police!" I yelled at Mother as Peter and I took off after Schuler.

"Wait!" Mother called after us. "Take the gun!"

But there wasn't time to fish it out from behind the couch. We'd already heard him going out the back door, and couldn't afford to give him any more of a head start. Besides, he was now unarmed. We raced out the back door just in time to see Schuler going out the gate next to the garage.

We ran after him, Peter and I pretty much keeping neck and neck with each other. We crossed the yard, went through the gate and out into the alley. There was no sign of Schuler.

"He headed that way!" Peter said, pointing east. We'd seen that much before we got to the alley. We took to our heels and when we reached the end of the alley we stopped and looked both ways. To the right we saw Schuler disappearing around the corner onto Fullerton, still heading east.

"Let's go!" I said as we ran after him.

We made it the short half block in record time, and turned onto Fullerton. It was after one o'clock in the morning and the sidewalk was only dimly lit by the spillover from the periodic street lamps. We stopped and peered down the sidewalk, but couldn't see any sign of him.

After standing there for several seconds, straining our eyes against the darkness so hard they hurt, Peter exclaimed, "Look! I think that's him!"

He pointed toward a distant spot on the opposite side of the

216

street. At first I didn't see anything, but that didn't keep me from following Peter as he ran. It wasn't long before I could see what he was going after: something that appeared to be a shadow was scurrying up the sidewalk. Once we'd made it across the street and were directly in its wake, I could make out it was Schuler, mainly by the black coat flapping behind him as he passed in and out of the range of the street lights.

He seemed to get farther away from us as we panted after him. I don't like to think we were slower than he was, just that he had the prospect of saving his life adding wind to his heels. And I was unfortunately discovering that you can run faster when you're being pursued. This was the first time in our short, lamented career with the government that we'd been the chasers rather than the "chasees." I was astounded at the distance he'd gained when he passed into the more fully illuminated business area.

"I think he's headed for the El!" Peter gasped out.

Sure enough, even though we were over a block away when he got to the tracks suspended over the street, Schuler disappeared. Worse yet, in the distance we could hear the distinctive metallic screeching of an approaching train. We both redoubled our efforts and picked up speed. I still can't believe how fast we covered the last block. You would've thought we were regular commuters trying to get to work.

The train was considerably nearer as we turned into the station and were faced with the damnable turnstiles. Although both of us are loath to do such a thing, there just wasn't time to go fishing in our pockets for those blasted fare cards that I normally find so convenient. In unison, we leapt the turnstiles and ran into the concrete area where twin staircases spiral away from each other, one to the platform for trains going north, the other for south. The station guard yelled and started to come after us.

"Oh, Jesus!" I exclaimed. "Which one?"

"It's a southbound train!" Peter yelled, figuring that Schuler was after the train, not caring which direction it was headed.

The noise from its approach was so loud now that we could tell it was just about into the station. We sped up the stairs two at a time and came onto the platform. There was a surprising number of people there, given the late hour, all facing in the direction of the oncoming train. We waded through them, hampered by the noise and our exhaustion, but after several moments of frantic searching we spotted Schuler. He was just beyond the crowd, half-collapsed against a post with his back to us, trying to catch his breath. We started for him, but he looked back over his shoulder while we were still at a distance, and panic crossed his face.

The train was just speeding into the range of the platform. Schuler looked from us to the train, then across at the platform on the opposite side of the tracks. It would be impossible to reach the other platform in a jump, but it might be possible to for him to clear the first tracks and then climb to the other side. He appeared to be desperately trying to gauge whether or not he could do it.

We rushed toward him, the train now barreling into the station, and just as we reached him he jumped. I grabbed at him and caught the end of his coat. I don't know if it was actually that I pulled at him, or that he was so startled he hadn't given full power to his leap, but he didn't clear the first set of tracks. The train hit him full force while he was in mid-jump. He was thrown forward onto the tracks, and then disappeared beneath the train with a shriek.

Some of the passengers waiting on the platform screamed in horror as the train ground itself to a halt on top of him. When the doors opened, chaos broke out.

There was only a short wait before the police showed up. Before their arrival, we'd tried to figure out what—and how much—to tell them, but this had been perhaps the longest day of our lives, and our brains were so fatigued we were finding it hard to come up with anything even halfway convincing to explain why we'd chased this man up onto the platform and into a speeding train.

As it turned out, we received some help from a very unexpected quarter.

The people who'd been waiting for the train, as well as some who'd gotten off it, were huddled in various groups on the platform when the first of the police arrived. Two uniformed officers were brought up by the guard who'd followed us when we jumped the turnstiles. His interest in our petty larceny at that time had been lost in the pandemonium that followed the tragedy. But when he brought up the police, he pointed us out to them.

"Oh, Christ!" I whispered to Peter.

However, just as the officers were starting for us, a young woman, wide-eyed with shock, grabbed one of them by the arm and said loudly, "Did you see what happened?"

"No," said the cop, "what?"

"That guy over there!" she replied, pointing at me, "He tried to save that man's life!"

I was astonished, and from the looks on their faces, so were the officers. They both looked from the woman toward us, and then back at the woman.

She said, "He tried to stop that man from jumping in front of the train."

"Really?" said the other officer.

If this had come from just the one woman, he might not have believed her, but several other people concurred. One older man said, "Yeah. Risked his own life. You don't think you'd see anything like that in this day and age, do you?"

When the officers finally made it over to us and asked us what had happened, I deferred to Peter. He told them that the dead man was John Schuler, Charles Clarke's campaign manager, and that he'd been over at our house. He said that Schuler had been talking about suicide and had run out of the house, and we followed him. And that the chase had culminated in our trying to stop him from throwing himself in front of the train. Unsuccessfully. With so many of the people on the platform willing to swear that that was exactly what they'd seen, there didn't seem any reason not to believe us.

I didn't see any reason not to believe us, either. It was a very plausible lie verified by strangers. It was just as I'd said to Frank the day before: The truth just sounded too crazy.

FOURTEEN

Mother, Peter, and I had hoped to be able to stay in bed very, very late, since having our sleep interrupted two nights in a row by attempts on our lives had left us feeling "rather flat," as Mother put it. But it was not to be.

Agent Henry and Agent Raymond showed up on our doorstep at nine o'clock Sunday morning, one week to the day since Charles Clarke's office was destroyed. They were insistent enough about the doorbell that we decided they weren't going to go away, so Peter and I donned our bathrobes and trundled down the stairs to let them in. Mother followed not long after, apparently having forgotten to care about what the neighbors might think if they saw her receiving g-men in her bed clothes. Even with little more than four hours sleep she managed to look fresh and well rested. As she flowed down the stairs in an elaborate virginal-white dressing gown, she looked like she was on her way to atomize the boudoir rather than be questioned by the Feds.

We explained to the agents what had really happened the previous night. Or most of it. We told them that Schuler had admitted to killing Jody because she'd found out that he'd made videotapes of himself having sex and was insisting that he resign. And that

Schuler had tried to kill us because he mistakenly thought we knew about the tapes, too. All of which was true.

But we didn't tell them that Mary-Linn Hadden had put us on the scent of the tapes to begin with, or that Ned Turner had been the one to verify their existence and claim he could get hold of one. We figured there was no point in causing trouble for anyone else.

We also didn't tell the agents about the tape we had.

Henry and Raymond left only partly satisfied. It's possible they didn't believe us, but I suspect they were disappointed that the case had been cleared by a pair of Nancy boys and the queen Mother.

When they'd gone, we retired to the kitchen and Mother made some tea. None of us was hungry.

"I wonder why he didn't kill Mary," Peter said, once we were situated around the table.

"Huh?"

"Mary Linn-Hadden. I wonder why Schuler didn't kill her. I would've thought he'd believe she'd be the first one Jody would tell what was on the tape."

I took a sip of tea. "My guess is that he figured Jody wouldn't tell anybody—not even Mary—what was on it until she was sure of it. And apparently she didn't. Remember, Mary assumed it was a tape of the Republican candidate, just like we did. It also would've looked awfully suspicious if Mary had been killed right away. It would've proved to the Feds that Jody and Mary were the targets, rather than Clarke's campaign."

"Do you really think Jody didn't tell Mary about something so important?" Mother asked.

"I think that's exactly the kind of relationship they had. Mary was really the 'little woman' in it. She's like one of those house-wives from the fifties who doesn't know anything about paying the bills or the checking account, or anything. Jody took care of every-thing. I don't think Jody would've told Mary anything upsetting. At least, not until she had to."

"And Schuler must've known the dynamics of their relation-ship," said Peter. "He worked closely enough with them."

We quietly drank our tea for a while, then Mother set her mug on the table and cleared her throat. "Well, darlings, we have to decide what to do with that tape."

Peter looked across the table at me. "You know how I feel about outing people. Especially in a case like this. We don't know what that tape means. It could've been a one-time thing. He could've been experimenting. It could've just been his bad luck that he chose to experiment with that pig."

I sighed heavily. "I know, I know. I can't use his sex life against him. At least, not to out him. But I think we have to do something about him."

Peter looked thoroughly surprised. "Why?"

"There's a couple of things you've forgotten, and we can't over-look them." I explained what I meant. When I was done Peter sat back in his chair.

"You're right."

I turned to Mother. "And we're not exactly welcome in the Clarke camp, so we're going to need your help."

It wasn't until later Sunday morning that news of John Schuler's death hit the airwaves, creating the sensation that one would expect. Reporters speculated on what reason he might have had for committing suicide, and on what his death might mean to the Clarke campaign. This naturally led the news people to the next logical step in the story: Clarke's chances of winning the Democratic nomination. They already had results showing Clarke had risen even higher in the polls in the few hours since news of Schuler's death had broken. It seemed Clarke was rising on a ladder of dead bodies.

We decided to wait until Monday, after we'd been able to get some rest, to put our plan into action.

Monday was the day before the primary, and the Clarke campaign moved into the Piedmont Hotel on south Michigan Avenue to prepare for the big day. Mother, Peter, and I took a cab to the hotel late in the morning. We paid off the driver and walked briskly through one of the building's oversized revolving doors.

Like many of the city's older hotels, the Piedmont has a sort of faded elegance that no amount of upgrading can completely erase. The lobby is full of marble statues—mostly nudes discreetly covering the naughty bits—and a thick red carpet that seems to unfurl as you walk on it. Down a short hall to the right of the entrance is the Grand Ballroom, which would be the site of Clarke's victory celebration. The doors stood open, and there was a flurry of activity inside.

"Why don't we try there first?" I suggested.

Mother shrugged and we went down the hallway.

The Grand Ballroom was not quite so large as I'd expected, but it would look impressive on television. Hotel staff, all dressed in identical white shirts and black pants, were setting up tables and chairs, and testing the sound system. Some of Clarke's volunteers were busy decorating the room with huge red, white, and blue banners. Apparently they'd learned from footage of Peterson's rallies.

"What are you doing here?" Shawn Stillman demanded as he bustled up to us. He was in his shirtsleeves, clipboard in hand, and looked frazzled.

"Hello, Shawn. This is my mother," I said.

"I'm ... pleased to meet you," he replied falteringly. He seemed rather nonplussed to have his question met with an introduction. He turned back to me. "What are you doing here?"

"We're here to see Clarke."

"You've got to be kidding! The day before the primary? Haven't you caused enough trouble? They told me you weren't supposed to be anywhere near the campaign anymore."

"We need to talk to him about John Schuler," said Peter.

Shawn's face fell. "John! Isn't it unbelievable! Suicide! Jesus!"

"We were there when it happened," I said. "And we need to talk to Clarke about it. Do you know where he is?"

He looked at Mother, then back at me. "What's going on?"

"It's important, Shawn."

He closed his eyes and shook his head. "I don't think I want to know what's going on." His eyes slid open. "Charlie should be up in his suite. It's number 1407. But I don't think you'll be able to get in."

"Thanks."

We were going back down the hallway to find the elevators when my attention was caught by movement in a small alcove that gave way to the bathrooms. Two men were locked in a very passionate kiss. I stopped in my tracks when I saw who it was.

"Mickey!" I exclaimed. Mother and Peter came to a halt beside me.

The two men broke from their embrace and looked out at us.

"Oh, hi guys!" he said with his usual effervescence. "You know Joe, don't you?"

Joe Gardner pulled away from him slightly and blushed as he mumbled a greeting.

"Looks like Ann Landers was right!" Mickey continued. "I volunteered to try and find a man, and it looks like I got what I was looking for!"

Joe rolled his eyes, only for the first time it was with amused weariness. "I'll make him politically aware yet!"

"Nice to see you," I said mechanically. Then we continued down the hall and left the lovebirds to it.

"I don't believe it!" I said. "Mickey Downs and Joe Gardner! Those are the *last* people I expected to see together. I thought they hated each other!"

"You know how weird mating rituals can be," said Peter.

"But what about that kiss that Joe gave Tony Milano at the party? That was only a few days ago."

Peter considered this for a moment, then burst out laughing. "We really are idiots!"

"What?"

"You remember he looked over at us, and we thought he wanted to make sure we were watching?"

"Yeah?"

"Think about it, Alex. What were we doing when he did that?"

It took an effort to recall the scene, but it finally came to me. "Talking to Mickey!"

Peter nodded. "Right! Joe must've been trying to make him jealous."

"God, I'm glad we're not that young anymore!" I exclaimed.

"I don't think we ever were!"

The elevators were on the opposite side of the lobby from the Grand Ballroom. We rode up to the fourteenth floor to the accompaniment of a Muzak version of "Rhythm Nation." When we stepped off the elevator, there was no doubt about which suite was 1407. There was an armed guard sitting on a chair to the left of the door.

"Well, Mother, do your stuff," I whispered.

She looked down her regal nose at me. "This won't require 'stuff,' dear."

We went down the hall to the guard, who got up as we approached, bringing with him a legal pad that had been sitting beside his chair.

"We're here to see Mr. Clarke," said Mother.

"Names?" the guard replied.

"My name is Jean Reynolds, my son Alex, and Peter Livesay."

He glanced over at us as if he'd heard the names before, but wasn't sure where, then looked down at his pad. "I don't have your names here."

"Could you tell Mr. Clarke that I want to see him?"

"He's not seeing anyone who's not on the list."

"Oh, he'll see me," said Mother, "I'm British."

The guard's brow furrowed, and for a time he looked as if he thought her reasoning should make sense to him. He started to say something else, but Mother cut him off. "If you could just tell him that we're here. He knows who we are. Tell him we would like to speak to him about John Schuler."

He stared at her a little longer, then turned and went into the suite. A moment later he opened the door again and ushered us in. The "living room" was awash with people, some of whom I recognized, and some I didn't. Clarke was in the middle of a little group of them around a low round table by the window, pretending that he wasn't intensely interested in our presence. He could almost have made me believe he hadn't already been told we were about to come in. He made a show of "noticing" us for the first time, then came over and shook our hands.

"Hello, hello," he said in that openfaced way that had made him so popular with the people. "I'm . . . well, I'd be lying if I didn't say I was surprised to see you. I thought we'd made it fairly clear where we all stood at our last meeting."

I glanced over his shoulder and saw his wife, Wendy, sitting on a pink satin chair in a corner of the room. Her hands were folded in her lap and she was looking over at us warily.

"We'd like to speak to you in private," said Mother. "It's very, very important. And it's about John Schuler."

The was a split second of silence before he said, "Yes, yes, follow me."

He led us into the bedroom, in which a few people were standing by the dresser holding a huddled conversation. He asked them to leave, then closed the door behind them.

"It was tragic about John, just tragic," said Clarke, not managing to meet any of our eyes. "It's a sad thing. I don't know what I'll do without him."

"Really?" I said. "I would think you'd be relieved."

He looked up sharply. "I don't know why you say that. John might have had his faults, but he was a good friend." He paused, staring at me as if daring me to challenge him. Then he softened somewhat. "The men from the FBI talked to me yesterday. I know, as you do, that John didn't really commit suicide. And I can't tell you how sorry I am that he dragged you into whatever he was doing. Despite our friendship, I have to admit that he was a very troubled young man. I don't know exactly what he was up to, or why he would make an attempt on your life the way he did, but I want you to know how sorry that I am that I have, in however small a way, been the cause of your having come into a dangerous position."

Until that moment, I don't think I ever realized just how

226

quickly your opinion of someone can change. If he had fessed up to his own part in it right then and there, I think I could've almost forgiven him.

"Mother?" I said.

She reached into her shoulder bag, pulled out the videocassette, and threw it onto the bed. The black plastic case lay there like a dark blot against the stark white coverlet. Clarke glared at it with bugged out eyes as if he recognized it for the next bomb that would explode his campaign.

"We've watched this," said Mother. "It made very interesting viewing."

He cleared his throat and raised his head, although once again he found it difficult to look any of us in the eye. "You have to understand—"

"Drop out of the race," I said simply.

There was a shocked silence.

"What?"

"Drop out of the race."

He pointed at the tape. "Because of that? I would think you of all people would understand—"

"*You* don't understand," I said, cutting him off again. "We don't care. We don't care about your sex life. But you need to drop out of the race."

Sweat started to pour off him at such a rate that you could feel the humidity in the room go up. "You can't mean that! You don't realize the amount of good I can do for your people."

"Our people?" said Peter.

Clarke ignored him. "One indiscretion doesn't . . . whatever faults I might have, I think they're far outweighed by the good that I can do."

"Thanks, but we don't need you. There are other Democratic candidates."

"But nobody that's as much on your side as I am!"

I couldn't believe it. Even Clarke thought that gay rights was our only issue. I was getting tired of Joe Gardner being proven right.

"They'll do," I intoned. "You don't get it, do you? This isn't about your sex life. I wouldn't care if you were breaking into Lincoln Park and fucking monkeys if that's what made you happy. That's not what we're talking about here."

He looked thoroughly confused and, for once, frightened. "What . . . what are we talking about?"

"Two things," said Peter. "Someone has already been able to blackmail you to get you to act. That makes you more dangerous than you're worth if you were to get into office. Someone else could come up with a copy of this tape, want you to vote their way and what would that mean? Suddenly you'd forget all the promises you made to 'our people.' "

"That's not true!" he protested lamely. "It was one thing with John. I knew him. But nobody else has this tape. You could just forget about it. It would be like it never existed."

"But we couldn't forget about Jody," said Mother.

"Jody?" He tried hard to look like he didn't know what was coming, but the effort it was taking made him transparent. "What about her?"

"You knew that Schuler killed her," said Peter.

Clarke turned on him. "No, I didn't!"

"Of course you did," I said. "You might not have known at first. You might have honestly thought the bombing was done by some run-of-the-mill terrorist. And the ironic thing is that her death helped your campaign, in more ways than one!"

"You're doing wonderfully well at the polls," Mother interjected sardonically.

"But you knew later. You knew after the attempt was made on our lives. That's when you knew it was Schuler, didn't you?"

"How could I know that?"

"Because of the tape," said Peter. "You knew it was Schuler the minute you heard we'd asked about the tape."

"How would I have known about the tape?"

I sighed. "Because Schuler told you."

Clarke's face froze. "How do you know that?"

"You see, Jody didn't know that you were on one of the videotapes until Schuler told her. All she knew was that he'd made tapes

228

of himself with other guys, and she wanted him to resign. We found out that her death had something to do with a video, but we thought it was a tape of Fritz Peterson. When we asked Schuler about it, he mistakenly believed that we were confronting him about *that* tape." I pointed to the one on the bed.

"That doesn't mean I knew about any of this!" Clarke said angrily.

"Right after we talked to him he made a beeline for your office. At the time we thought he was just going to fill you in on what we'd said. But it was more than that. He knew there were only two people on earth who knew about that particular tape, you and him. And he knew he hadn't told us."

Clarke looked down at the floor. "You're very observant, aren't you?"

"We keep our eyes and ears open," said Peter.

"He went to your office and accused you of having told somebody, didn't he?"

Clarke didn't answer.

"It doesn't matter whether you confirm it or not," I said, "because when Schuler threatened to kill us, he said that he knew that you hadn't told us."

"As if I would," Clarke said quietly. "He was crazy. He thought . . . He was just crazy."

Peter picked up the story. "You might have only suspected before, but when the FBI told you about the attempt on our lives, you knew Schuler had done it."

There was a very long silence, then Clarke slowly sat on the edge of the bed. "I should've stopped it all," he said weakly. "I should have stopped it all the minute he showed me that videotape."

"Yes, you probably should have," said Mother.

"I should've known it was all over. But it didn't seem fair. It didn't seem fair that my whole career should end before it started just because we . . . I . . ."

"Now you know how we feel," I said.

He looked up. "I didn't know it was John, really."

"You suspected."

He shook his head. "Not at first. I had no idea he had anything to do with Jody. But when I heard about you, I suspected. *Suspected*. I didn't know. What was I supposed to do? Tell the FBI that I thought my campaign manager might be a murderer? I didn't have any facts to go by. And doing it would've ruined me."

I sighed. It didn't sound much different than our reluctance to report anyone's behavior to the FBI. But this went beyond that.

"But you had to have done more than suspect when someone tried to kill us right after we asked about a tape," said Peter.

He nodded, finally conceding the point. "Nobody else knew about the tape. Just me and John." He sounded supremely sad, as if something other than his career had just been ruined. "But I still didn't know anything for sure."

"It would be a lot easier for me to believe you if it wasn't for that elaborate charade you and John played out for us in your office when you fired us. You acted surprised when we told you Schuler had known what Jody was doing. And then the two of you acted out that little scene when you confronted him. You're a very plausible liar, Mr. Clarke."

He looked up at me. "But that's all over now. John is gone, there's nobody else who can blackmail me, and there's still so much good I can do!"

"You're forgetting about us," said Mother.

His face hardened. "So you're planning to blackmail me now?"

I looked down at him. "You can walk away without ever having this 'indiscretion' of yours exposed, with your family and your . . . dignity . . ." I hadn't meant to stumble on the word, but I couldn't help it: I couldn't think of another to use and that one caught in my throat. "Your dignity intact. Without anyone every knowing. But you have to leave the race. I don't care how you live your life in private, but I won't have you as our representative in public. Your judgment is impaired, don't you see that? You've betrayed us already—heck, not just us, everyone."

"You can easily say that you're backing out because it's become too dangerous," Mother said helpfully. "And that you don't want to endanger your family. Both of which would be true, by the way. Or that it has simply become too much for you with two of your workers dead. There isn't a caring human being in this state who wouldn't understand, and feel for you."

"But whatever you do," I said, "you'll have to drop out. If you don't, we'll use the tape."

There didn't seem to be anything more to say on our part, and the once-articulate Clarke no longer looked capable of speech. On our way out the door, I gestured at the tape and added, "By the way, you can keep that one. We made copies."

We were fortunate enough to get an elevator to ourselves on the way down.

"You know what really, really pisses me off?" I said. "When the media gets hold of the real story on Schuler, it'll make us all look bad. The Religious Reich will have a field day!"

"The Religious Reich?" Peter said with surprise. "You're beginning to sound like Jody."

"She had her good points," I said after a beat.

"I don't think you have to worry about what'll happen," Peter replied. "Everyone thinks Schuler committed suicide. When Ned Turner outs him—as he's sure to do now that Schuler's dead—everyone will know that the 'truth' about Schuler was imminent, and chalk it up to another case of the pressures placed on gays to stay in the closet!"

Mother sighed deeply. "In't awful?"

"Would you really have used that tape?" said Peter.

"Naw, of course not."

"You sounded awfully convincing."

I smiled. "For all you know, I could've meant we'd use it as a marital aid."

"As if we ever needed one."

The elevator doors opened at the lobby and we stepped off.

"Well, that certainly made for an interesting morning!" said Mother. "I'm famished. Why don't I take us all out for the biggest and best lunch we can find!"

"Any place but at this hotel," I said.

"I'd love it," said Peter.

As we approached the revolving doors, Mother said, "Oh, by the way, did I tell you that Simon called yesterday? He's not going to be able to stay on after all. His company's called him back to London."

"Really?" I said.

"Yes. Isn't that a shame? I had such a good time with him. I'll miss him."

"Will you really?"

"Oh, yes! He was great fun to be with. And he really knew how to treat a lady, which you can't say of a lot of men these days." She paused and sighed. "If only he hadn't been such a gigolo."

I stopped abruptly. "You *knew* about him?"

She looked at me as if I'd slipped a cog. She drew her pursed lips to one side, eyed me affectionately, and said, "Oh, Alex, *really!*"

She then dove into the revolving door. Peter and I were a few steps behind her.

As usual.